# Kingdom of Dragons

## Book Three of The War-Torn Kingdom

By Timothy L. Cerepaka

*An Annulus Publishing Book*

*Annulus Publishing, Cherokee, Texas, 2016*

Published by Annulus Publishing

Contact: timothy@timothylcerepaka.com

Cover design by Elaina Lee of For the Muse Design

ISBN-13: 978-0692735534

ISBN-10: 0692735534

# Acknowledgements

I would like to thank my uncle, James Wilhite, for helping me get this manuscript into publishable shape. I'd also like to thank the rest of my family for supporting me while I wrote this novel. You guys rock.

# Chapter One

*Forty years ago ...*

**K**ING RIUNO, THE KING of Lamaira, stood in the Royal Garden of Castle Lamai, hiding inside a grove of trees that kept him hidden from view from anyone else who might be in the Garden. It was cool and shady inside, which was nice, because today was easily the hottest day of the summer and Riuno would have been sweating hard otherwise.

Today, Riuno probably should have been back in the Castle, discussing trade relations with countries like Hasfar and the Rameen Empire with his advisers, or perhaps listening to his Minister of the Border update him on the progress of the border wall in the west. Or maybe discuss with his Minister of the Public how to more efficiently direct tax revenue.

Riuno fully intended to do all of that, because he knew that it was his duty as King of Lamaira to focus on those important matters, but first, he wanted to have a little bit of fun before getting into the drudgery of the day.

*Where is she?* Riuno thought. *If she doesn't show up soon ...*

But then Riuno heard light footsteps as they walked across the soft, neatly-trimmed grass of the Garden. He knew those footsteps anywhere, because he had spent many a day listening to those footsteps as they walked across the Garden lawn. He savored the sound, because he knew who they belonged to and what their presence here meant.

Yet Riuno did not let the good feelings he was experiencing distract him. He tightened his grip on the tree that he stood by, waiting for just the right moment to reveal himself to his lover, who sounded like she was making her way there.

Then he heard her voice whisper, as sweetly and softly as a cool breeze on a hot summer's day, "Riuno? Where are you?"

Riuno smiled before jumping out of his hiding place and landing in front of her. He held up his hands and shouted, "Boo!" startling the woman before him, who jumped backwards in shock, her hand on her chest and her expression as startled as a deer.

The woman standing before him had skin as pale as snow, with long dark hair that was as beautiful as midnight. But right now, she looked terrified, causing Riuno to laugh.

"Ha!" Riuno said. He pointed at her face. "Got you. You should see the look on your face. It's priceless."

The woman's beautiful face quickly turned from surprised to annoyance. "Riuno, you know I don't like it when you jump me like that. You know how strong I am. I could have reacted instinctively and broken your neck without even thinking about it. How would you feel then?"

Riuno shook his head. "Not very much, because I would be dead, but come on, you have to admit that it was a great prank. Better than the gag necklace I gave you that one time, right?"

Despite herself, the woman—whose name was Tananeen—smiled. "Or the time you and I scared that nasty old man who was being mean to the kids. He must have lost half of what little life he had left when he heard the growl of a dragon come from the throat of a young woman like myself."

Riuno chuckled at that. "Oh, yeah. I remember that. Or what about the time we took that bread, stuffed it with sand, and gave it to Sir Renas? He still doesn't accept any bread I offer to him, even if it doesn't have any sand in it."

Tananeen laughed, which made Riuno smile even more. "Yes, that was certainly amusing. Perhaps I was a little too hasty before. I should have been less offended by your prank and more amused."

"No, it's all right," said Riuno, waving off her apology. "But anyway, come in here with me. I don't want anyone seeing us together, because we're technically not supposed to be seeing each other."

Tananeen nodded and followed Riuno into the grove of trees where he had been hiding just moments before. As soon as they were hidden from view, Riuno took Tananeen into his arms and held her close as he could. She hugged him even more tightly, but not tightly enough to harm him with her immense strength.

"We never get to do this enough," said Riuno with a sigh. "One of the perils of being the King of Lamaira, I suppose."

Tananeen nodded again, her head rested against his chest. "Yes. But you know what your people would do if they know you and I were seeing each other. They would be angry, maybe even angry enough to kill me."

"That's because my people are foolish and narrow-minded," said Riuno as he ran his fingers through her beautiful hair. "They don't understand the bond between us. Maybe you are not entirely human, but I know that you are far more human than some of the other woman that my father has attempted to convince me to marry."

Tananeen chuckled. "And you are far braver and nobler than any of the Dracone males I've known. My mother has never understood why I don't seek a mate among my people, but then, she doesn't think very highly of humans in general. 'Weak and scrawny little things that need to wear the ores of the earth to protect themselves in combat,' she always says."

"You don't believe that, do you?" said Riuno, looking down at Tananeen with a questioning look.

Tananeen looked up at Riuno. Her green eyes were beautiful; they looked human, but behind them, Riuno saw a fire that existed in no ordinary human. It was a fire to match the fire in his own body, a fire he felt for her anytime he saw her or thought about her, a fire which would have made him fight for her life if she was ever in danger.

"I used to, before I met you," said Tananeen. She stroked his beard. "But then I learned that humans, while not as strong as my people, have the kind of fortitude and mental strength that I don't always see among Dracones. It's the kind of strength that helped you humans survive the earliest days of Creation, despite being surrounded by beings you cannot hope to match in terms of strength."

"Unfortunately, not all humans have that strength," said Riuno with a sigh. "Many humans are cowardly and easily frightened. They put on a show of strength, but cower at the slightest sign of danger. I feel nothing but pity for those fools, especially because I rule over a good chunk of them."

"But who cares about the cowards and deceivers?" said Tananeen. "What matters is that we're together and that we will always be together no matter what happens."

With that, Tananeen kissed Riuno. Riuno returned the kiss, which was warm and firm. But, despite how enjoyable it was, Riuno sensed a tenseness in Tananeen's lips and her body. He usually paid no attention to it, because their frequent trysts were always a little tense due to the fact that they were not supposed to be together. That actually added to the excitement of their secret meetings, but this tenseness, he could tell, was not due to excitement.

Pulling away from Tananeen, Riuno looked in her eyes and said, "What's the matter?"

Tananeen looked at Riuno in confusion. "What do you mean?"

"You seem worried about something," said Riuno. "I felt it in your body. Is something worrying you? Did you hear about some bad news that is making you worry for the future—*our* future, I should say?"

Tananeen looked away from Riuno, which was not a good sign. "I would say that it's nothing, but I know that you know me well enough by now to know when I'm lying. But I still don't want to talk about this with you, because if I do, I fear that you will be just as worried as I am, and I don't want you to worry about anything that you can't do anything about."

"I understand, Tana, but I want to share your burden with you, whatever it is," said Riuno. "We're lovers—and if it were acceptable to the people of Lamaira, we'd be spouses—and lovers share their worries and burdens with each other, no matter how heavy they may be."

Thankfully, Tananeen looked at Riuno again. Her eyes were full of worry, but that hardly detracted from their beauty. "I was talking with my mother a few weeks ago. She told me that she did not really approve of my relationship with you, that she wished I would pick out a handsome mate from among my people instead, and to forget about humanity."

Riuno rolled his eyes. "Doesn't you mother always say that? Honestly, I feel like I could make you the Queen of Lamaira, give you a castle of gold and a city of silver to rule over, and your mother would still insist that you marry another Dracone who lives in dirt and squalor and sees you as nothing more than a way to continue his own lineage. She's ridiculous."

"I know, but she's still my mother and I know that she only wants what's best for me, even if I don't always agree with it," said Tananeen. "But this time was a little different. She told me that, while she didn't really approve of our relationship, that she believed it might work out for the better in the end."

Riuno raised an eyebrow. "Really? Are you sure this is your mother we're talking about or is this a mimic who has taken her place? Because your mother has never approved of our relationship before."

"She told me that she senses an ancient evil rising," said Tananeen. "A deep evil, one that has been locked away for centuries. She says it's an evil that humans and Dracones once worked together to stop a long time ago, but now it is rising again and the only way to stop it is for humans and Dracones to work together again."

"Again?" Riuno said. "When have humans and Dracones ever worked together? We've always hated each other, even before my father drove your people out of Lamaira. And what is this 'ancient evil' she speaks of?"

"I don't know," said Tananeen, shaking her head. She held Riuno tighter, like she wanted him to protect her. "She just said that if you and I marry, then the humans and Dracones might stand a chance against this evil. She didn't say when or where it would rise, but she did say that to combat it, the combined might of humanity and the Dracones would be necessary to ensure the survival of both of our peoples."

"That's an odd thing for your human-hating mother to say," said Riuno. "In fact, I'd say that confirms my earlier theory that that wasn't your mother at all, but instead some malicious mimic who took your mother's form in order to confuse and frighten you, though for what reason, I cannot say."

Tananeen pushed him a little. "Stop that. My mother hasn't been replaced by any mimics. I don't think that anyone could mimic my mother very convincingly anyway, at least if they hoped to fool me."

"It was just a joke," said Riuno. "But I do find your mother's words curious nonetheless. And you know, I actually agree that we humans and Dracones would be better together. At least, I think you and I would be better together."

Tananeen smiled despite herself. "I know. But I'm still worried about what my mother said. Despite her prejudices, she is a wise woman and leader of my people. She knows more about the past than anyone and her ability to predict the future before it happens is almost uncanny."

"Well, I'm surprised that she did not see our love blooming, then, if her ability to predict the future is so good," said Riuno.

"Anyway, I still have some time before I need to return to my kingly duties. Why don't we spend that time doing a little less talking? We can worry about this 'ancient evil' later."

"All right," said Tananeen. She wrapped her arms around his neck and leaned in for another kiss.

Soon they both forgot about their worries and fears, for they were consumed by their passion for each other, a passion that overrode everything else at the moment. And when they stopped and went their separate ways for the day, Riuno soon forgot about what Tananeen's mother had said as the day's work consumed his focus, although deep in the back of his mind he worried about what Tananeen's mother's warning was and hoped that this ancient evil, whatever it was, would not rise during his reign at least.

# Chapter Two

*Forty years later ...*

A LOUD RUMBLING IN the sky above woke Keo. He sat up in his tent, blinking rapidly as the rumbling outside grew louder and louder. At first, he thought that it was a thunderstorm building—the sky had become grayer and cloudier the farther north that he and his friends traveled—but the rumbling didn't sound quite like lightning. It sounded more like the rumbling of a roar deep in the throat of some massive creature, which confused Keo, because he had been dreaming about that just moments before, though now he was wondering whether he had been dreaming that at all or if he had in fact been listening to the creature rumbling in his sleep.

But even now, sitting up in his tent, his legs covered by the blanket of his bedroll, Keo still believed that this might be a dream. Everything around him looked a little fuzzy, like it usually did in his dreams, so he thought that all he needed to do was go back to sleep and he could wake up again later.

Then, somewhere above his tent, he heard an earsplitting roar. A second later, the flap to his tent opened and Dlaine—one of his traveling companions—stuck his head through it. The older man's hair was messy, like he had just woken up, and there was an urgency in his eyes that told Keo that this was no dream.

"Dlaine?" said Keo, yawning and rubbing the sleep out of his eyes. "What was that?"

"A dragon," said Dlaine. His face was pale. "A *big* one, too."

Keo's eyes widened. "A dragon? I thought we wouldn't see any Dracones until we got deeper into the Upper Mountains."

"Same here, but there's one flying above our heads at the moment and it seems angry," said Dlaine. "Just grab Gildshine. You're going to need it."

With that, Dlaine pulled his head out of the tent. Keo immediately grabbed his magical sword, Gildshine, which lay in its sheath to his right. He crawled out of the tent as quickly as he could and stood up, drawing Gildshine from its sheath as he did so.

The cold air of the Upper Mountains hit him hard, making him shiver, but Keo tried to ignore it as he looked up at the gray sky above. At first, he did not see anything out of the ordinary due to the thick cloud cover, but then a dragon swooped out of the clouds.

It was indeed a big dragon. Keo had only seen one dragon before, and he had thought it quite large, but this one was easily twice as large as that dragon. This one had crimson scales and wings as wide as a lake. Large spikes ran along its back and tail and its mouth was large enough that it could probably snap Keo in half with no effort if it wanted. Its eyes glowed orange, like fire, and its talons looked as sharp as swords.

But the dragon was visible for only a moment before returning to the clouds above out of sight. Still, Keo kept Gildshine out, mostly because he doubted that the dragon had decided to leave them alone.

Then someone shouted, "Keo!" and Keo looked down to see Maryal, Dlaine, and Easan running toward him. Maryal wore her Magician's robes, as she always did, though they looked like they had been hastily thrown on, no doubt because she had been awakened just as abruptly as he had. Dlaine also looked a little frazzled, while Easan seemed to be the only one who hadn't been awakened abruptly, at least if the state of his long, dark hair was any indication. Keo figured Jola was also among them, but he could not see her due to her constant invisibility.

Keo's friends stopped a few feet from him, prompting Keo to say, "Are any of you hurt?"

"No," said Maryal, shaking her head and yawning. She looked up at the sky, but the dragon was still hidden from view in the clouds. "But that dragon is still there and it will probably try to kill us if we don't fight it off."

"How long has it been there?" said Keo, glancing up at the sky again.

"I don't know," said Maryal, shaking her head. "It just appeared out of nowhere a few minutes ago. It must have been hiding in the mountains or something."

"Do you think it was following us?" said Keo.

"I doubt it," said Dlaine with a snort. "How can something that big have followed us without us noticing?"

"The Dracones are said to have magic that humans don't," said Keo. "But regardless, we need to try to talk with it. If it hasn't attacked us yet, then maybe that means it doesn't want to kill us."

"Talk with it?" said Easan, staring at Keo in disbelief. "Did you hear its roar? It's a monster. I imagine the only reason it hasn't attacked us yet is because we woke up and ruined its surprise attack."

Keo sighed. "Easan, remember, the whole reason we're here is to establish an alliance with the Dracones. If we attack it, that won't make us look good in the eyes of its people."

Easan folded his arms across his chest. "So what are you saying, that we just stand here and wait for it to come down and have a nice chat?"

"I'm saying we try to talk with him," said Keo. "And we attack only if it attacks—"

Keo was interrupted by another roar and, in the next instant, the red dragon flew down straight to the earth. As it flew toward them, it opened its mouth and unleashed a stream of blazing fire at them, causing Keo to shout, "Separate!"

Everyone ran in a different direction as the dragon's fire breath cut a large swath through their camp. Keo's tent was burned into ashes and those ashes were crushed when the dragon landed hard on top of them, scattering the ashes to the wind as it turned around to face Keo.

Up close, the dragon was even larger than it had been from a distance. The dragon easily towered over Keo, making him feel small, but he did not run or show any fear toward it even as smoke rose from its nostrils and muscles rippled under its skin.

Holding Gildshine before him, Keo said, "Dragon! We are not your enemies. We came because we wished to speak with—"

Again, Keo was interrupted, but this time, it was not by the dragon, but by a large burst of golden flames flying over his head and striking the dragon in the face. The golden flames hardly left a scratch on the dragon's face, but it shook its head anyway and let out a deep growl from its throat that told Keo that it wasn't happy about that sudden attack.

Keo risked a glance over his shoulder to see Easan standing there, aiming his own sword, Shadowbane, at the dragon. Shadowbane was covered in those same golden flames and it wasn't hard for Keo to guess that Easan had shot those at the dragon.

"Easan!" Keo said. "What are you even thinking?"

"What?" said Easan. "Didn't you say we could fight back if it attacked us?"

Keo ground his teeth. More than once over their two month journey to the Upper Mountains, Easan had shown this same kind of annoying attitude that seemed designed to annoy Keo more than anything. Keo was still not sure if Easan was behaving dense on purpose or if he was genuinely confused about it, but he had no time to dwell on his frustrations with Easan at the moment, because a loud roar in front of him caused him to look at the dragon again just in time to see burning flame rising from the dragon's throat.

Instinctively, Keo jumped to the side as the dragon unleashed another fiery stream of destruction. Easan also dodged it, but unlike Keo, he responded by firing another burst of golden fire. This also hit the dragon, causing it to shake its head again and glare at Easan.

"That's right," Easan shouted, waving Shadowbane at the dragon mockingly. "*I* hit you, so why don't you come over here and fight me like a man? I can take you. I can take anything."

Rising from the dirt, Keo watched as the dragon turned to face

Easan. Keo immediately knew that there was no way that Easan could beat the dragon on his own, which made him wonder why Easan seemed obsessed with fighting it by himself.

*He must be suicidal or something,* Keo thought.

But again, he had to ignore those thoughts for now. He raised Gildshine, which caught fire with its own golden flames, and shot his own burst of fire at the dragon. His flames hit the dragon's head, but had about the same effect as Easan's; that is, they succeeded only in angering the dragon, which turned its head to look at Keo now.

Then Maryal appeared out of nowhere and unleashed a large blast of wind at the dragon. The wind blast struck the dragon in the side, which actually made it stagger slightly, but rather than shoot Maryal with its fire, it swiped at her with its long tail. Maryal shot a blast of wind under her feet, sending her flying into the sky above the dragon's tail, which swept under her without even touching her. Then Maryal landed on the ground gracefully, but retreated from the dragon, which was clearly too strong for her spells to harm.

Now the dragon was looking in every direction, trying to focus on Keo, Easan, and Maryal at once. It seemed unable to decide who was the bigger threat, which was good, because that gave them more time to figure out a way to beat it. Not that Keo could think of a way to beat it, however, because the dragon seemed completely immune to all of their attacks.

Then Keo heard Jola's voice in his head say, *Keo, Dlaine and I have figured out a way to beat the dragon. Just draw it away from the camp toward the nearest valley.*

An image appeared in Keo's mind of the valley that was

behind him. It was a little ways away from where he stood, but he knew that he could lure the dragon there. In fact, knew that he had to, because he was quite sure at this point that the dragon was not in any mood to talk to any of them.

*All right,* Keo said. *What are you guys going to do to defeat it?*

*You'll see,* said Jola. *Just get its attention and we'll do the rest.*

Keo didn't like doing plans without knowing the full details, but with the dragon slowly getting over its confusion, he decided that he would just have to trust that Jola and Dlaine knew what they were doing.

So Keo pointed Gildshine at the dragon and shouted, "Hey! Come after me, you ugly beast!" and fired a larger than normal blast of fire at the dragon, striking it dead on in the face.

Once more, the dragon roared in anger, but this time, it wasn't confused about who to attack. Keo immediately ran toward the narrow valley where Jola had directed him. He heard the dragon running after him, its massive feet creating tremors in the ground with every step, but he didn't stop to look over his shoulder at it because he might slow down and right now he was doing all he could to keep ahead of the dragon. Unfortunately, he could hear the dragon gaining behind him, which was bad because Keo could not run any faster than he was now.

As he ran, Keo glanced up at the valley ahead. It was fairly narrow, though Keo would have no trouble passing through it. The dragon might have to slow down, although it might also just need to fold its wings closed against its back. Keo wasn't sure what Dlaine and Jola were planning, but he gave it no more thought because he heard the dragon's roar again, which sounded far too close now for comfort.

Keo dashed through the short and narrow valley and passed through to the other side quickly. The dragon, on the other hand, rammed straight into the valley, but got stuck. It hissed and growled as it attempted to free itself, but before the dragon could do anything else, a couple of loud explosions went off on the mountain peaks on either side. The dragon looked up just as two massive rock slides rolled across the mountain's face toward it, but the dragon couldn't dodge it.

The rock slides fell with an earsplitting crash onto the dragon, knocking it down to its belly and causing it to roar in agony and anger. But the dragon's roars were nothing more than angry sounds, because the dragon was trapped by the narrow valley and the enormous amount of rock and dirt that covered its body. It struggled hard against the trap, but despite the dragon's obvious physical strength, it couldn't even budge the rocks and dirt piled on top of it.

Still, Keo kept a good distance from it, because the dragon had a long neck and could still breathe fire if it so chose. He wasn't sure how far its fire breathe ranged, but he didn't want to find out.

Then Keo heard someone running to him and looked to his right to see Dlaine running toward him. Dlaine stopped a few feet from Keo and rested his hands on his knees, panting as he did so, like he had run a mile.

"Where were you?" said Keo, looking at Dlaine in confusion.

"Helping Jola make sure that her plan worked, of course," said Dlaine. He stood up, dusting off the shoulders of his coat, and glanced at the dragon, which was still preoccupied with freeing itself. "Looks like it did. Smart girl, as always."

"What did she do, exactly?" said Keo. "I heard some explosions and saw the rock slides happen, but I don't quite follow what happened."

"Exactly what you saw," said Dlaine. He gestured at the mountainsides where the rock slides had fallen from. "Jola used her magic to set two explosive spells for when that dragon would attempt to pass through the valley. She designed the spells to send the maximum amount of rocks and dirt falling down on the dragon, which I estimate to be a ton or two."

"So the dragon is stuck and won't be able to escape?" said Keo, glancing at the dragon, which was still too distracted by the rocks and dirt covering it to focus on Keo or Dlaine.

"We don't know for sure because we don't really know how strong the dragon is," said Dlaine. "But clearly, since it hasn't escaped yet, I think it's safe to say that it won't be able to escape for a while."

Keo sighed in relief. "That's good to know. Now we just need to figure out how to communicate with it so we can—"

Keo was interrupted by the sound of shifting rock, causing him to look at the dragon. It was trying to stand up, trying to move the rock and dirt off of its body, and actually seemed to be having some success. Keo and Dlaine watched as the dragon twisted and turned its body, each movement dislodging more and more rocks, until the dragon jerked forward and broke through the remaining rocks and dirt with a roar of triumph.

"Shit," said Dlaine. He looked at Keo. "Run?"

"Run," said Keo.

The two turned and ran, giving them a head start on the

dragon, but that head start turned out to be useless, because the dragon flew overhead and then landed in their path. Keo and Dlaine skid to a stop, but before they could turn to run back the way they came, the dragon's long tail appeared behind them, effectively trapping them between the dragon's head and its tail.

Keo fired another burst of golden flame at the dragon, but the dragon dodged it. Smoke rose from the dragon's nostrils as it prepared to fire its burning breathe at them, but there was nowhere for Keo or Dlaine to run now.

Keo looked at Dlaine. "Any ideas?"

"Nope," said Dlaine, shaking his head, though he raised his fists anyway. "Except try not to get turned into this thing's dinner."

Keo gulped and looked up at the dragon. Its throat was lighting up due to the flame building up inside it, which Keo knew would kill them instantly if they did not avoid it. Yet there was no way they could escape and he had just about given up hope before the roar of another dragon split the air suddenly.

A second later, a second dragon—this one smaller and black, in contrast to the crimson of the first dragon—clamped its teeth around the red dragon's neck and yanked it backwards. The red dragon choked, but despite being bigger and stronger than the other dragon, it allowed itself to be pulled away from Keo and Dlaine. The black dragon threw the red dragon to the ground, but the red dragon got back up on its feet and snarled at the black dragon.

"Where the hell did *that* dragon come from?" said Dlaine, looking around in confusion. "I didn't even hear it coming."

Keo, however, was too busy watching the two dragons as they

snarled and growled at each other. The black dragon looked very familiar to Keo, but he could not remember where he might have seen it until he saw its green eyes and the memories came roaring back to the forefront of his mind.

"Dlaine!" said Keo, looking at Dlaine in excitement. "That's the Dracone woman from Tain, the one who killed Aster and Shadow."

"It is?" said Dlaine, looking at the black dragon in surprise. "By golly, I'd say you're right. That looks just like her, though she looks even nastier now than she did back there."

Dlaine wasn't kidding. The black dragon was snarling and hissing at the red dragon, who despite being larger than her, she did not seem to fear at all. The two dragons circled each other, their nostrils smoking, as they looked for an opening in which to strike down the other.

Then the red dragon suddenly launched forward, but the black dragon ducked, allowing the red dragon to soar over her head. The red dragon fell with a crash onto the ground, but before it could get back up, the black dragon was on top of it. She slammed her fore claws into the red dragon's neck, keeping its head down as the red dragon struggled to break free, but it was clear that she had it in a headlock that it couldn't free itself from no matter what.

The red dragon tried to raise its head, but the black dragon slammed it back down and snarled. This time, however, Keo thought he understood that the black dragon was telling the red dragon to stay down and stop fighting. It wasn't like he was translating its snarls into Lamairan, but he found himself understanding the basic idea nonetheless.

"Is she trying to kill him?" said Dlaine. "Not that I'm complaining, but she certainly looks like that's what she's trying to do."

Keo shook his head. "Not kill him, no. Just get him to submit to her authority."

Dlaine looked at Keo, a puzzled look on his face. "How do you know that? Are you a dragon whisperer now or something?"

Keo rolled his eyes. "She hasn't dealt him any mortal blows yet. If she was trying to kill him, he would be dead already. It's pretty obvious to me."

"Well, it ain't obvious to me," said Dlaine. "But I'll take your word for it."

The red dragon tried to get up again, but as before, the black dragon slammed his head down and let out an inhumanly loud hiss that made Keo's arm hairs stand up on end. The red dragon froze completely when it heard the black dragon's hiss, which then turned into a much softer growl, although it still made Keo a lot more wary of the black dragon than he had been before.

Then, before Keo and Dlaine's startled eyes, the red dragon and the black dragon started to change. Their bodies shrunk, their wings retracted into their bodies, and their long snouts pulled back into their faces.

In seconds, the two dragons had been replaced by two humans. One of them was the Dracone woman who, with her black hair, robes, and pale skin, looked the same as she had back in Tain, while the other one under her foot was a young man in red armor who looked annoyed at being pinned to the ground.

Then the Dracone woman looked at Keo and Dlaine and smiled. "Long time, no see, Keo. And welcome to the Upper

Mountains, the home of the Dracones, though I wish I could have welcomed you here in a far less confrontational way."

# Chapter Three

S EE?" SAID KEO TO Dlaine, a satisfied smile on his face. "It is her, like I said."

"When did I ever doubt that?" said Dlaine. He looked at the Dracone woman, whose foot was still planted firmly on the back of the young man on the ground. "Thanks for saving us."

"It was no problem," said the Dracone woman with a shrug. She nodded at the sullen young man underfoot. "Veta here didn't know who you and your friends were. He's never seen any of you before and has only seen a few humans in his life, so please excuse him for attacking you like that."

"I was only doing my duty," the young Dracone man, named Veta, snapped from underneath her foot. "Protecting the clan from invading humans when you interrupted me."

"Five humans is hardly what I'd call an invading force," said the Dracone woman. Then her eyes narrowed and she said, in a far more threatening voice, "And don't speak so disrespectfully to me again, youngling. You know how you are supposed to behave toward your elders."

"I also know how I am supposed to behave toward human-lovers," the Dracone man muttered, though Keo heard him just fine.

An inhuman growl emitted from the Dracone woman's throat and she pressed down harder on the man's back, causing him to shout, "Ow! I am sorry. I did not mean to insult the Dragon Princess so. Please let me go. I will not harm the humans, nor will I insult you or treat you with disrespect ever again."

The Dracone woman looked skeptical of Veta's promise, but then she nodded and said, "Very well. When we return to the Nest, I will inform your parents about your disrespectful behavior and let them determine the appropriate punishment for a youngling as disrespectful as yourself."

Based on Veta's sullen silence, Keo guessed that the Dracones did not give light punishments to younglings who disrespected their elders.

As the Dracone woman removed her foot from the back of Veta, Keo heard people running toward him and looked to his left to see Maryal and Easan running toward him and Dlaine. They stopped a couple of feet away from them, with Maryal looking tired from the running, while Easan looked ready for battle.

"Where's the dragon, Keo?" said Easan, looking in every direction, with Shadowbane in both hands, though its flames were out at the moment. "We heard the rock slides and saw it escape, but didn't see where it went. Did it fly back into the clouds again?"

Keo shook his head and pointed at Veta, who was rising to his feet and dusting dirt off his red armor. "That's the dragon."

Easan looked over at Veta and frowned. "But that doesn't look like a dragon at all. Are you trying to fool me or something?"

"He's a Dracone," said Dlaine. He nodded at the Dracone woman. "Like her, who I'm sure you recognize."

Maryal gasped when she saw the Dracone woman, though it was a happy gasp rather than a scared one. "Hey, it's her! Where did she come from?"

"She saved us," said Keo. He gestured at Veta. "Stopped the younger dragon from killing us and forced him to take on a human form."

"Then this is the perfect opportunity to kill him," said Easan. He raised Shadowbane. "He's probably easier to kill in human form than in dragon form, I bet."

Keo glared at Easan. "No. We are not killing him or the woman. She's already made him promise not to harm us. Remember, we came here to *talk* with the Dracones, not kill them."

Easan looked highly disappointed by that, but he lowered Shadowbane and said, "All right. But if he tries to attack us, then I'll take his head clean off his shoulders."

"With a toy like that?" said Veta, who Keo had not noticed approaching them with the Dracone woman by his side. He sneered at Shadowbane. "You humans are truly delusional. Even in my human form, it would take a much larger and stronger blade than that to even scratch me."

Easan glared at Veta, while Keo observed the youngling more closely. Veta was a tall and muscular young man in appearance, perhaps a few years older than Keo at most. In contrast to the Dracone woman's black robes, he wore plated red armor that looked like the scales of his dragon form. The gauntlets of his armor were tipped with claws, just like the claws of his dragon form, and his body radiated heat that Keo felt even from a distance. He looked capable of smashing boulders with his fists and didn't seem to carry any weapons, which made sense, because Veta's dragon form was probably the only weapon he needed. Veta was also bald, though that did not take away from his strong appearance.

"Again, welcome to the Upper Mountains," said the Dracone woman as she and Veta approached. She bowed at them, which caused Veta to look rather offended, though she didn't look at him as she stood up. "I am pleased to see that you made it to these Mountains unharmed. Was your journey north dangerous?"

"Not really," said Keo. "We didn't run into any demons along the way and mostly took known routes, though climbing the Mountains themselves has been hard due to how steep they are. The only problem was crossing the Bloody Gorge, but we managed to cross it without any casualties."

"You will have to tell us all about your adventures sometime," said the Dracone woman. "But I forgot that you have not introduced yourselves to Veta yet."

"All right," said Keo. He looked at Veta and pointed at himself and each one of his friends as he spoke. "I'm Keo and this is Dlaine, Maryal, Easan, and Jola, but Jola is invisible, so if you can't see her, that's why."

Veta's eyes narrowed. "Did you say your name was Keo?"

Keo blinked. "Yes, I did. Why? Have you heard the name before?"

"It's a word in the Dracone language that means 'miracle,'" said Veta. "But why does a human have a Dracone name? It is an insult to the pride of our clan."

"Hey, I didn't name myself," said Keo in annoyance. "My parents did, and because they're dead, I can't ask them why they named me after a word from your language, either."

Veta still looked offended by the idea that a human was running around with a name from his language, but he didn't press the issue further. The Dracone woman, on the other hand, looked heartbroken for a moment before her normal expression returned, which made Keo wonder what she had been so worried about before.

Veta looked at the Dracone woman with disapproval. "Dracone Princess, how do you know these humans? They have never been here before."

"I met them in the human city of Tain a couple months ago," said the Dracone woman. "I suppose I forgot to tell you about that."

"Oh, I know all about your excursions into the human lands, Princess," said Veta. He wrinkled his nose, like he smelled something awful. "I also know that the Queen doesn't approve of them at all. But I didn't realize that you had actually interacted with the humans there. I thought that you simply observed humans because of your strange fascination with them."

The Dracone woman's expression turned hard for a second before she shook her head and said, "I know what the Queen thinks of my excursions and I have already made it clear to her over the years that I don't care."

Veta snorted, causing smoke to rise from his nostrils. "Weren't you just lecturing me about showing respect to my elders a few minutes ago?"

The Dracone woman growled at Veta again, that same inhuman growl that she always made, which caused Veta to step back. "Know your place, youngling."

"Fine, fine," said Veta with a shrug. "But when the Queen demands to know who let these humans into our territory, I'll make sure that she'll know that you are responsible."

"You seem to have mistaken me for someone who cares," said the Dracone woman, her tone icy.

"Wait a minute," said Keo, before Veta could respond. He pointed at the Dracone woman. "Are you royalty? Because Veta just called you the Dracone Princess."

"Yes, I am," said the Dracone woman, nodding, although she didn't sound excited about it. "I'm the daughter of Queen Sayot, the current matriarch and leader of the Dracones."

"What is your name?" said Keo. "You never told it to us back in Tain. Can you tell it to us now?"

The Dracone woman hesitated, like she was deciding whether or not Keo and his friends could be trusted with a deep secret known only to a chosen few, but then she said, "Tananeen. My name is Tananeen."

Keo nodded. "Tananeen … got it."

The way Tananeen looked at Keo, it seemed like she was expecting him to recognize the name, but Keo had never heard it in all of his life. And based on the expressions of the others, his friends had never heard it, either. He wondered why Tananeen expected him to know the name, because he had not known any other Dracones until he met her just a couple of months ago and therefore did not know anyone else with Dracone names (aside from himself, and he didn't even know the origin of his name until literally a few minutes ago).

"Will you be taking us to the rest of your people?" asked Maryal. "After all, the whole reason we came here was because we wanted to offer an alliance with your people."

Veta made a face like he was sick to his stomach. "Form an alliance? Between humans and Dracones?" He looked at Tananeen in annoyance. "When did you agree to that?"

"I told them to come here to speak with us about forming an alliance in order to battle the demons," said Tananeen, "who will rise again in two months' time unless we can stop them before then."

Veta shook his head. "I know that the demons are returning, but I am skeptical that an alliance with humans would be wise, given our ... history with them."

"It will, if we do it right," said Tananeen. "What you don't realize is that Keo here is the next King of Lamaira. He has no ill intentions for our people."

Veta looked at Keo with deep skepticism in his dragon-like eyes. "None of the stories I've heard ever describe humans as being kind to us Dracones, except for the Human King."

"Who?" said Keo.

"You call him the Good King in your language," said Tananeen. "We call him the Human King because he is the only human king who is listed in our oral histories, the only one who has ever left a significant impact on our people."

"Aside from the Murderer, of course," said Veta in a disgusted voice.

"Who?" said Keo, glancing at his friends in confusion, although they seemed just as confused as he was.

"We'll tell you more about that later," said Tananeen. "For now, you can follow us to the Nest, where the rest of our people are."

Veta growled in surprise. "What? Princess Tananeen, you do remember that humans are not allowed in the Nest, don't you?"

"I know, but I don't care," said Tananeen. She gestured at Keo and his friends. "If our people are going to survive the upcoming war with the demons, then we will have to be willing to put aside even our most ancient of laws and traditions if that will ensure our survival as a species. And if the Queen has any problems with that, then she can bring it up with me."

Veta looked like he wanted to argue the point further, but then he shook his head and mumbled something in a language that Keo did not recognize.

But Maryal, who was rubbing her hands together like she always did whenever she was anxious, said, "We aren't going to be meals for your people, are we, Tananeen?"

"No," said Tananeen, shaking her head. "I will protect all of you from any Dracones who may wish to harm you. Our traditions might state that humans are never allowed in the Nest, but my fellow Dracones respect my authority too much to try to harm those I have put under my protection."

Veta snorted again, earning him a glare from Tananeen, but she said nothing. That made Keo wonder whether the rest of the Dracones actually respected Tananeen's authority or not. He hoped that they did, because if they didn't, then he had a feeling that he and the others were going to be someone's dinner tonight.

"Anyway, the others have no doubt noticed our absence by now, so let us go before the Queen sends anyone to find us," said Tananeen. She turned around and gestured for Keo and his friends to follow. "Follow me and Veta. The Nest isn't far from here, but it is hard to find if you are not a Dracone, so just stick close to us until we get there."

With that, Tananeen started walking north. Veta glared at Keo one last time before turning to follow Tananeen, and soon Keo and his friends were following the two Dracones, though they kept a respectful distance from Veta just to be safe.

# Chapter Four

THE PATH TO THE Nest took them higher up into the mountains, where the air became thinner and thinner, although Keo wasn't as badly affected by it as the others. Dlaine and Maryal both looked rather sick, while Easan was putting on a strong face, although with the way his lips trembled at the edges, Keo knew that he was just faking it. He could not see or hear Jola, but he doubted she looked much better.

Tananeen and Veta, of course, did not seem sick at all. They walked along the rocky, twisting pathway without showing even the slightest bit of concern about how high they were going. Keo supposed that, because they were both Dracones, they could fly if they accidentally fell, though he still felt a bit worried that they might fall if they weren't careful just the same.

Not only that, but the air became colder the higher they went. Keo and his friends had been told by the Keepers back in Tain that the Upper Mountains were known for their cold weather, which was why they all wore warm clothing, but even with their wool shirts and thick coats, the cold air made Keo shiver. Again, neither Tananeen nor Veta seemed bothered by it, but Keo assumed that the Dracones constantly generated heat in their bodies at all times, which explained why the cold did not seem to bother them. He still wondered why the Dracones lived here in the Upper Mountains, though, because he doubted that the Dracones liked the cold that much.

Up and up they went, walking along the very rough, almost unnoticeable path to the Nest. Tananeen said that this path had not been used in decades because very few humans ever came this way, while the Dracones almost exclusively flew from the Nest whenever they needed to leave it or flew back into it when returning from a trip or hunting expedition. Veta actually seemed surprised to learn that there was a path for humans to reach the Upper Mountains, as if he had never been told about it before, which was a sign of just how unused it was.

As they climbed higher, Keo noticed various hints that there were dragons nearby. Spots of blackened earth, created by dragon fire, were everywhere, though none of them particularly recent based on how cold they were. Sheep and goat bones were scattered here and there, most likely leftover from meals that the dragons ate, while deep claw marks in the earth showed that at least a few dragons had been here. Some of the marks were even bigger than Veta's claws in his dragon form, which made Keo wonder just how large Dracones could grow. He had thought that Veta represented the upper size of what Dracones could grow to, yet if these claw marks were correct, then there was at least one other Dracone that was much larger than Veta. Keo just hoped that this Dracone was dead, because he didn't relish the thought of running into a Dracone that was larger and possibly unfriendlier than Veta.

Eventually, they reached a large set of iron gates that looked very old, like they had been constructed ages ago. The gates were built into a narrow space between the Mountains, almost like they were a part of the Mountains themselves. Huge, thick chains ran through the gates' handles, chains that were as thick as Keo's bicep, if not more so. The gates themselves had images of dragons carved into them, although many of them were either faded from years of exposure to the elements or covered in rust.

As they approached the gates, Veta raised a hand and said, "I'll knock these gates down. No need to mess with the lock."

But Tananeen grabbed Veta's arm and glared at him. "No. We will not knock down the gates created by our ancestors. Unless you want to put them back up yourself, of course."

Based on Veta's reluctant expression, Keo guessed that Veta didn't know how to fix the gates if he broke them.

"Fine," said Veta, wrenching his arm out of Tananeen's grasp and glaring at her. "Then why don't we transform into dragons and fly them over the gates instead?"

"Because that is not how humans are supposed to enter the Nest," said Tananeen. "And I do not want a human riding me, anyway, at least not without the proper safety equipment, which we don't have."

"Hey, now that I think about it, why didn't you just fly us to the Upper Mountains when you were back in Tain?" said Keo, causing Tananeen and Veta to look at him over their shoulders. "Wouldn't that have been faster than having us walk across the Old Kingdom and much of the Upper Mountains, too?"

"As I said, I lack the saddles and other things you would need to fly comfortably on my back," said Tananeen. "Flying is dangerous for humans anyway. It was much safer for you to travel on foot."

"Why is flying so dangerous for humans?" said Keo. He gulped. "Because we could fall off your back?"

Tananeen's expression darkened. "Let's just say that there are things in the sky that even we Dracones have to look out for, and leave it at that."

Keo glanced up at the sky, but all he saw was the dark clouds that looked like they were about to either rain or snow. He wondered what kind of things could live in the sky that could be so dangerous to beings as powerful as Dracones, but decided that it was one of those things in life that he didn't need to worry about. Instead, he decided to be grateful that those things, whatever they were, had not yet decided to come down from the sky to terrorize humanity.

Then Keo looked at Tananeen as she walked up to the gates. She raised her hands before the gates and spread them wide.

A second later, the massive chains rumbled and parted by themselves, which was a strange sight to behold. In seconds, the gates were unchained, allowing Veta—who appeared hardly impressed by the sight of the chains moving on their own—to pull open the gates. They looked extremely heavy, and indeed, Veta struggled at first to open them, though Keo thought it was less to do with the gates' weight and more to do with the fact that they had not been opened in a long time and were therefore probably quite rusted.

Nonetheless, Veta succeeded in pulling them open with a loud creaking sound that made Keo and his friends cringe. Once the gates were open wide enough, Tananeen gestured for them to follow her and Veta, who passed through the gates without another word. Keo exchanged concerned looks with his friends, but since Tananeen had said she would protect them from her fellow Dracones, Keo led his friends through the open gates and onto the other side.

Upon passing through the gates, Keo stopped and looked down at the large valley that spread out before them. So did the others, who all looked surprised at what they saw.

Down below, spreading out for quite a ways, was a valley full of dragons. Large stone pillars rose from the earth, their tips full of nests that appeared to have gigantic eggs in them. Many of these pillars had dragons sitting upon them, dragons which were about the same size as Tananeen's own dragon form, although their colors and wings looked different. Their colors ranged from black to brown to red and even blue and green in one case and most of them appeared to be adults, although Keo spotted a few baby dragons poking their heads out from underneath the safety of their mothers' wings.

On the valley walls were massive cave openings that appeared to have been carved out of the rock. Dragons—again, mostly females from what Keo could see, though he saw a few males as well—flew in and out of those caves, which he assumed were more nests. He saw one female dragon carrying a dead goat in her mouth, which she dropped into the mouths of her hungry babies, which immediately started fighting over the dead goat, tearing the corpse apart with their tiny teeth and claws as easily as if it was made of paper.

There were a few dragons on the floor of the valley, but they appeared to be adolescents, because they did not look as large or as well-developed as the adults that flew or sat in their nests. Two of the adolescent dragons were wrestling with each other, snapping and clawing at each other's hides, but none of the adults bothered to break them up, perhaps because that was considered normal behavior for growing dragons like them.

At the other end of the valley was a huge cave mouth, but Keo did not know what lay inside it. All he knew was that the other dragons kept a respectful distance from the huge cave mouth, as if they were afraid of whatever was inside it. That made Keo hope that they would not go into that cave.

"Here we are," said Tananeen, spreading her hands as if to encompass the entire valley. "The Nest of the Dracones, our home and our country, where we have lived for decades."

"Wow," said Maryal, watching the dragons with wide eyes. "I didn't realize that so many Dracones still existed."

Tananeen lowered her hands and a frown appeared across her face. "Unless we act quickly, I am afraid that they will not."

Keo nodded, understanding that Tananeen was talking about the demons. He didn't see how the demons could possibly pose a threat to the Dracones, seeing as the Dracones were so powerful and strong, but perhaps the demons were stronger than they appeared or they knew of the Dracones' weakness, whatever that was.

"How many Dracones are there?" said Easan, though unlike Maryal, he was looking at the Nest with wariness, like he expected the entire valley to attack them.

"Five hundred, with slightly over six hundred infants and unborn," said Tananeen. "It is a small number from our heyday, when we numbered in the thousands and lived all across Lamaira, but we are a strong and united people regardless."

Keo looked at Tananeen in shock. "You mean there used to be

thousands of Dracones in Lamaira? What happened to them?"

"You mean you honestly don't know?" said Veta in disbelief. "Didn't your people tell you about what you did to us?"

Keo was about to say no, but then Tananeen held up a hand to interrupt him and he nodded at her to speak.

"That is something I will tell you more about later," said Tananeen. She nodded at the massive cave mouth on the other end of the Nest. "For now, we must go to Queen Sayot so you may speak with her about forming that alliance we spoke of earlier."

"Did you tell her that we are coming?" said Keo. "Have you already spoken with her about it?"

Tananeen scowled suddenly and looked back toward the cavern on the other side of the valley, as if she was remembering some bad memories. "No, but my mother will see you anyway. I will *make* her see you, whether she wants to or not."

"If I recall correctly, hasn't the Queen said that she wants nothing to do with humans?" said Veta. "Unless you plan to offer them to her as a meal, of course."

"My mother always listens to me, no matter what," said Tananeen. "And don't you dare suggest that I feed them to her. I would never feed the last hope of our people to my mother or any of the other dragons in this valley. If you even joke about that in front of me again, I will make sure you never joke again."

Veta said nothing in response to that, although his demeanor became more sullen than ever. He just said, "Do I have to go with you? Or can I go back to my nest?"

"Do what you want," said Tananeen, waving in a random direction. "I don't care. Just don't harm Keo or his friends while they're here."

Veta nodded and, in an instant, transformed into his dragon form again and took off into the sky. The wind created by his wings taking off blew Keo's hair around and sent dust into his eyes and lungs, making him and his friends, who also got dust in their lungs, cough, while Tananeen just watched as Veta flew toward one of the openings in the valley walls.

"What do we do now?" said Maryal, who was readjusting her robes, which had messed up by the gust of wind created by Veta's wings.

"Meet my mother the Queen, of course," said Tananeen, pointing at the cave on the other end of the Nest. "She lives in that cave. She doesn't come out anymore due to her old age. We'll have to go in to meet her."

"And you are certain she'll want to see us?" said Keo.

"I don't know if she'll *want* to, but I will make sure that she does regardless," said Tananeen. "Unlike Veta, my mother is less prejudiced against humans, though she still does not like them very much."

Dlaine gulped when he looked down into the valley. "Are we going to have to walk across the valley to get there? With all of those dragons flying around and watching us?"

"We will, but don't worry, they know better than to attack any humans under my protection," said Tananeen. "Now come. We have no time to lose, because every minute we spend here is another minute that we don't spend crafting the alliance between humans and Dracones that will be necessary for the survival of both our peoples."

With that, Tananeen walked down into the valley, and Keo and his friends followed her again. This time, they followed her more closely than before, because none of them felt safe among the large, deadly-looking dragons that were present in the valley. Keo did, however, briefly wonder about why they had not run into any demons since leaving Tain two months ago, but decided that the demons had probably not gotten this far north yet and hopefully never would, if Queen Sayot agreed to the human/Dracone alliance.

As they walked across the valley floor, the other Dracones started to take notice of the visitors. Dozens of large, glowing eyes followed Keo and the others as they made their way to the Queen's cave on the other end of the Nest. Mother dragons sitting on their nests crouched low over their unborn and babies, as if to protect them from the humans, while the male dragons flew high overhead or hissed and snarled from a distance. None of the dragons appeared likely to attack Keo or any of his friends, probably because they were being led by Tananeen, but Keo kept his hand on Gildshine's hilt anyway, even though he knew that Gildshine wouldn't be of much use against five hundred full-grown dragons. Easan, also kept his hand on Shadowbane's hilt, but unlike Keo, his hand was wrapped firmly around the sword's hilt, like he intended to draw it at some point.

They passed by the two wrestling younglings that Keo had seen earlier, who immediately stopped wrestling when they passed. One of the younglings—which had green scales and a long, whip-like tail—stepped forward as if to investigate Keo and the others, but Tananeen glared and growled at them, causing both younglings to turn and fly away immediately. But Keo noticed that the two did not leave entirely; instead, they followed Tananeen, Keo, and his friends from a safe distance.

As they walked, Keo picked up the pace until he was walking by Tananeen's side and said, "Tananeen? Can I ask a question?"

"Yes?" said Tananeen, glancing at him as they walked. She seemed oblivious to the glares and threatening looks from the other dragons, though perhaps she was just ignoring them. "What is it?"

"I've noticed that Dracones can change form, from human to dragon and back again," said Keo. "But I don't see any other Dracones in their human form aside from you in here. Why is that?"

Tananeen frowned, like Keo had just stepped into a sore subject. "Most of us Dracones find our human forms weak and inefficient, particularly for the harsh weather of the Upper Mountains. I mean, of course, even in our human forms, we are much stronger than normal humans, but most of the time we prefer our dragon forms due to their strength and resilience."

"Oh," said Keo. He glanced up at a nest as they walked and saw a couple of baby dragons peeking their tiny heads over the side to watch them pass. "Is it an inborn ability that all Dracones possess?"

"Yes," said Tananeen. "But it takes a lot of practice and training before you can easily change forms at will. And not all of us are equally good at it; some can only do it partway, while others will always have little telltale signs, like sharp fingernails or rough skin, to indicate their true nature. Some never bother with it at all due to their hatred of humans."

"How much control do you guys have over your forms?" said Keo. "Can you make your human forms look however you like?"

"No," said Tananeen, who didn't seem at all bothered by Keo's questions. "Our human forms, like our dragon forms, are set from birth. We even have clothes that our scales turn into during transformation, so we never have to worry about nudity or finding clothes to wear whenever we transform."

Keo nodded, but said nothing else in response. He was starting to worry that all of his questions might be annoying Tananeen, even though she seemed to enjoy speaking with him. He was just worried that the other dragons might be listening in, although it was impossible to tell whether they understood what he was saying or not.

But it wasn't until they were about halfway across the Nest that any of the dragons decided to do more than just snarl and look scary. A massive male dragon, with yellow scales, flew down from nowhere and landed directly in their path. This dragon was slightly bigger than Veta, but looked older, although his age did not detract from his vicious appearance. The yellow dragon had huge red eyes and sword-like teeth, a low growl emitting from its throat.

Tananeen stopped, forcing Keo and the others to stop as well. Tananeen hardly seemed fazed by the large yellow dragon, which was glaring down at her like she had done something wrong. But a quick glance at his friends showed Keo that they appeared apprehensive in the face of this yellow dragon, even though Tananeen had said she would protect them, especially Easan, who had partially drawn Shadowbane from its sheath.

"Weret," said Tananeen, her voice direct and authoritative. She gestured to the right. "Move aside. These humans are with me and I have brought them to speak with my mother the Queen regarding a possible alliance between humanity and our people."

The yellow dragon, apparently named Weret, growled in response, but then started to transform. In seconds, the huge dragon was gone, replaced instead by a man who might have been in his early thirties. His eyes were now more orange than red, but they looked as harsh as ever. Like Veta, he wore armor, only his was yellow and pitted and scarred, like he had fought in dozens of battles. His hair was short and blond, which matched the color of his clawed gauntlets.

"What do you mean, you have brought them to speak with the Queen?" said Weret. His voice was deep and booming, making him sound like a dragon even in his human form. "I was not informed of this."

"Because I knew you'd respond like this if I told you about it ahead of time," said Tananeen, shaking her head. "Anyway, Weret, I asked you to move aside. I have made my decision and am not in the mood to debate it, so go away."

"Um, excuse me?" said Keo, causing Tananeen to look over her shoulder at him. "But who is this guy?"

"This guy?" said Weret in an offended tone. He patted his wide chest. "I am Captain Weret, Defender of the Nest. I am the Captain of the Queen's Legion of Wyverns and the Nest's security. No one—human or Dracone—enters or exits this place without my knowledge or approval."

Weret put a heavy emphasis on the word *approval* and looked at Tananeen when he said that.

Tananeen, however, merely said, "I am the Dracone Princess, which puts me above you in terms of authority. And as Princess, I have every right to invite whoever I wish into the Nest *without* first seeking your approval."

"Yes, but these are *humans*," said Weret, gesturing at Keo and the others like they were something filthy he had found on the underside of the rock. "We have not had any humans in the Nest since … by the ancestors, I cannot even remember the last time we had a human here. In fact, I don't think we have ever had any humans in the Nest before, not even once."

"That isn't exactly true," said Tananeen. "The Human King visited this place once, though that was before we Dracones made it into our home."

"Precisely," said Weret. "There is no precedent behind this at all. That is why I am worried, Princess."

"Trust me, Weret, these humans can be trusted," said Tananeen, nodding at Keo and his friends. "They only wish to speak with the Queen about forming an alliance with us to fight the demons, which are rising again."

Weret didn't seem to believe that, but he stepped aside and said, "All right. I must defer to your authority. But if any of these humans tries to harm any of our people—especially any of the unborn or infants—I will tear them apart with my own claws."

"Fair enough," said Tananeen, "though I sincerely doubt that you will need to worry about them. They are very well-behaved and even heroic humans."

Weret, again, looked skeptical, as if he expected Keo and his friends to start killing every unborn and infant dragon in the Nest. But he did not attack them or try to argue with Tananeen. He just watched as Tananeen resumed leading them across the valley, which made Keo feel a little uncomfortable, but he did not show it, because he had a feeling that the Dracones did not respect people—particularly humans—who showed weakness. Easan, however, tossed a glare back at Weret, as if offended by Weret's worries that they might kill the children.

Soon reached the Queen's cave, which was even larger up close. In fact, now that Keo looked at it, he thought that the cavern mouth was shaped like the mouth of a dragon, with stalactites and stalagmites that resembled dragon teeth. He wondered if the Dracones had intentionally designed it that way or if this was a natural rock formation.

But Keo did not wonder about it any more, because Tananeen walked inside without hesitation. So Keo and his friends followed, if only so they would not remain outside with the dragons that kept looking at them with hostility.

# Chapter Five

THE INTERIOR OF THE cave was pitch-black, but before they went in very deep, a small blue flame appeared suddenly at the front of the group. Keo realized that the blue flame was floating in the palm of Tananeen's hand, which meant that she had summoned it herself. He hadn't known that Dracones could summon fire in their hands like that, which made him wonder what other powers and abilities the Dracones had that Tananeen had not yet told them about.

But even Tananeen's blue flame did not illuminate the interior of the large cave entirely, although it illuminated enough of the cave for Keo to see the path they walked upon was marked with claw marks, dozens and dozens of them, no doubt from many dragons entering and exiting the place. Yet it was very quiet in this place, which made Keo wonder if the Queen was asleep. In any case, Tananeen did not seem bothered or disturbed by this, so he simply assumed that the silence was normal for the cave.

As they walked, however, the cave became lighter and lighter, thanks to a series of glowing stones in the walls and ceiling that looked to be about as big as Keo's head. The stones glowed a whitish light, which made it easier to see that the walls had carvings on them. These carvings resembled the carvings on the gates, depicting dragons fighting against an enemy Keo didn't recognize, but which were probably the demons of old. He didn't ask about them, however, because he didn't think it was relevant to their current situation.

Before Keo could ask how much longer until they reached the Queen, Tananeen pointed up ahead and said, "We're here."

Keo looked ahead. They seemed to have reached the back of the cave, because Keo saw a massive stone wall ahead, with no openings or doors to lead them out. In front of the wall was a large nest on an even large platform, which rose a few feet above their heads.

Curled up in the nest was the largest—and oldest—dragon Keo had seen yet. It was even bigger than Weret, its scales faded, cracked, and missing in some places. Its wings clung to its back, but he could tell that they were a lot thinner and web-like than the wings of the younger dragons. Its head lay on its front claws, its skin and scales a dead gray color, which made it looked like a corpse. A strong smell like death permeated from the dragon, noticeable even from a distance.

"Looks like a dead dragon walking," Dlaine muttered.

"My mother is old, the oldest dragon still alive in our clan, but she is not dead," said Tananeen. "She is, however, asleep. She usually sleeps because she wears out easily due to her old age."

"Maybe your mother was alive the last time you saw her, but can you be sure she didn't die sometime between the time you and Veta found us and now?" said Dlaine. "I mean, I'm not trying to be a downer or anything, but—"

A deep, guttural growl suddenly echoed throughout the cavern, coming from the nest where the Queen lay. Dlaine and

Maryal jumped in surprise, while Keo and Easan reached for their swords before Tananeen said, "Fear not, my friends. My mother is merely awakening, no doubt due to hearing our voices."

The Queen raised her head, but she did not open her eyes. She sniffed the air and looked down at them. Tiny wisps of white smoke rose from her nostrils with a snort.

"Awakening, my daughter?" said the Queen. Her voice was dry and brittle, like she was an ancient statue at risk of shattering under the slightest pressure. Yet there was also an authoritative undercurrent, obvious despite her age. "I was merely napping. But I will admit that the stench of humans and their irritatingly high voices did not help me rest."

"Irritatingly high voices?" Easan repeated. "My voice is *not* —"

Tananeen held up a hand and said, "Silent, Easan. Let me speak with my mother. She is slightly less abrasive toward me than she is toward humans."

Easan closed his mouth and folded his arms over his chest, looking unhappy about not being allowed to challenge the Queen. Keo understood, but deep down he was happy that Tananeen had silenced Easan, because Queen Sayot gave him the impression that she did not tolerate dissent or criticism from her inferiors, particularly if those inferiors were human.

Then Tananeen stepped forward and said, "Queen Mother, I have returned with the humans I told you about recently, the next King of Lamaira and his friends. They have come to discuss a possible alliance between humans and Dracones to prepare against the demons."

The Queen—who still had not opened her eyes—let out a low

growl, but then nodded her large head very slowly and said, "Fine. Let the next King of Lamaira speak, then. I will hear his offer and consider it."

Tananeen looked surprised at her own mother's agreement, but then she nodded at Keo to step forward and speak.

Nodding in return, Keo stepped forward and looked up at Queen Sayot, who was now looking at him. 'Looking,' however, was not the best word, because the Queen's eyes were closed shut and did not seem likely to open again anytime soon.

"Hello, Queen Sayot, Queen of the Dracones," said Keo, bowing once, even though he was not sure that she could see him at all. "I am Keo of the Sword. I come from South Lamaira and am the Rightful Heir to the Throne of the Kingdom of Lamaira."

Queen Sayot tilted her head slightly, as if intrigued. "The Rightful Heir? Does that mean you are Riuno's son?"

Keo blinked in surprise, but kept speaking. "Yes, though I never knew my father, because he died when I was only a few months old. I was raised instead by a master swordsman living alone in the Low Woods and only recently learned the identity of my real father. Did you know King Riuno?"

Queen Sayot snorted, causing more white smoke to shoot out of her nostrils. "No, but my daughter knew him, in more ways than one."

Surprised, Keo looked at Tananeen. Tananeen looked horrified by the Queen's words, as if Queen Sayot had just revealed a terrible secret that was never supposed to be revealed to anyone.

"You mean Tananeen?" said Keo, looking at Queen Sayot again. "She never mentioned knowing my father."

Queen Sayot chuckled. "I see that Tananeen hasn't told you

everything, has she? Of course she hasn't. My daughter is very good at keeping secrets. But tell me, did you ever learn your mother's identity?"

Keo shook his head. "No. My mother died after my father's death. I don't even know her name."

Queen Sayot let out a bark of a roar that Keo realized was a laugh. "So that is what they told you, then? I am not surprised. You humans have never wanted to acknowledge the accomplishments, or even the existence, of us Dracones. I imagine they told you that your mother is dead for the same reasons."

"Hold on," said Keo. "Are you telling me that my mother was a Dracone? And that she's still alive?"

"That is exactly what I am saying, son of Riuno," said Queen Sayot.

Keo stepped closer, his eyes fixed on the Queen's ancient face, his hands balled into fists. "Where is she? Can I meet her?"

"You have already met your mother," said Queen Sayot. "In fact, she is standing right next to you."

"What do you—" Keo looked to his left and saw Tananeen standing there. He stopped mid-sentence as he grasped Queen Sayot meaning. "No way. You mean that Tananeen—"

"Is your mother, yes," said Queen Sayot, though her voice was full of disapproval and disappointment, "which makes *you* half-Dracone, if I am not mistaken."

Tananeen was not looking at Keo or anyone else. She seemed angry about something, probably angry about how Queen Sayot had just revealed that secret to Keo. As for Keo's friends, they all seemed just as astonished by this revelation as he was, particularly Easan, who looked both surprised and envious.

"I'm … half-Dracone?" said Keo, looking back up at Queen Sayot. "But … what? I don't understand."

"Tananeen is obviously not going to explain, so I shall explain it quickly," said Queen Sayot. "Some forty years ago, your mother traveled from the Nest to the Kingdom of Lamaira, breaking the taboo that my people had placed on travel to human lands in the process. She met your father, who was a young man at the time, and they fell in love, though they kept their love a secret because of the disapproval they would face from both humans and Dracones if it was known. And at some point, dear Tananeen became pregnant with you and gave birth to you shortly before the death of your father."

Keo looked at Tananeen again. "You mean all this time … you were my mother and you didn't even tell me? Why?"

Tananeen looked up at Keo. Her eyes were full of sadness, but Keo could not tell if she was sad about having to spend so long separated from Keo or if the Queen's story was bringing back sad memories that she had not thought about in a while.

"I didn't want to distract you from your mission," said Tananeen. "And I was afraid that you wouldn't believe me, because we don't look very much alike. I thought you might even reject me, because you were raised among humans who hated Dracones and so I thought you might have inherited their hatred for us."

"How long have you known I was your son?" said Keo. His hands shook despite himself. "Why didn't you come looking for me after my father's death?"

"I didn't think my people would accept you," Tananeen

admitted. "I asked your father's most trusted servants to spirit you away from the chaos that enveloped Tain after Riuno's death. I wanted to ensure that your father's enemies would not know where you were so they could not hunt you down and kill you before you had a chance to grow."

Keo blinked back the tears burning in his eyes. He didn't want to cry—hadn't even felt like it even a few seconds ago—but this revelation had touched something in him that he hadn't felt in a long time, if ever.

Keeping his voice level, Keo said, "Then how long have you been following me? Were you watching me as Master Tiram raised and trained me to become the swordsman I am today?"

"I didn't know where you were for two decades," Tananeen said. She brushed back some of her hair. "I even thought you might have died in the wilderness somewhere, but then I sensed that the demons were coming back, and if the demons were returning, then I thought it was only a matter of time before you, the *shelmai*, returned as well. So I went to Tain, where I thought you would arrive at sooner or later, and hid there for a few months until you and your friends arrived, at which point I knew that you were my son."

"This ..." Keo wasn't sure what to say. "I thought you were dead, but instead you were here in the Nest, having forgotten all about me for twenty years?"

"I *never* forgot about you, Keo," said Tananeen. She stepped forward, putting her hands together as if in prayer. "Never. Not one day passed where I wouldn't think about you and ask the ancestors to watch after you. I prayed and hoped every day that you would grow up to become a strong and wise young man who would save us from the demons, and I believe that every last one of my prayers has been answered."

Tananeen sounded like she meant every word she said, but Keo still stepped away from her. He didn't know how to handle all of this information at once. It all sounded totally implausible to him, even impossible, but neither Queen Sayot nor Tananeen seemed to be lying. He had no way of denying anything they said, which just made him all the more confused.

He looked down at his fists. "But … if I'm half-Dracone, then why do I look entirely human?"

"No one ever taught you how to transform, of course," said Tananeen. "You were raised among humans who knew nothing about us. But I can teach you, Keo. I can teach you everything you need to know about the other half of your lineage, if you want."

"Assuming the halfbreed inherited that particular ability from you," said Queen Sayot. "Or that I allow him to stay here and learn our ways."

"Why wouldn't you?" said Keo, looking up at Queen Sayot again. "If I'm half-Dracone, doesn't that mean I am one of you?"

Queen Sayot let out a loud, ferocious snarl that even made Keo jump. "But you were raised among *humans*. You smell of humans, you talk like a human, you behave like a human. For all intents and purposes, you are far, far more human than Dracone. You therefore have no claim to kin in the clan."

"But I'm your grandson," said Keo. "Doesn't that mean anything to you?"

"I have many grandsons and granddaughters," said Queen Sayot in a harsh voice. "Grandchildren who are far more Dracone in their ways than you could ever hope to be."

"Wait, does that mean you had more children besides me?" said Keo, looking at Tananeen again.

Tananeen nodded, though reluctantly. "Yes, but only because it was part of my duty as a female member of the clan. Because of our small numbers, no female dragon is exempt from having children and I have had to bear the children of many male dragons over the years. But believe me, Keo, that you are still my son through and through, regardless of what my own mother thinks."

"He is an ugly runt of a halfbreed is what he is," said Queen Sayot. "Even with my blindness, I can just tell that he is a weakling, as all humans are. He could never continue the lineage of our people, not if he lived to be a thousand years and became wiser than King Yeornas."

Keo had never heard such vitriol in the voice of anyone before. He didn't know what he'd done to earn Queen Sayot's wrath, the wrath of his own grandmother if Tananeen was telling the truth about being his mother. As far as he could tell, the only problem was that he had had the wrong father and that wasn't his fault.

"Hey, Keo is a good kid," said Dlaine, patting Keo on the shoulder. He was glaring up at Queen Sayot. "If he was *my* grandson, I'd be the proudest grandpa around. But I guess you can't see that because you're a blind old bat."

Another deep growl emitted from Queen Sayot's throat, this one far more threatening than her previous ones. "And who do you think you are, speaking to me as if I were another human like yourself? I should order the Nest to tear you apart for your insolence."

"You will not," said Tananeen. She gestured at Keo and his friends. "Keo and his friends are under my protection. I will not let you or the others kill them, no matter how disrespectful they may behave."

Queen Sayot snorted more smoke from her nostrils and genuinely seemed to be on the verge of ignoring her daughter's warning and attacking.

But then Queen Sayot let out a long, tired sigh and said, "Very well. I suppose I was acting too unkind earlier. The ancient evil arising that I sensed years ago is stronger than ever. We can discuss this later; for now, we must focus on our common foe."

"Ancient evil?" said Keo, somewhat surprised by Queen Sayot's sudden change in attitude. "Do you mean the demons?"

"Yes," said Queen Sayot, nodding. "That is what I mean."

"You mean you Dracones have known about them for a long time?" said Keo. "How long have you known about the demons?"

"Ever since the reign of your grandfather, King Murza, or as we call him, the Murderer," said Queen Sayot, her tone angry again. "I sensed the demons' return because we Dracones have a closer connection to the demons' seal than humans do. At first, I thought it was nothing, but the feeling has grown stronger and stronger every year, until now it consumes my every waking moment."

"Why do you Dracones have that connection to the demons' seal?" said Keo. "I thought that the Good King had sealed them away. I didn't think you Dracones had anything to do with the demons' defeat."

Another deep growl emitted from Queen Sayot's throat. She even stood up, revealing her full, considerable height. "How dare you say such a thing to my face. If it wasn't for us Dracones, the demons would have completely destroyed humanity ages ago, yet your oversized ego forces you to pretend that humanity and humanity alone defeated and sealed the demons away one thousand years ago."

Queen Sayot's large, ancient frame shook with rage and wrath dripped from every word. She looked ready to climb out of her nest and attack Keo and his friends for that insult, but then she lay back down and coughed, like she had overexerted herself.

"But none of the old legends even mention the Dracones," said Dlaine, who had his hands in his pockets. "All of our legends say that humanity and the Dracones have always hated each other. We have a ton of stories of big scary Dracones flying around destroying villages and rampaging through cities, killing off hundreds upon thousands of people."

"That is mostly propaganda," said Tananeen. She sounded quite angry herself, though not nearly as angry as the Queen. "While it is true that there have always been Dracones who viewed humans as little more than cattle to be slaughtered or hunted, the truth of the matter is that humanity and Dracones were originally friends and allies, even lovers in some cases."

"Then what, may I ask, happened to change that?" said Easan, scratching the side of his neck. "Did you Dracones get fed up with us and leave?"

"Unfortunately, it wasn't quite so simple or peaceful," said Tananeen. "It happened many decades ago, before any of you were born. I myself was a much younger woman when it happened, as was my mother. Do any of you remember the king before Riuno, King Murza the First?"

Only Dlaine nodded. "I remember my own parents lived during his reign, but I was born after Riuno took the Throne. My parents told me that he was a warmonger."

"A warmonger is a kind term for the monster who ruled over you humans for almost half a century," said the Queen. She coughed again. "We call him the Murderer."

"Why?" said Keo. "Was he that bad?"

"He was the bloodiest king that Lamaira had ever seen," said Tananeen, the anger in her voice obvious. "He spent thousands, perhaps even millions, of lems on funding his own wars with neighboring countries like Hasfar to the south and Teka to the west. He wanted to expand the Kingdom, turn it into an empire, with himself as its first emperor, hence why he called himself King Murza the First."

"I guess he didn't succeed, then," said Keo.

"No, he did not," said Tananeen, shaking her head. "Each war was a complete disaster as the Lamairan Army was driven out of each country it invaded. As a result, the Kingdom was in deep debt, with no obvious way to pay for it except to raise taxes, but Murza did not want to admit that the wars had been lost or that he had mismanaged the Kingdom's treasury."

"What did he do, then?" said Keo.

"Blamed the Dracones, of course," said Queen Sayot. She snorted more smoke from her nostrils. "He said we were to blame for the country's economic woes and military failures. He convinced the people that he needed to raise taxes in order to get money to kill off the Dracones."

"And he succeeded," Tananeen said, looking down at her feet in sadness. "The people were angry, so they went along with it.

Murza sent his Knights and Magicians to kill off as many Dracones as they could find. And while we Dracones are stronger than you humans, you humans have always been more populous than us, so you overwhelmed our people with a combination of numbers, intelligence, tactics, magic, and brute force."

"I was one of the few survivors," said Queen Sayot. "So I gathered what survivors I could find and then led them out of Lamaira, to the Upper Mountains, where we founded the Nest. Other survivors heard about the Nest and trickled in over the next several months, but none of us ever returned to Lamaira and we killed off any humans that got too close to our territory. It is how I became the Queen; my father, the King of the Dracones, was one of the first slain, murdered in cold blood by Murza himself when that deceitful human invited him to a banquet in his castle."

Maryal covered her mouth with her hands. "That's awful. I had always heard that Murza was one of the most brutal kings to rule Lamaira, but I never thought he would commit genocide."

"He did more than that," said Tananeen. "He went through and systematically rewrote the history books and legends to omit the Dracones and everything we have done to help humanity. He took the stories about the bad Dracones and based all of our depictions on those ones, making us look like bloodthirsty beasts that couldn't be reasoned with and would annihilate humanity if given the chance."

"By the Good King's name," said Dlaine, stroking his chin in surprise. "King Murza really was an old bastard, wasn't he?"

"He was a monster through and through," said Queen Sayot. "And a coward who refused to take responsibility for his own actions. He is the prime reason we Dracones hate humans, because there is nothing you humans can do to make up for the near annihilation of our entire species."

"But you said that Dracones and humans used to be friends?" said Keo. "When? For how long?"

"Since the Good King's time," said Tananeen, folding her hands behind her back. "You see, Keo, in those days, the humans and the Dracones both suffered from oppression at the hands of the demons. The two peoples originally did not work together, due to our differences in language and thinking, but the Good King was the first human to attempt to communicate with us. Our legends state that the Good King believed that the combined might of the humans and the Dracones would be enough to overthrow the demons, so he came to King Yeornas, our first King, and convinced him to work with him to defeat the demons."

"They were an effective team," said Queen Sayot. "By working together, Yeornas and the Good King successfully killed a demon, the very first demon to be killed by humans and Dracones. News of their victory spread far and wide among both humans and Dracones, leading to similar partnerships forming between the two peoples that led to the deaths of more and more demons, until soon an all-out war between the demons on one side and humanity and the Dracones on the other had started."

"The combined might of humanity and the Dracones was indeed strong enough to defeat the demons," said Tananeen. "The Good King and Yeornas then banished the King of Demons and his remaining minions far beneath the earth, where the demons have remained until just recently, and where, hopefully, the demons will never escape from again."

"Wow," said Keo. "I didn't know any of that."

"Now you do," said Tananeen. "I hope you also understand why it is important that humans and Dracones work together. You humans believe that you need only a new King on the Throne to keep the seal blocked, but you fail to understand that you also need the Dracones."

"Why?" said Keo.

"Because, as we said, defeating the demons the first time was a combined effort between the humans and the Dragons," said Tananeen, gesturing at herself and Keo. "And the seal was maintained by humans and Dragons together. The seal can only work if there is a descendent of the Good King on the Throne and if the current leader of the Dracones is also in the land."

"So you mean that if I had decided to stay in Tain and become the King of Lamaira, that the demons would have still risen?" said Keo. "Even if I reunited the entire Kingdom under my rule?"

"Unfortunately, yes," said Tananeen. "That is something your grandfather never understood. Murza was aware of the seal keeping the demons locked away, but he thought that only the current King of Lamaira was needed to maintain it and that we Dracones were unnecessary."

"I see," said Keo, stroking his chin. "Now I understand why you wanted me to come here to form an alliance with your people. Did you also want to train me to use my Dracone powers?"

"I was hoping for that, too, yes," said Tananeen. "But later." She looked up at Queen Sayot, who still lay with her front claws folded over each other. "First, my mother must agree to form an alliance between humanity and the Dracones."

Keo nodded and also looked up at Queen Sayot. "All right,

Queen Sayot. You heard all of that, so I know you understand the importance of forming an alliance between our people and yours. Will you agree to work with us to stop the demons from rising again?"

Queen Sayot was silent for a moment. She seemed to be thinking over Keo's offer, but it was hard to tell because she was very still and her dragon face was difficult to read. Her closed eyes also made it even harder to tell what she was thinking, but Keo was confident that she would accept his offer. After all, the demons were a threat to both peoples, so there was no reason for Queen Sayot to say no.

In fact, Keo was already thinking about how the humans and Dracones would work together when Queen Sayot said, in a surprisingly firm voice, "No."

Keo did a double-take. "What? I'm sorry, but I don't think I heard you correctly, Queen Sayot."

"I said no," said Queen Sayot. "Must I repeat myself? I thought that the young had clearer ears than the old, but then, the young always refuse to listen to their elders, rarely to their benefit."

"But ..." Keo was almost too shocked to respond. "But the demons are rising again. The only way to stop them is for humanity and the Dracones to work together. We have no choice."

Queen Sayot scratched her snout with one of her claws, seemingly uninterested in anything Keo was saying. "Actually, we have plenty of choices. And I have chosen to reject your offer to form a human/Dracone alliance."

Tananeen stepped forward, a deep growl in her throat. "Mother, do you even know what you are saying? Are you even thinking about the greater good? About the long-term health of our people? You remember the stories about what the demons did to our ancestors. They'll repeat it here if they are allowed to rise again, except even worse, because they've had a thousand years to stew in their anger toward us for beating them the first time."

"I *am* thinking about the long-term health of our people, Tananeen," said Queen Sayot with a snarl. "I am thinking that allying with humanity, even to stop the demons, would be a grave mistake. How can I know that Keo will not turn on us as soon as the demons are no longer a threat, and finish the job that his grandfather started?"

"I would never do that," said Keo, putting one hand on his chest. "I'm not my grandfather. I don't hate Dracones the way he did. And if any humans *did* give you or any other Dracones trouble for no reason, I would defend you just the same as anyone else being treated unfairly."

Queen Sayot shook her head. "I cannot know that you are telling the truth about that. I have learned that humans often have two faces: The one they show you when they want to trick you into trusting you, and then the one they show you when they stab you in the back."

"Mother, Keo is a trustworthy person," said Tananeen, gesturing at him. "I observed him in Tain and know that he can be trusted. He would never stab us in the back for any reason. That is not the kind of human he is."

"Even if you are correct, I still fail to see why we should help the humans," said Queen Sayot. "I say that the humans deserve to be oppressed and slaughtered by the demons. We owe you nothing. We Dracones will stay here in the Upper Mountains, and if any demons do come this way, we will kill them just like we did in the days of the Good King. But otherwise, we will remain out of the conflict. And that is my final answer."

With that, Queen Sayot turned around on her nest, hiding her face from everyone else. Her tail curled around her body and she let out one last snort that sent the largest smoke plumes up from her nose yet into the air, a clear sign that she did not want to talk with them anymore.

"Is that really your final answer?" said Keo. "Don't you realize that the demons won't leave you alone if they rise again? And if they succeed in destroying humanity, they will do the same to you. You Dracones may be stronger than us, but are you strong enough to handle the might of the—"

"Leave!" Queen Sayot roared, interrupting Keo before he could finish speaking. "Or I will have Weret and the Legion kill you all for trespassing upon my domain."

Keo wanted to continue to argue with her, but Queen Sayot spoke with a finality that even he could not deny. Still, he opened his mouth to keep arguing, but then Tananeen rested a hand on his shoulder and said, "Keo, don't. My mother clearly does not want to speak with you or anyone else right now. Let us leave. Trust me, it is all we can do."

As much as Keo didn't want to admit it, Tananeen had a point. Queen Sayot was very clearly not interested in being convinced to change her mind. Even if he thought that Queen Sayot was behaving in an utterly foolish and irrational manner, he knew that there was not a word he could say to convince her to change her mind.

So Keo nodded and bowed at the Queen, saying, "Thank you

for listening to my offer, Queen Sayot. I wish that you had accepted it, but if that is your final answer, then my friends and I will leave the Nest and continue our quest to stop the demons elsewhere on our own."

Queen Sayot did not answer, though Keo knew that she had to be listening. He wished that she would answer, but he knew better than to expect an answer from her now.

So Keo stood up, turned around, and walked past his friends back the way they came. His friends fell into step behind him, while Tananeen walked by his side. She didn't say anything, either, probably because there was nothing she could say to change her mother's mind.

# Chapter Six

WHAT A RUDE WOMAN," said Easan as Keo and the others walked through the cave. He was looking over his shoulder as he said that, a look of disgust on his face. "Refusing to help us purely out of spite for something that happened before any of us were even born … what a spiteful woman."

"It's understandable, given what Murza did to the Dracones, but I agree that it's bad," said Maryal. She looked at Keo as they walked. "Are we really going to leave the Nest?"

"Yes," said Keo. "We're going to West Lamaira, where the Divinians are. We're going to convince them to ally with the Old Kingdom against the Magicians."

"But we just got here," said Dlaine. He picked up speed until he was walking by Keo's side, his hands in his pockets. "Don't you think we should stay just a little while longer, at least?"

"Why?" said Keo, glancing at Dlaine. "You heard her. You know what the Dracones think about us humans. If we stay, they'll just use that as an excuse to kill us. We can't beat the demons and reunite the Kingdom if we're dead."

"But didn't she just say that we couldn't restore the seal unless we had the Dracones on our side?" said Maryal. "How are we supposed to stop the demons without the Dracones?"

Keo shook his head. "I don't know. We'll think of something, I'm sure."

He looked at Tananeen as they walked. Tananeen had been quiet since they had left Queen Sayot's nest. She seemed angry about Queen Sayot's decision, which made Keo feel a little better, because he was angry as well. He may not have displayed it to the others, but he was quite angry at the Queen for her stubbornness. He just didn't see any point in risking their lives and wasting time trying to convince Queen Sayot to change her mind, especially when she had made it clear that she wasn't going to change her mind anytime soon, if ever.

But more importantly, Keo found himself unsure what to say to Tananeen. Now that he knew that she was his mother, he wasn't sure how to react to that. He had lived his whole life believing that both of his parents had died shortly after his birth, yet here was his mother now walking by his side, as alive as anyone else. Perhaps that was another reason for Tananeen's silence; she didn't know what to say to him, either, now that he knew that he was her son.

Part of Keo felt angry at her, even though he tried to ignore the anger. He remembered what she had told him about why she had sent him off when he was so young, and he supposed it had worked out for the best in the end, seeing as he was still alive, but a part of him was angry that she had not even bothered to look for him until years later.

*What would my life have been like, I wonder, if Tananeen had searched for me much earlier than she did?* Keo thought. *Would I already be the King of Lamaira and have succeeded in reuniting the Kingdom and stopping the demons before they became too powerful? Would I have been able to save Nesma from being manipulated by the demons, too?*

Keo looked down at his hands. He wondered just what the extent of his own Dracone powers were. Could he also transform into a dragon? Could he breathe fire? The only fire he ever felt inside himself was the fire that created the golden flames around Gildshine, but he hadn't tried to shoot it from his mouth before, and he was hesitant to do so, because he feared that he might just melt his own mouth off. Even so, Keo could see the benefits of learning to control his dragon powers, even if the Dracones did not accept him as one of their own or his offer to form an alliance with them.

He also wondered if Master Tiram had known about this. Tiram had claimed that he didn't know who Keo's parents were, but could Tiram have been lying? That didn't seem likely to Keo, because Tiram had always been honest with him, but it did make him wonder exactly how much Tiram knew about his true parentage. He supposed he would never know for sure, at least for a while, because right now Master Tiram was back in the Low Woods, hundreds of miles away from the Upper Mountains. Still, Keo made a mental note to ask Tiram about this later, when he returned home.

Then Tananeen said, "Keo?"

Keo snapped out of his thoughts and looked at her. She held a blue fire in her hands, which helped to illuminate the darkness of the cave, the glow of its blue flames making her face look blue itself.

"Yes?" said Keo. "What is it?"

"I want to apologize for my mother," said Tananeen, shaking her head. "She has always been as stubborn as a mule, even before you were born. But I never imagined that she would outright reject your offer like that. It worries me more than I'd like to admit."

"Like I said, it's fine," said Keo. "We'll just find another way to stop the demons. We've done all right against them on our own. I'm sure we'll continue to beat them as we head to West Lamaira."

"I am not so sure about that," said Tananeen. "The demons will only grow more and more powerful as the seal weakens. You yourself know that humans cannot kill demons on their own, at least without magic or magical weapons like Gildshine."

"I know, but I still believe that we'll succeed, one way or another," said Keo. "Anyway, there's no point in talking about this. Sayot made it clear she's not changing her mind, so I'd rather focus on what we can do, like go to West Lamaira and speak with the Divinians."

"Are you certain that you don't want to stay here instead and learn how to control your Dracone powers?" said Tananeen. "I could teach you. I've had to help many young Dracones learn how to control their shape-shifting and fire powers over the years. I could easily teach you without any problem."

"Are you sure that we would be allowed to stay here and learn?" said Keo, glancing over his shoulder at the darkness of the cave behind them. "I know you're the Princess, but Sayot is the Queen. And, while I'm no expert on Dracone clan dynamics, I know that a Queen's word is always more authoritative than a Princess's, so if she says we're not allowed to be here, then we have to leave regardless of how we feel."

"I know," said Tananeen, "but I might be able to convince her to let you stay long enough to train. She might not want anything to do with you, but if I promise to keep you and your friends separated from the rest of the clan—"

"No, it's fine," said Keo, holding up one hand to silence her. "Don't waste your time. The demons are still going to rise in two months. It would be better for us to spend our time reuniting the Kingdom than convincing your mother to put aside her prejudices and help us."

Tananeen bit her lower lip. "What about your powers, then? How will you learn how to use your Dracone powers to their fullest extent if you don't have a teacher to train you?"

Keo thought about that for a moment as they walked. He glanced at the others for a moment before looking at Tananeen again and saying, "Why don't you come with us?"

Tananeen looked at him in surprise. "You mean travel with you and your friends?"

"Sure," said Keo, nodding. "Having a Dracone on our side would be useful, especially if you train me. Plus, you are my mother, so this can be a good way for us to get to catch up with each other."

Keo meant every word he said. While he still wasn't entirely sure how he felt about Tananeen, he was starting to decide that he might not be so angry with her after all. She might not have been the best mother in the world, but she was his mother, the only parent he had. And even if she wasn't his mother, the fact that she was a powerful and experienced Dracone alone made her worth inviting to join the team. He was certain that the others would not object, except perhaps for Easan, but Keo didn't really care what

Easan thought.

Before Tananeen could respond, there was the sudden sound of flapping wings ahead of them, and in the next second a medium-sized dragon with green scales—possibly an adolescent by his size—flew out of the shadows. The dragon immediately spotted Tananeen and fell to the ground before them, sending up small clouds of dust around its feet upon impact.

The sudden appearance of the youngling made Keo and the others jump back in surprise, but Tananeen merely tilted her head and said, "Serwa? What is the problem? You look like you are in a hurry."

Serwa opened his mouth to speak, but all that came out was a series of growls and snarls. It sounded threatening to Keo, but Tananeen looked like she was listening to his every word. Her expression, however, became more and more serious the more she listened, although Keo was unable to translate Serwa's growls and snarls into anything meaningful.

"I understand," said Tananeen, after Serwa finished speaking. Tananeen sounded deadly serious, as if Serwa had just given her some very grim news. "I will let Keo and his friends know what you just told me. But while we do that, go and tell my mother about this. She needs to know about the situation, even if she can't do anything about it."

Serwa nodded and then looked at Keo. It was an angry look, like Keo had somehow wronged him, even though Keo had not even met this particular Dracone before. Keo met Serwa's gaze, trying not to break it, because he had a feeling that that would be showing weakness and the Dracones clearly did not tolerate weakness, whether among themselves or among humans.

Then Serwa jumped into the air and flew over them, heading toward the back of the cave, where Queen Sayot was. Keo and his friends watched in confusion as Serwa flew away, but before anyone could say anything, Tananeen grabbed Keo's arm and started dragging him to the exit.

"Hey!" said Keo, struggling to regain his balance as Tananeen dragged him along. "Where are we going? What did Serwa say?"

Tananeen stopped and looked at Keo and his friends with urgency in her eyes. "Serwa said that a group of humans have taken several of the unborn hostage and are threatening to kill them unless you give yourself over to them."

"What?" said Keo. "Who are these humans? Where did they come from? Why do they want me?"

"Serwa didn't know," said Tananeen. "He just said that the other adults haven't been able to save the unborn because the humans have taken them inside a nearby cave that's too small for the adults to fit inside. That's why he came here to tell us."

"I don't like the sound of this at all," said Dlaine. "What should we do?"

"We have to check this out," said Keo. "As much as I'd like to go to the Divinians now, I don't want these unborn baby dragons killed, not if I can help it."

"But we don't owe the Dracones anything," said Easan, folding his arms across his chest. "Even if you are half-Dracone yourself, Keo, this smells like a trap to me."

"Even if it is, so what?" said Keo. "This could be a good way to win over the Dracones. If they see me coming to save their unborn children, then they might treat us with less hostility than before and maybe Queen Sayot will rethink our offer."

"Good point," said Maryal. "But I still wonder just who these guys are and where they came from."

"Let's find out," said Tananeen. "And quickly. Serwa made it sound like the humans who stole our unborn were very serious about smashing the eggs if you don't show up soon. Follow me."

It wasn't long before Keo, Tananeen, and his friends reached the cave where the mysterious group of humans was supposed to be. It wasn't hard to find, because there were at least a dozen fully-grown adult Dracones, all male and all in dragon form, flying or standing around it. The cave opening itself was indeed too small for any of the dragons to fit more than their snouts through, if even that, but the adult Dracones still flew around it anyway, as if hoping that the kidnappers might eventually come out on their own where they could get them.

As Keo, Tananeen, and the others approached the cave, a large yellow dragon—who Keo recognized as Weret—flew over and landed in front of them. He immediately transformed back into his human form, an urgent look on his human features.

"Princess!" said Weret. "Did you receive the message I sent you through Serwa?"

"Yes," said Tananeen, nodding. "He said that a group of humans kidnapped some of our unborn and are holding them hostage, correct?"

"That's correct," said Weret. "And don't ask me where these humans came from or how they stole the eggs before we noticed, because I don't know and no one else does, either. I suspect they used some of their human magic to do it, because I've heard that human magic can hide humans from detection and allow them to enter places they normally cannot."

"Do you know if any of them are Magicians?" said Keo. "Because if they are, that would explain a lot."

"I don't know," said Weret. Then he glared at Keo. "But I do know that they said that they wanted to speak with you. They said that they will give us back all seven of the eggs they stole unharmed if you would just enter the cave alone."

Keo raised an eyebrow. "Did they identify themselves or say why they wanted me?"

"No, they did not," said Weret. He stepped toward Keo, his hands twitching like he wanted to grab him. "But if you will not hand yourself over to them, then I will do it myself, because I value our unborn far more than I value your human life."

"That won't be necessary," said Keo quickly, holding up his hands in warning. "I came because I wanted to help rescue your unborn. You don't need to force me to do anything."

Weret raised his eyebrows in surprise. "Why are you risking your own life for the lives of our unborn?"

"Because it's the right thing to do," said Keo. "Anyone who threatens the lives of unborn children like that—even if these unborn children are Dracones—is scum no matter what species they are. So don't worry, because we'll have them out in a second."

Keo stepped toward the cave with his friends, but Weret got in their way again.

"Sorry, but the kidnappers said that they only wanted Keo, not the rest of you," said Weret, glaring at Keo's friends. "They said that if Keo did not enter alone, they'd kill all our unborn."

"But what if it's a trap?" said Maryal. "Keo might need our

help."

"It doesn't matter if it's a trap or not," said Weret. "I am not going to risk the lives of our unborn children just to make a *human* feel safe."

Weret said the word *human* like it was the worst insult he could think of.

Maryal opened her mouth to argue, but then Keo raised his hand and said, "No, Maryal, it's fine. As much as I'd appreciate having some backup, I don't want to risk the destruction of those eggs. I'll be fine on my own."

Maryal looked like she didn't like that at all, but then she nodded and said, "Okay. But why can't Jola go with you, at least? She's invisible, so they won't be able to see her and therefore won't know that you didn't come in alone."

Keo stroked his chin. He glanced down at the ground to Dlaine's right, which was where he thought Jola was standing, because that was where she usually stood.

"That's not a bad idea," said Keo. "I only worry that they might somehow be able to sense her presence, assuming any of them are Magicians."

*Don't worry, Keo,* said Jola's voice in his head. *I've made it impossible for Magicians to sense me with their magic. Only unusually powerful Magicians would be able to sense me now, but I doubt that any of them are that powerful.*

"One of you is invisible?" said Weret curiously, looking over Keo's friends with a frown. "What human trickery is this?"

"It's not trickery, it's magic," said Keo. "Regardless, letting Jola come with me is a good idea. But Jola, you'll need to be very, very quiet, because if they even suspect that I brought one of you with it, they'll probably smash every last Dracone egg in their possession."

*No need to tell me that,* said Jola. *Silence is another one of my specialties.*

Jola sounded confident enough, which was good, because Keo suspected that the egg thieves were likely very dangerous. After all, how many humans would risk breaking into a valley full of angry, powerful, human-hating dragons that had no qualms with killing even innocent humans who trespassed upon their domain and steal not just one or two, but seven, eggs from these same dragons, who were also highly protective of their children, both born and unborn?

*They are either insane or dangerous,* Keo thought. *Or both.*

# Chapter Seven

THE DARK CAVE WAS much smaller than Queen Sayot's cave was, with a lower ceiling that didn't quite force Keo to bend over, but did make him feel slightly claustrophobic. The place had a putrid reek, like droppings, and there were claw marks on the floor and walls, which made him wonder if perhaps baby dragons came in here to play and explore. He figured that a baby dragon would be able to fit without any problem, but he knew that there were no baby dragons in here right now, except for the unborn that were still in their eggs. It was also warm, despite the lack of sunlight, which was likely due to the baby dragons practicing their fire breaths in here.

Because of the cave's narrow walls and low ceiling, Keo was able to see the tunnel without needing a lot of light. He didn't see any humans, but he heard movement somewhere in the back. He listened hard, but it was impossible to tell just who or what was moving back there based on sound alone. Still, Keo gripped the hilt of Gildshine, ready to draw it in case anyone came barreling out of the darkness at them, even though he wasn't sure he would have enough room to draw Gildshine in this place.

"See anything?" Keo muttered under his breath to Jola, who was right beside him.

*Nothing that you don't,* said Jola. *Should I go ahead and scout the rest of the tunnel?*

"No," Keo whispered, keeping his voice as low as possible so the kidnappers ahead wouldn't be able to hear him. "I don't want to risk the kidnappers hearing you, which would ruin our plan. But if you do see or hear anything unusual or dangerous, let me know."

*Sure,* said Jola, although she sounded a little reluctant about it. Most likely she disagreed with Keo's order to stay by his side, probably because she believed that her invisibility and silence made her impossible to sense, but Keo did not want to take any unnecessary risks, at least until they had a better idea of who these kidnappers were and what they wanted, anyway.

So Keo and Jola slowly made their way forward, both of them as quiet as possible. Keo listened as hard as he could, but the kidnappers must have been just as quiet as Jola, because he no longer heard the movement back there that he did moments ago. He wondered if the kidnappers were lying in wait, ready to ambush Keo as soon as they saw him.

It wasn't long before they reached the end of the tunnel and emerged into a much larger and much more open cave, although it was still nowhere near as big as Queen Sayot's.

There were about four or five other tunnel entrances along the walls, which seemed to lead deeper into the underground tunnel system that existed underneath the Nest. In the center of the room were seven dragon eggs—ranging in color from red to blue to green and more—gathered together in a makeshift nest. The eggs looked unharmed, while the kidnappers themselves were nowhere to be seen.

*Where did the kidnappers go?* said Jola, who sounded just as worried as Keo felt. *Did they run away?*

*Why would they do that?* Keo replied in his mind. *Unless they're really just a bunch of cowards, but I doubt—*

Suddenly, three things fell from the ceiling and landed on the floor between Keo and Jola and the eggs. Keo immediately drew Gildshine, holding it before him as the three things rose to their full height.

The three 'things' that had fallen from the ceiling were not merely 'things,' but human beings. They appeared to be brothers, perhaps even triplets, because they all shared the same lanky body structure and all wore red-and-white Magician's robes. Their most striking feature, however, was their white lips, which would have made them look like walking corpses had their orange eyes not been so bright and alive.

All three of the kidnappers appeared unarmed, but Keo wasn't going to let down his guard around them. They were all obviously Magicians, but beyond that, Keo knew nothing else about the triplets.

"Are you the kidnappers that the Dracones told me about?" said Keo, watching the three kidnappers carefully.

"That's us," said the middle kidnapper. His voice was high and manic, like he was hyped on some kind of drug. "And you are Keo of the Sword, the angel killer, right?"

Keo scowled. "Angel killer? That was a ... hold on, how do you know about that?"

"Magician Nesma told us," said the middle kidnapper. "When she contacted us to do a job for her, she told us that you had killed an angel. Not that it really matters to us, of course. We just want our money, and the Magical Council always pays well."

"Nesma?" said Keo in shock. "So you're working for her? Did she send you to kill me?"

"More or less," said the middle kidnapper. "But allow me to introduce us. We are the Brothers White Blood, the most skilled and successful assassins in all of South Lamaira. My name is Ankem and these are my brothers, Karem and Pokol."

Neither Karem nor Pokol spoke, but that didn't make them appear any less threatening. But it was hard for Keo to keep an eye on all three of them, so he just focused on Ankem for now.

"How did you even find me?" said Keo. "I didn't tell Nesma I was going to the Upper Mountains."

"Nesma told us that she's been tracking your movement ever since you left South Lamaira a couple of months ago," said Ankem. "But it doesn't really matter how she found you. She told us that she needed us to kill you, so we followed you and your group of friends to this place."

"Why didn't you attack us before?" said Keo. "Why did you wait until we entered the Nest before you struck?"

"You were always one step ahead of us due to your constant traveling, so we never even got a chance to attack you until just a few hours ago," said Ankem. "Of course, it seemed like we would never get a chance to kill you when you entered the Dracones' territory, but then Pokol here came up with the brilliant idea of taking some of the eggs and holding them hostage until the Dracones handed you over to us."

Ankem patted his brother on the shoulder, causing Pokol to smirk, as if he was very proud that his plan had worked out so well.

"This way, we get you, while avoiding the wrath of the Dracones," said Ankem. "It is a brilliant plan that I wished I had come up with on my own, but that's why I work with my brothers. Three heads are better than one."

"I know," said Keo. "So is that what you want, then? To put down my sword and let you kill me in cold blood?"

"That's more or less the plan," said Ankem. He licked his lips. "Though we might have some fun with your corpse before we take it to Nesma. We haven't had lunch yet, after all, and we're all big eaters, despite our thin bodies. You look like you've got a lot of meat on your bones, perhaps enough for all three of us."

Keo shuddered at the implication. "What if I fight you instead?"

"We'll smash the eggs and still kill you," said Ankem without missing a beat. "But if you let us kill you, we'll let the Dracones have their unborn back. We've never really liked eggs anyway, so it isn't a loss to us."

Keo gulped. He could not hear Jola, but he knew that she had to be doing something about the Brothers. He hoped that she had some kind of plan, because he wasn't sure how much longer he could keep these assassins distracted until they got bored and decided to go straight for the kill.

So Keo said, "How did you even get past the gates without the Dracones knowing?"

"We took the tunnels, of course," said Ankem, gesturing at the openings that Keo had noticed earlier. "There's an entire tunnel system underneath the Dracones' little territory. We found an entrance outside and followed it until it led us here. We kept expecting to run into some kind of guard or trap, but the Dracones apparently never thought that anyone would ever attempt to enter their territory this way. Quite foolish, if you ask me."

Keo agreed, but he wasn't going to say that, because he was still listening for Jola. He wanted to get a clue about what she was going to do, but so far he had not heard anything from her. He supposed that she was being quiet so that the Brothers wouldn't hear her, but he would have appreciated it if Jola had at least telepathically told him what she was about to do.

"But enough talking," said Ankem. "We Brothers did not gain our fearsome reputation from talking our targets to death. Drop your sword and stand still long enough for us to kill you, unless you want these eggs to be smashed, of course."

Ankem gestured at the seven eggs behind him and his brothers. Keo considered simply attacking the three Brothers, because they seemed close enough that he could attack them before they destroyed the eggs, but at the same time he hesitated. He knew nothing about the magical abilities of the Brothers or how fast they were, though he had a feeling that they were not weak.

*Come on, Jola, what are you doing?* Keo thought, even though he wasn't sure that Jola could hear him right now. *Are you going to help me or not?*

"Keo?" said Ankem. His tone became as cold as ice. "Are you going to put your sword down or not? I promise that your death will be quick, albeit not painless, if you put your sword down."

Keo gritted his teeth. He'd just have to trust that Jola was doing what she needed to do, whatever it was.

So he said, "Why don't you come and *take* Gildshine from me? If you're so powerful, you should be able to do that without any problem, right?"

Ankem, Karem, and Pokol scowled and Ankem said, "So the destruction of the eggs it is, then. Very well. But you are correct. We shouldn't have any trouble killing you, even if you don't put down your—"

A rock flew out of nowhere toward the back of Ankem's head, which Keo immediately recognized as Jola's work. He watched as the rock flew toward Ankem's head, with Ankem seemingly unaware that it was going to bash his brain in.

But then, without warning, Ankem whirled around and held up one hand at the rock. It stopped and exploded in midair, turning into dust, which shocked Keo, because he had not thought that Ankem had heard the rock coming.

Then Ankem punched forward with his other hand and something materialized into existence several feet away from him and flew backwards into the back wall of the cave. The thing, whatever it was, hit the back wall and fell to the floor of the cave, stunned by the blow. It took Keo a second to realize that the 'thing' had been Jola, whose invisibility had been deactivated somehow, but he didn't waste time thinking about how that was possible.

Holding Gildshine in both hands, Keo ran at the Brothers, aiming to cut down Ankem, whose back was still to him. But Karem and Pokol stepped in front of their Brother and slashed at Keo with their hands.

Despite the fact that neither Karem nor Pokol made contact with Keo, Keo felt dozens of claws tearing at his flesh. Cuts appeared in his arms, hands, chest, and even on his face, causing him to cry out in pain and stop. Blood leaked out of these cuts as

Keo staggered backwards. The pain and blood was clouding his mind, making it harder to focus on the Brothers, but he forced himself to focus anyway because he could not afford to be distracted.

Then Karem and Pokol were in front of him. Karem grabbed Keo's wrists and twisted them hard, making Keo drop Gildshine. In the next second, Karem slammed Keo onto the ground and then Pokol jumped on him. Even though Pokol wasn't very large or heavy, he was heavy enough that Keo could not throw him off easily.

Pokol wrapped his hands around Keo's throat and started constricting, a mad glee in his eyes. Keo gasped for air and reacted instinctively, punching Pokol straight in the face with his bloody fist. The blow knocked Pokol off of him, but Karem's boot came out of nowhere and struck Keo in the side of the head.

The blow created stars in Keo's eyes, but he rolled to the side anyway, and just in the nick of time, because he heard a sudden cracking of rock that was too close for comfort. Shaking his head, Keo got back to his feet and looked to see a thick stone pillar standing in the place where he had been lying just moments before, having apparently been summoned by Karem or Pokol.

Not that Keo had any time to analyze the pillar, because Karem slashed at him again. This time, Keo jumped to the side, though he felt the harsh wind of something sharp and painful flying past him and he saw Karem's spell strike the wall on the other side of the room, cutting into it as easily as if it were flesh.

Then Pokol charged at Keo. He swung his fists at him, but Keo dodged the blows. Pokol's hasty attack left an opening, which Keo exploited by punching the assassin straight in the stomach.

But when his fist met Pokol's stomach, a loud *clang* echoed and pain shot up Keo's fist. Surprised, Keo did not see Pokol's fist coming at his face, and by the time he did, it was too late to dodge.

Pokol's fist crashed into Keo's face, creating more stars in his eyes and sending him staggering backwards again. Shaking his head, Keo's vision cleared just enough for him to see both Karem and Pokol bearing down on him, while Ankem was walking over to the other side of the room, where Jola still lay unconscious.

But Keo could not rescue her. He tried to punch Karem, but the assassin dodged his punch easily enough and slashed his hands at him again. More cuts appeared in Keo's skin and clothes, making more bloody wounds and causing Keo to fall down to his hands and knees. He tried to get back up, but Pokol slammed a boot down on his back, knocking Keo down onto the ground and pinning him to the floor.

"No, no, no," said Pokol, whose voice was deeper than Ankem's. "You aren't getting away that easily, target."

Keo gritted his teeth. He was wounded, tired, and angry, but there was no way that he could save himself, Jola, and the eggs. In fact, he didn't think he could save anyone. The Brothers White Blood had already shown themselves to be smarter and stronger than him. They would finish him and Jola off any second now and it would be all his fault.

That made him angrier than ever, mostly at himself for his failure to protect him and his friend. He tried rising again, but as before, Pokol pushed him down and snarled, "Stay down. There's no escape."

Still gritting his teeth, Keo felt a powerful fire rising deep inside him and he said, in the strongest voice that he could muster in his beaten state, "Yes ... I ... can ..."

Again, he tried to rise, but Pokol once more slammed his boot onto Keo's back, shouting, "No, you cannot!"

But, though Pokol was as strong as ever, his boot failed to pin Keo down. He heard Pokol and Karem gasp in surprise, but Keo did not let them have any time in which to react. He pushed up again, this time harder than ever, and sent Pokol staggering backwards.

Rising to his feet, with the fire now burning powerfully through his veins, Keo looked at his two opponents. Karem took a step backwards, a surprised look on his pale face, while Pokol was looking at Keo with apprehension. Keo wasn't quite sure why until he noticed that his skin was glowing golden, which he hadn't even realized until just this moment.

"Glowing skin?" Karem said, glancing at Pokol. "Did Magician Nesma say anything about Keo being able to do that?"

"No, but it doesn't matter," said Pokol. "We are the Brothers White Blood. We've killed kings and priests. We won't be stopped by a stupid kid."

Keo growled at that insult, a literal, dragon-like growl. "Stupid kid? Very well. You were asking for it."

Without thinking, Keo raised his hands and unleashed streams of golden flame at the two assassins. Both Karem and Pokol had only a brief second to shout before the golden flames completely enveloped them, cutting off their screams, which were replaced by the roar of the fire that ate away at their flesh and clothes.

Ankem—who had been standing over Jola, reaching down to

her with a sinister smirk on his face—suddenly looked up, his mouth hanging open in shock. "What is that?"

Keo could not answer, partly because he didn't understand it himself, but also because all rational thought had been dispelled from his mind, replaced instead by an almost primal desire to defend himself and his friend from their enemies.

But Keo lowered his hands anyway, breaking off the continuous stream of flame that ate Karem and Pokol. When the flames vanished, it revealed two blackened skeletons, stripped completely to the bone, standing where the two Brothers had been, though only for a moment. In the next, the skeletons fell to the ground together and smashed into pieces.

"Karem! Pokol!" Ankem shouted, standing up and seemingly forgetting all about Jola. "No!"

Keo smiled, his hands still burning with golden flame. "Oops. Looks like I melted your brothers. Sorry."

Ankem stepped over Jola, anger on his face. "Drop the snark, Keo of the Sword. No one gets away with harming—much less outright *killing*—even one Brother, much less two at once. I will completely and utterly destroy you so much that even your own mother won't be able to recognize you."

Keo smirked. "Bring it, then, weakling."

Ankem shouted and thrust his arms forward. More slashes hurled through the air toward Keo, but instead of dodging them, he merely raised his arms to protect his face. The slashes cut through him, but left no wounds or anything else to indicate that they had hit him. He didn't even feel them, though he did hear the slashes cut through the stone wall behind him.

"What?" said Ankem. Fear and panic were in his voice now,

evident in the way he stepped backwards. "Impossible. That was my strongest slash spell. You should be nothing more than a pile of sliced meat now."

Keo chuckled, which surprised even himself. "If that's your strongest spell, then I guess it's game over for you."

Keo rushed toward Ankem, moving far faster than he was normally capable of. With his fist burning, Keo punched Ankem directly in the face.

The blow knocked Ankem flat off his feet and he didn't move again. Even the awful burn in the shape of Keo's fist on the side of Ankem's face didn't seem to wake him out of his stupor.

Keo raised his fist to finish Ankem off, but then he heard a familiar voice in his head say, *Keo?*

Keo looked down to see Jola lying at his feet. She was no longer invisible, which meant that this was the first time Keo had ever actually seen her body.

She was incredibly small, no bigger than an eight-year-old girl. She had short red hair and deep black skin, which looked unnatural on her for some reason. She wore a simple brown jacket and white shirt underneath and a pair of shorts for pants, though she didn't wear any shoes on her feet. She was looking up at him with large green eyes, as if astonished by what she saw. Not that Keo understood, seeing as his appearance had hardly changed, but he was too surprised by finally seeing her appearance to react right away.

"Jola?" said Keo in surprise. He shook his head. "Listen, I'll check on you later. I have to finish off Ankem before—"

Without warning, Ankem's eyes snapped open and he raised his hands. A cloud of smoke suddenly shot out of his hands and into the air, blinding Keo and causing him to cough and hack as the smoke entered his lungs. He heard Ankem get up and fully expected the assassin to take advantage of his blindness to strike him down, but when Ankem did not attack, Keo wondered what happened to him until a wind, courtesy of Jola, blew through and scattered the smoke everywhere.

Once the smoke was gone, Keo looked and saw that Ankem was nowhere to be seen. He wasn't even on the ceiling. It was like he had magically vanished.

Blinking the tears out of his eyes created by the smoke, Keo felt the fire within him starting to die down, his skin returning back to its normal color. He felt far more exhausted than he had even just a couple of seconds ago, nearly as exhausted as he usually felt after using Gildshine's special cutting ability, but he managed to stay conscious.

"Where did he go?" said Keo, looking around the cave again, even though he knew that Ankem was no longer there.

*He must have escaped through one of the other tunnels,* Jola said, gesturing at the other tunnel entrances that Keo had noticed earlier. *The only question is, which one?*

"It doesn't matter," said Keo. "If we went after him now, we'd never find him. He could have gone through any of those paths and we'd waste a ton of time and effort searching for him, time and effort that could be better spent on other things."

*You're right,* said Jola. She rose to her feet, looking none the worse for having been blasted backwards by Ankem's magic. She looked up at Keo again. *But he is going to come after us again, no doubt.*

"No doubt," said Keo, nodding in agreement. "But for now,

we need to return these eggs to their parents. Can you walk?"

Jola nodded. She looked down at her scrawny form for a moment, as if surprised by her own appearance.

"What's the matter?" said Keo. "You seem surprised about something."

Then Jola looked up at him again, except this time Keo saw self-loathing in her eyes, like she hated her own body. She shook her head. *It's nothing. I just am not used to seeing my own body is all.*

"I'm not used to seeing it, either," said Keo. "Is there a reason you're always invisible?"

*Yes,* said Jola. *Now let me go back to it. You don't need to see me.*

With that, Jola's form turned invisible, startling Keo, who hadn't been expecting that. He heard her walking, however, and then saw the eggs float upwards on their own, which would have been a spooky sight if he had not known that Jola was using her own magical powers to raise the Dracone eggs.

*Ready to go back and tell the Dracones that our mission was successful?* Jola asked.

Keo nodded, even though he wondered why Jola apparently hated her own body like that. He decided not to bring it up, however, because Jola hardly seemed to be in the mood to talk about it. Besides, he had his own questions to worry about, such as why he was able to turn golden and why he could shoot fire from his hands like that.

So Keo followed Jola and the floating eggs toward the cave's exit, his mind still puzzling over these questions.

# Chapter Eight

WHEN THEY EMERGED FROM the cave, they were immediately greeted by the mother of the eggs, a Dracone with purple scales who immediately took the eggs away from them without so much as a thank you. Nonetheless, Keo thought that their mission had been successful, at least until Weret said that the Brothers White Blood had stolen *eight* eggs, not seven, which meant that there was an eighth one still missing. But Weret informed Keo that they would send some of the younglings into the tunnels after Ankem, who had most likely taken the eighth egg with him, though to where and why, no one knew.

Regardless, the Dracones were happy when they learned that two of the kidnappers were dead and the third was badly injured and on the run. While none of them thanked Keo and Jola for their actions, Keo could tell that the Dracones no longer looked at him and the others with quite as much hate or distrust as before. They probably still saw Keo and the others as their inferiors, but at least now it seemed like the Dracones were content to leave Keo and his friends in peace, rather than growl and snarl at them like they had before.

In fact, Keo and his friends were even allowed to stay in the

Nest overnight, as per the Queen's orders. Apparently the Queen had heard about Keo and Jola rescuing the unborn and decided to reward him by allowing him and his friends spend the night in the Nest. Although the Queen had made it clear in her message that she was not going to rethink her rejection of Keo's offer to form a human/Dracone alliance, she said that she believed in rewarding heroism even if performed by a human, which was why she was letting him and the others stay for the night. That was fine by Keo, because the sun was already starting to go down and traveling in the Upper Mountains at night was never a wise idea.

Keo and his friends were taken to Tananeen's nest, which was located in one of the caves in the valley walls. It was a large, warm place, much better than the coldness of the tents that Keo and his friends had slept in during their journey to the Upper Mountains. Tananeen made beds of straw and hay for them to sleep on and also created a large fire to keep them warm during the night. The reason they were staying at Tananeen's nest was because she was the only Dracone who was willing to let them stay with her, because the other Dracones—even the ones that were appreciative of Keo and Jola rescuing the unborn—had zero interest in sharing their nests with a bunch of humans.

Because they had had a long day, Keo's friends went to sleep quickly. Dlaine was the first to nod off, curled up into a ball on his hay bed, snoring softly, while Maryal followed soon after. Easan seemed to be trying to stay awake because he didn't trust the Dracones, but eventually exhaustion must have overtaken him, too, because when his eyes closed, he immediately started snoring. Keo didn't see or hear Jola sleep, but he figured that she was probably planning to spend the night awake, because she always acted as the night watch. Though Keo didn't see any reason for her to stay awake now, because he felt safe in Tananeen's nest. But he didn't tell her to go to sleep, mostly because he knew that she wouldn't listen.

Keo also tried to go to sleep, but despite his exhaustion from the events of the day, he found it impossible to rest. He was thinking about how savagely he had acted earlier. It was like he had discovered an entirely new part of himself, a side of him he hadn't even suspected existed until then. Not only had he killed two other humans, he would have made that three if Ankem hadn't managed to escape.

Keo had never killed any other human beings before. He had killed plenty of demons, which never weighed on his conscience at all, but there was something different about killing other human beings. He tried to tell himself that it was completely justified, that he had killed them only in self-defense, and he knew that was true and that no one, not even his worst enemies, could hold that against him, but even so, Keo had not even hesitated to kill those two as easily as any demon. He thought it might be harder to kill humans, even if in self-defense, than demons, but apparently it was not.

Keo looked at Tananeen. She was sitting in her human form by the fire to his left, staring into the golden flames that burned warmly. She didn't seem likely to be going to sleep anytime soon, either, so Keo decided to take this moment to ask her a few questions.

Sitting up, Keo said to Tananeen, "Not tired?"

Tananeen looked at him. In the light of the fire, she looked much older than she normally did. Now Tananeen never looked quite as young as, say, Maryal, but it seemed like she had aged a decade over the day. Keo wondered if that had to do with the stress of recent events.

"Not really," said Tananeen. "Dracones can go without sleep for a much longer time than humans. The last time I slept a full eight hours was two days ago, but it still hasn't affected me as badly as it would a human. I will have to sleep again tomorrow, though, otherwise I'll suffer the same sleep deprivation symptoms that humans do."

"Why do I have to adhere to a normal human sleep schedule, then?" said Keo, glancing down at his body. "I'm half-Dracone. Shouldn't I be able to go longer without sleep than normal humans?"

"I do not know," said Tananeen. "There is still a lot I don't know about you, because there have been few human/Dracone hybrids in history. You are, to my knowledge, the only human/Dracone hybrid who is even still alive."

"So I'm unique, then," said Keo. "Who was the last human/Dracone hybrid?"

"I cannot remember," said Tananeen, shaking her head. "Most human/Dracone hybrids don't live to be as old as you. Most die young, often during childbirth, because human and Dracone blood doesn't usually mix. That you survived and have grown up to be such a handsome, strong young man is a miracle in itself, and a testament, I think, more to your father's blood than mine."

Keo looked down at his hands. "I don't feel miraculous. I feel more like a freak than anything. My friends haven't rejected me, but I am not so sure that the rest of humanity will accept me if they learn about my truth after we leave this place."

"Humans often have a hard time accepting things that are different from them," said Tananeen, nodding. "But then, we Dracones are hardly one to talk, considering how coldly most of my people have treated you and your friends, even after you rescued our unborn."

"I think they're upset that we didn't save all of the eggs," said Keo. "Ankem got away with one, but I don't know where it is or what he's planning to do with it."

Tananeen scowled, a deep but short growl emitting from her throat. "He won't get far. The younglings have excellent noses. They should be able to find him no matter what hole he's crawled into. And once they do, he will wish that you had been the one to finish him off."

Tananeen's tone—harsh and beast-like—made Keo look at her in surprise. "I didn't think you wished death on your enemies like that."

"You don't understand," said Tananeen. She sighed and brushed back some of her dark hair. "It is of utmost importance that every unborn Dracone child is saved. Do you know why?"

Keo shook his head. "No, I don't."

"Because we are a much smaller people than we were before your grandfather slaughtered us," said Tananeen. She sounded bitter about that. "I don't remember it as well as my mother because I was born after we were driven out, but she told me there used to be thousands of us. Never quite as large as humanity, but enough that we were never on the verge of extinction, enough that every Dracone could find a clan to be with, a family to be born into and cared for."

Tananeen sounded nostalgic for it, even though she had not

been born at the time. Keo supposed she got it from her mother.

"But when your grandfather turned on us, our numbers dwindled down to a few hundred, which forced my mother—who was pregnant with me at the time—to lead us here, to these cursed mountains," said Tananeen. "Our numbers have grown since then, but even after seventy years of survival, we still are nowhere near as large as we once were. Our growth is constrained by the Nest, which we are afraid to leave because it is the only territory we own and can control. We fear that if we tried to expand our territory, that the humans will fight back and maybe even invade and destroy the Nest and our unborn."

"Then that's all the more reason for you to join us," said Keo, resting his hands on his knees. "Once I am King of Lamaira, I could give you more land to live on, more land to grow your clan. Doesn't Sayot understand that?"

"My mother doesn't, sadly enough," said Tananeen. She hung her head. "It has been decades since she has spoken with a human being, so she only remembers Murza and his followers and supporters, who gleefully butchered us with their magic and weapons. I fear that that is all she will ever remember humans as, that she will never be able to put her prejudices behind her so that both peoples can survive."

Keo nodded, but then a question occurred to him. He wasn't sure at first if he should ask it, seeing as it was rather personal, but then he decided that it was just as personal to him as it was to her, so he thought it would be safe to ask.

So Keo said, "Can I ask you a question? About my father?"

Tananeen looked at Keo. She looked eager to hear the question, but also a little worried, like she wasn't sure that she wanted to hear it. "Certainly. What is it?"

"I want to know why you fell in love with him," said Keo. "I mean, why don't you hate humans as much as your mother? What piqued your interest in them?"

Tananeen bit her lower lip and looked back at the burning fire. "I've always been different from my fellow Dracones, even from female Dracones. Even though I was aware that humans had killed my own father, I was nonetheless curious about them and how they survived without our own powers and strength. On the pretext of hunting, I'd travel from the Upper Mountains to the farms and towns in the foothills and fields at the Mountains' foot, just to see humans working and living."

"Did anyone ever see you?" said Keo.

"Not in my dragon form," said Tananeen. "Often, I'd take on my human form and walk among the humans, amazed at what I saw. I never liked hearing the slurs and derogatory jokes made about my people—there were a lot of those back then—but I found humans fascinating anyway, how they could eat, live, work, and survive without any of our natural advantages as Dracones."

"Do humans still fascinate you?" said Keo.

"They still do," said Tananeen, though she still didn't look at Keo. "On one of these trips, I met a dashing young prince named Riuno on one of his northern hunting expeditions. He and a group of his friends and servants were resting at a tavern in one of the towns, which I was visiting because I had grown to like the taste of human beer. We met in that tavern and fell in love immediately."

Tananeen spoke fondly of that day, like she was still sitting in the tavern with Riuno even then. She didn't even seem to be looking at the fire. Instead, her eyes were looking at the past filtered through her memories, which made her look happier than Keo had yet seen her.

"Did my father know you were a Dracone?" said Keo, scratching the back of his neck.

"Not at first," said Tananeen. "He originally believed that I was just a pretty peasant girl, but after about a year, I told him what I really was. It absolutely frightened me and I thought that he was going to reject me, maybe even kill me outright. I had heard tales about other Dracones who, in their human forms, fell in love with real humans, only to be murdered or chased away by their lovers when they revealed their true natures to them in a moment of vulnerability."

"But my father wasn't like that, was he?" said Keo.

"Of course not," said Tananeen. She gestured at Keo. "You are proof of that. Even though it was his father who had run a powerful propaganda campaign to turn the Dracones into the most hated species in the Kingdom, Riuno saw right through it. I think it's because in his youth, he often sat with Murza during meetings with his advisers and so got to see firsthand just what kind of horrible man his father was. He knew that we Dracones were not as bad as his father's propaganda claimed, so he had no trouble accepting me for who I was."

"How many people knew that you and he were seeing each other?" said Keo. "Did you ever get married?"

Tananeen smiled again, though there was something sad about it. "Your father and I kept our relationship a secret from everyone we knew, save for a handful of Riuno's most trusted servants. My mother found out eventually, but she could never keep me away from Riuno, even after she threatened to send the Legion to get me back. But Riuno's father never knew, even to the day of his death. But we did get married in secret, a private ceremony with only your father's most loyal servants in attendance."

"Wow," said Keo. "What did my father do after my grandfather's death?"

"When Riuno became King, I convinced him to try and restore relations with the Dracones," said Tananeen. "He sent envoys to my mother, but she killed every last one. It frustrated me greatly, but my mother merely saw Riuno as the son of Murza. Among us Dracones, we have a habit of treating parent and child as the same, no matter how different their personalities or beliefs are, and so my mother simply saw the return of Murza in Riuno, even though he couldn't have been any more different from his father even if he tried."

"Did my father eventually stop sending envoys?" said Keo.

"Eventually, yes," said Tananeen. "I tried to tell him that he just needed to keep doing it, but Riuno didn't want to keep wasting the lives of his servants trying to get an 'old hag,' as he called my mother, to listen to reason. It was your father who eventually forbade all travel to the Upper Mountains, because he did not want any of his people to be needlessly killed by mine."

"But what about you?" said Keo. "What did he do to you?"

"He still loved me, of course, and tried to spend as much time as he could with me, despite his duties as King of Lamaira taking up a huge portion of his time," said Tananeen. She sighed. "I became a lot more comfortable with being seen in public with Riuno, which led to rumors that I was his wife. But I always tried to avoid public appearances, because I knew that if word got out that Riuno was married to a Dracone, it would have led to the people demanding his head on a platter."

Keo's eyes widened. "Really? I didn't know that anti-Dracone hate was so strong back then."

"Hatred toward the Dracone has gone down since your father's death," said Tananeen, nodding. "Most people, particularly around your age, no longer even remember the Dracone, to the point where some believe we're just stories and nothing more. Still, the fact is that anti-Dracone hatred exists, which is why I had to hide my true nature back in the Old Kingdom."

"I see," said Keo. He looked at the fire for a moment before another question occurred to him and he looked at Tananeen again. "How did my father die?"

Tananeen looked at him again, this time with surprised eyes. "You mean no one ever told you?"

Keo shook his head. "No one did. I only ever hear that when my father died, the Kingdom shattered into the three major factions that continue to fight among each other today. But I don't know how that happened."

Tananeen pushed her hair back again. She seemed to be trying to figure out what to say to Keo, which made him wonder what she was going to say. Perhaps his father's death had been more complicated than he thought.

"Well, your father, the King, was murdered by a demon," said Tananeen.

Keo's mouth fell open. "What? A demon? But ... how? I thought that the demons hadn't been able to slip through the seal until recently."

"True, but the seal had been weakening for fifty years by the time of your father's death," said Tananeen. "Without the Dracones to reinforce its power, the Good King's bloodline was not enough to keep the demons behind the seal entirely. One demon managed to escape and made its way to Tain, where it slit your father's throat in his sleep and fled before I could stop it."

Tananeen sounded heartbroken now, almost too emotional to go on, causing Keo to say, "If you don't want to talk about this—"

Tananeen held up a hand, silencing Keo instantly. "No, I need to talk about this. You need to know it if you are to understand what has happened. If you are going to be the King of Lamaira, then you need to understand the past as well as the present and the future."

"Okay," said Keo. "But why did the Kingdom fall apart when my father died? Why weren't they able to choose a successor?"

Tananeen sighed. "Remember King Murza raising taxes and sending off the peoples' sons to die in pointless wars. That left a bitter taste in the mouths of many of your people, even after Murza blamed us Dracones and started a campaign of extermination against us. Even those who hated the Dracones knew that Murza was responsible for Lamaira's dismal state. They did not get a chance to kill Murza before he died of old age, so they took out their anger on Riuno instead."

"What do you mean?" said Keo. "I thought a demon killed my father."

"It did, but the demon had help from conspirators in the castle," said Tananeen. "To this day I still don't know for sure who summoned the demon, but I do know that the conspiracy fell apart when the Kingdom fell into bloody civil war, which the conspirators hadn't been expecting. Riuno's Magicians took over the south, because they felt that they had lost most of their best students in the wars and Dracone extermination campaign, while the Divinians took the west, because they were a religious minority who faced harsh persecution from Murza during his reign, because most of them had refused to participate in the pointless wars he had waged."

"And the Restorationists took the east, the Old Kingdom," said Keo, "in order to preserve the traditions and customs of my ancestors."

"Exactly," said Tananeen, nodding. "And you, of course, know the rest."

Keo looked at the fire again, thinking hard about what Tananeen had told him. "Then reuniting the Kingdom won't be as easy as I thought."

"Of course it won't," said Tananeen. "But you will have to do it anyway in order to stop the demons. Otherwise, no one, human or Dracone, will survive."

Keo nodded, his eyes still on the fire. Then he remembered something else and said, "Oh yeah. When I was fighting the Brothers White Blood earlier, my skin turned golden and I could shoot fire out of my hands. Golden fire, just like the golden flames I can summon around Gildshine. Do you know what that means?"

Tananeen tapped her chin in thought. "It sounds to me like you unconsciously accessed some of your Dracone powers. We Dracones can summon fire with our hands in our human forms, even though we usually prefer to breathe it from our mouths in our dragon forms. Your golden skin might have been you partially transforming into your own dragon form."

"What do you mean?" said Keo, looking at her again. "I thought transformations were always complete."

"Not necessarily," said Tananeen. "Young Dracones often have a hard time shifting forms during their early years. Many of them will get caught halfway, looking like a humanoid dragon or a dragon-like human. It's completely normal, though it can be uncomfortable at first."

"So I can transform into a dragon, then?" said Keo. "How do I do that?"

"Not here," said Tananeen, shaking her head. "Or now. But I could teach you in the morning, if you want, though I don't know how helpful I can be, seeing as I've never trained a half-Dracone before."

Keo thought about that. Learning how to transform into a dragon would be extremely useful. At the same time, though, Keo wasn't sure that it would be wise to spend more time here in the Nest than was necessary. They still needed to get to the Divinians and it would take them a long time to travel to the west, particularly on foot, and they needed every minute they could if they were going to get there before the demons rose again.

Then another idea occurred to Keo and he said, "Can't you come with us and teach me how to control my powers along the way to the Divinians? That way, we won't waste time that could be better spent going to them."

Tananeen sighed. She looked at the burning flames again before saying, "I would love to come with you and your friends, Keo, because as your mother I have spent far too much time away from you, more so than any mother should spend away from her child. But I cannot."

Without warning, anger rose in Keo, sheer, utter anger that almost made him shout, anger that he hadn't been expecting to feel. But he restrained his anger and said, in a calm voice, "Why not? You're my mother and you've always been a rebel. Why not do the right thing and come and help me and my friends?"

"Because I am still a Dracone," said Tananeen. "Not only that, but I am the Dracone Princess. My people need me. My mother is getting older and older every day. I may not always agree with her on everything, nor do I approve of the bigotry my own people showed toward you, but I am still a Dracone and I must be here to succeed my mother in case she dies or is forced to abdicate the throne for some unknown reason."

Keo leaned toward her. He tried to hide his anger, but his hands shook nonetheless. "But didn't you hear what your mother called me? She called me a halfbreed. And the rest of your people don't like me or my friends, either, even after we rescued several of their unborn. Why do you feel the need to be so loyal to them?"

Tananeen suddenly looked at Keo. There was anger in her eyes now, an almost primal anger that made Keo sit back in surprise.

"Weren't you listening?" said Tananeen. "I am the Dragon Princess. I cannot simply abandon my people, even to help my son. I hoped that you would understand this, but I can see that you still have a long way to go before you do."

"What is there to understand?" said Keo, who was feeling defensive under her harsh tone and words. "I'm your son. Shouldn't you care more about me than your people? You said you wanted to spend more time with me, but now you are rejecting the only opportunity that will allow you to do that? Are you even listening to yourself when you talk?"

"I know exactly what I am saying, Keo, but I don't think that *you* do," said Tananeen. "Perhaps once you have grown older, you will understand where I am coming from. Your father did. That's why he never asked me to come live in Tain with him. He knew I couldn't, even though we both loved each other more than anything else in the world."

"All I hear is a mother who is sending mixed messages to her son," said Keo. "But fine. If that's what you want to do, then do it. I don't need your training, either. In the morning, my friends and I will just go southwest, to the Divinians. Maybe they'll be more receptive to our message."

With that, Keo lay back down on his hay, turned so that his back was facing Tananeen, and closed his eyes. He heard Tananeen draw closer to him, heard her whisper his name, but he did not respond. Eventually, he heard her lie down on her hay as well and soon heard her snoring.

But Keo did not drift to sleep right away. He was too consumed by his anger toward his mother to relax, although eventually exhaustion won out over anger and he soon drifted into slumber.

# Chapter Nine

IN THE MORNING, KEO and his friends left soon after a quick but satisfying breakfast of dried meat and bread from their travel supplies. Neither Tananeen nor the other Dracones had any food edible for humans to offer them, aside from some cooked sheep that Tananeen had stolen from one of the farms near the foot of the Upper Mountains.

Because of Keo and Jola's rescue of the Dragon eggs, the group was permitted to leave without experiencing harassment from the Dracones, although they nonetheless received a lot of glares from the Dracones anyway, probably due to the fact that all five of them had committed the unforgivable crime of being human (or half-human, in Keo's case). Only the mother Dracone from yesterday, the one whose eggs had been stolen in the first place, looked upon Keo and his friends without any hostility as they passed her nest, but even she did not thank them, probably because she could not speak Lamairan.

It wasn't long, then, before Keo and his friends left the Nest and returned to the surrounding mountains. Instead of going back the way they came, however, they went around the Nest to the other side, which would take them south and eventually west, according to Tananeen, who had traveled to the Divinians' country before and so therefore knew the quickest way to get there.

It was the only bit of help that they received from Tananeen, or that Keo would accept, at least. He was still angry at her refusal to come with them, at how she was clearly more loyal to the Dracones than to him. He wasn't quite sure why this angered him, because he had not even known that she was his mother until yesterday. It probably had to do with the fact that he had never known his mother growing up, so learning that his mother cared more about her own people than him was hard to take.

Even worse, however, was the knowledge that the Dracones were firmly against working with the humans to stop the demons, especially knowing how important the Dracones were to the defeat of the demons. Keo tried to pretend that it didn't matter, especially whenever Maryal or Easan (who seemed to think that Keo was acting like an idiot for not trying to convince Queen Sayot to work with them) brought it up, but deep down he knew that this was a huge failure on their part. The Dracones could have been a mighty ally, but with Queen Sayot's stubborn refusal to work with them, the entire mission had been a huge failure. That depressed Keo, because he had left Tain after telling the Keepers and the other Tainians that he would return with the Dracones by his side.

But now, it was clear that Keo and his friends had wasted two months for nothing. The Dracones were going to remain isolated in the Upper Mountains, ignoring the rising threat of the demons that threatened to destroy them all. The only glimmer of hope was Queen Sayot dying of old age and then Tananeen succeeding her, but that seemed like an impossible thing to hope for at the moment, because even though the Queen was obviously old, she seemed to have too much fight in her to give up the ghost just yet.

The failure of the mission wasn't just affecting Keo, however. Maryal kept looking back toward the Nest the farther down the Mountains they traveled, even after the Nest itself was lost from view. Easan made no secret of his belief that Keo had failed in the negotiations, while Dlaine seemed to be both relieved and worried, as if he was unsure whether the fact that the Dracones had allowed them to leave alive was a good thing. As always, Keo could not see Jola, but he suspected that she was just as stressed out by this failure as he was, if not more so than the others due to how she had helped him save those eggs and had not received any real thanks from the Dracones for doing it.

But none of them suggested that they go back to the Dracones and try to talk with them again. That was because they knew that if they tried going back, the Dracones would not hesitate to kill them all. It was better to go to the Divinians, who the Keepers had promised to send messengers to announcing the return of the *shelmai* and thus preparing them for Keo's arrival, than go back and risk inciting the Dracones' collective wrath.

So they traveled down the Mountains for a couple of long, silent, and very cold days, during which no one said much and they didn't see much of anything. They did come across the skeletal remains of a few Dracones here and there, but they did not see any living Dracones at all. Nor did they want to, because Keo had a feeling that if they saw another Dracone, it would probably try to kill them even if Keo told it that he was the son of Tananeen.

Three days after they left the Nest, something of interest

finally happened. It was early in the morning, with the first rays of the sun poking over the mountain peaks, with the cold frosty air lingering around them. They had just finished breakfast and were preparing to resume their journey down the Upper Mountains when Keo heard the scraping of boots against rock.

That made Keo stand up from folding his tent and looked around their surroundings. They had camped in a fairly isolated portion of the Mountains, just off the main path they had been taking down to the foot of the Mountains. This portion was shaped like a square, with their tents set up around a fire in the center. Large boulders surrounded them on most sides, with a handful of cliffs and caves in the northern side. They had chosen to camp here because it was out of the winds and also because it was almost impossible to see from the main path, which meant that they were unlikely to be spotted by anyone traveling up or down the Mountains unless they were specifically looking for them.

But Keo thought he had heard the scraping of someone's boots against rock. He initially assumed it was Easan, Maryal, or Dlaine who had made that sound, but the boot scraping sound had come from a nearby cliff, whereas all of Keo's friends were in the same area as he was. He even thought that it might have been Jola, but Jola did not wear boots and certainly did not move so clumsily that you could hear her so easily like that.

All around Keo, the others were packing up their things, putting out the fire that had been used to warm them and make their food, and gather up their own possessions in their bags. None of them seemed to have heard the scraping sound, yet Keo was certain that he had. He looked around, but saw no one else in the area except for his friends and himself.

So Keo said, "Did anyone hear that?"

"Hear what?" said Easan, looking up from his bag in annoyance. "The failure of our mission?"

"No, not that," said Keo, shaking his head. "I heard someone's boots scraping against rock, and the sound didn't belong to any of you guys."

"Are you saying someone is hiding nearby?" said Maryal, who had just finished packing her things. She stood up and looked around the area, a frown on her face. "I don't see anyone."

"Jola?" said Dlaine. "Is there anyone around here who we don't know about?"

*I'm looking, but I think we're alone,* said Jola, whose voice Keo could hear in his head. *I didn't see anyone at all last night and there's no way someone could have sneaked up on us without*

—

A sudden *twang* interrupted Jola's words and an arrow shot past Keo's face and landed at his feet. Surprised, Keo jumped backwards, drawing Gildshine from its sheath at the same time, and looked up just in time to see someone with a bow disappear behind some rocks.

"What the hell?" said Easan, standing up and wielding Shadowbane in both hands as he looked for the archer. "Who was that?"

"I don't know," said Keo, his eyes scanning the rocks and cliffs around them, trying to spot the archer but failing. "But whoever he is, he almost hit me."

Dlaine ran over to Keo and plucked the arrow from the earth at his feet. He held up the arrow, which had a long shaft and silver tip, a frown on his older features.

"Huh," said Dlaine, turning the arrow over in his hands. "I don't think I've ever seen an arrow like this before. Head's sharp and thick, much sharper and thicker than it needs to be if the guy was just trying to kill a person or even an animal, and the shaft is designed to go all the way in. Very strange."

"I don't really care about the finer points of arrows," said Keo as he, Easan, and Maryal looked everywhere for sign of their assailant. "If that guy tries to shoot me again—"

Another *twang* and another arrow flew toward Keo, but he deflected it with Gildshine. This time, he saw his attacker: A young woman, wearing a red hood, standing atop some nearby rocks. There was a stunned expression on her face, like she was shocked that Keo had deflected the arrow, but Keo wasn't going to let her recover.

Gildshine exploded into golden flames as Keo pointed his sword at the woman. Burning fire shot from Gildshine's tip toward the woman, who belatedly attempted to move out of the way, only to trip and fall to the ground below. She fell on her back with a loud *crunch*, but Keo wasn't going to let her get off so easily.

He ran over to the woman as she sat up, shaking her head and rubbing her back. Keo raised Gildshine above his head at the same time that the young woman looked up at him in shock, her red hood falling back to reveal short blonde hair done in elaborate braids. But Keo could not care less about her hair, because he was going to kill her there and then with Gildshine, regardless of how she looked.

At least, that was the plan until he felt something sharp and hard press against the back of his neck. It felt like an arrow, an arrow that would pierce his neck and kill him if it was fired.

Then a harsh, male voice said in his ear, "Kill my sister and I kill you. Trust me, I've killed men for less than this before."

Keo gritted his teeth, but there was no way he could turn around in time to stop the man from shooting the arrow in his neck. He doubted his friends could save him, either, because they were probably not close enough to help.

He looked down at the young woman at his feet. She was staring up at Keo with surprise, as if she was shocked by Gildshine. Her eyes were drawn to its constantly burning golden flames, although Keo didn't find that odd, because that was how most people reacted whenever they saw the golden flames of the Rightful Heir.

"Are you going to lower your blade or not?" said the man. "Because my fingers are starting to slip, and whenever my fingers slip, someone usually gets an arrow straight through their heart. Or their head. Or their stomach. Or wherever I happen to be aiming it at the time."

Seeing that he had no other choice, Keo cut off the golden flames around Gildshine and sheathed the sword. At the same time, the young woman scrambled to her feet, picking up her fallen bow. She walked several feet away from Keo, looking both frightened and yet relieved that she was still alive.

"Aye, now," said the man, who Keo noticed had a strong accent he didn't recognize. "I'm going to take my arrow off your neck. But if you try to draw that weird burning sword of yours again to harm me or my sister, I will put my arrow through your skull again, and I don't believe either of us wants that, because that would be a waste of a perfectly good arrow for me and very painful and probably lethal for you. All right?"

Keo didn't like being at the mercy of this mysterious archer, but he nodded anyway and said, "Understood."

Then he felt the arrow's pressure on the back of his neck go away. Then someone in red dashed past him and Keo saw that a young man, close to him in age, was now standing by the young woman. Like the young woman, the young man wore a red hood, although his appeared older and more faded, like he had received it secondhand from someone else. Like the young woman, the man carried a bow, except his was longer and deadlier-looking than the young woman's. The young man also wore a long necklace with the teeth of some animal on it, which made Keo think that he must be some kind of hunter.

"Who are you?" said Keo as Dlaine, Maryal, and Easan ran over to him. "Why did you attack us?"

The young man had an arrow notched in his bow, the same arrow that Dlaine had noticed earlier. He glanced at his young sister and nodded at her once, probably to indicate that he should do all the talking. His sister didn't seem to mind. She even stepped back behind him, like she thought that Keo and the others would attack her if she did not have her brother's protection.

"We thought you were bandits," said the young man. His eyes darted from Keo to his friends' faces, like he was trying to read their minds. "Around here, we kill bandits and anyone else who intrudes upon our territory."

"Well, we aren't bandits, and we didn't know that anyone owned this place," said Keo, gesturing at their camp area. "We thought that it was part of nature."

"No part of this mountain is purely part of nature," said the young man, shaking his head. "'Tis all under the protection of the Great Mountain Man."

"The Great Mountain what?" said Easan.

"The Great Mountain Man," the young man repeated. He gestured at the ground under their feet. "He is the man who created the foundations of the Upper Mountains. He is not with us at the moment, but he does protect the Upper Mountains from all threats."

Keo frowned. "The Dracones didn't mention the Great Mountain Man when we visited them."

Keo immediately knew that he must have said something wrong, because the young man's suspicious glare turned into an outright scowl, while his sister hid closer behind him and looked up at the sky, as if she expected boulders to start raining down upon them.

"Did you just mention the Dracones?" said the young man with a snarl.

"Uh, yes," said Keo, nodding, although he found that he didn't like he young man's sudden hostility at all. He didn't think the young man was going to attack them, but he didn't think the young man was going to sit down and have a nice chat with them, either.

"You have met the Dracones?" said the young man. "When?"

"A few days ago," said Keo. "Why?"

The young man immediately aimed his bow at them, causing Easan to raise Shadowbane defensively and Maryal to raise her hands to cast a defensive spell. Yet the young man did not shoot them just yet, although he was clearly ready and willing.

"Are … are any of you Dracones?" said the young man, looking at them suspiciously. "The elders say that the Dracones can take on the guises of humans. Are you really human or are you deceivers attempting to trick us into becoming your next meals?"

Keo blinked. He opened his mouth to explain that only he had any Dracone blood in him before Dlaine stepped forward and said, "Nope. None of us are Dracones. There isn't a single drop of Dracone blood flowing through any of our veins. We merely visited them. That is all."

Keo looked at Dlaine in surprise, but Dlaine shot him a look that quite clearly said, *Shut up. I got this.*

The young man relaxed slightly when he heard Dlaine's words, but he did not lower his arrow at all. "Why did you visit the Dracones? What business could a group of humans like you have with those monsters?"

"Monsters?" said Keo in annoyance. "The Dracones aren't monsters. They're—"

"Keo," said Dlaine, holding up a hand. "Let me answer the young man's question, okay?"

Keo was about to say no, but then he realized that Dlaine had a plan to ensure that none of them got skewered by the unusually strong arrows that these two strangers had. So he nodded in affirmation, although that didn't stop him from feeling offended by the young man's description of the Dracones as 'monsters.'

"All right," said Dlaine, looking at the young man, "to answer your question, we visited the Dracones because we were trying to form an alliance with them to fight a threat against the Kingdom of Lamaira."

The young man exchanged a quick but puzzled look with his sister before returning his attention back to Keo and the others. "So you are allied with the Dracones? Then that makes you our enemy."

Dlaine held up his hands quickly, before the young man could shoot. "Whoa, there. I didn't say we're allies. Notice I said 'trying.' We didn't succeed."

"Largely due to our luckless leader here," Easan muttered, causing Keo to glare at him.

"But the mere fact that you tried to form an alliance with the evil beasts of the Mountains means that we cannot trust you," said the young man. "Anyone who seeks union with the Dracones is obviously evil."

"You don't understand," said Dlaine, shaking his head. "The Dracones may or may not be evil, but we needed their help to combat that threat to Lamaira that I mentioned earlier."

"Lamaira?" the young man repeated. "What's Lamaira? I've never heard of it."

Keo, Easan, and Maryal looked at each other in confusion, while Dlaine, who seemed to be trying to hide his own confusion, said, "What do you mean, you've never heard of it?"

"I have never heard of any kingdom called Lamaira," said the young man. "And neither has my sister. Are you lying to us?"

"We're not lying to you or your sister," said Dlaine. He pointed south. "South of these mountains lies a land that was once the great Kingdom of Lamaira, which is currently divided into three smaller kingdoms that are at war with each other. Didn't your parents, at least, tell you about Lamaira?"

"None of the elders ever mentioned this 'Lamaira' before,"

said the young man. "Right, sister?"

His sister nodded, but she still didn't say anything. She seemed a lot more timid than her brother, although Keo suspected that it was all an act, seeing as she had shown no timidity earlier when she tried to kill him with one of her arrows.

"Then I take it that you haven't heard of the *shelmai*, the Rightful Heir who is supposed to reunite the entire Kingdom?" said Dlaine. He pointed at Keo. "Who, by the way, is this guy right here."

"Never," said the young man, shaking his head. "All I have known is that the people who don't live on the Mountains are to be trusted even less than the Dracones." He gestured with his bow in the opposite direction. "Now leave. We have no interest in entertaining foreigners like yourselves, and if you don't leave, then prepare to find an arrow in your—"

"Brother," said his sister suddenly, grabbing his arm. Her voice was very soft. "Don't shoot them just yet."

The young man looked at his sister, but he did not aim his bow away from them just yet. "What is the problem, sister? Didn't they knock you down from the boulder and try to kill you?"

His sister looked at Keo, almost like she recognized him, and then said, "What that old man said about the *shelmai*. Doesn't that word sound similar to the name of the Great Mountain Man's son, Sheli?"

"Sheli?" said the young man. "Sister, you know that Sheli was said to have died ages ago. That is why the sky sometimes rains, because it is the Great Mountain Man crying over the death of his one and only son."

"Yes, but the legends also say that Sheli will one day

reincarnate to save us from the Dracones," said his sister. She pointed at Keo. "What if that young man over there is the reincarnation of Sheli?"

"I find that far-fetched, sister," said the young man. "Would the real Sheli ever try to form an alliance with the Dracones? I doubt it."

"But maybe he doesn't remember who he is," his sister said. "The legends said that Sheli might not remember his true identity at first, but maybe if we take him to the elders, they could help him remember who he is."

"Sister, you do realize that this man tried to kill you with a burning sword, yes?" said the young man. "What if he tries to do it again, except this time at the village itself?"

Keo didn't like the way the young man talked about him, like he was some kind of volatile murderer who had to be watched very carefully lest he snap and start killing people. But a look from Dlaine convinced Keo to keep his mouth shut. Dlaine seemed to think that the young man and his sister might be of help, though he didn't see what they could gain from working with these two.

"He only attacked me because I attacked him," said his sister. "Otherwise, he probably wouldn't have even touched me. It was in self-defense, which the real Sheli was said to do all the time whenever someone attacked him."

"I suppose you have a point, but I still don't trust this man or his friends," said the young man. "Nor do I feel comfortable leading them to the village. What if they try to harm the others?"

"We can stop them if necessary," said his sister. "There are a lot of strong men in the village who can stop them if they try to harm anyone."

"I still don't know," said the young man. "It seems like a risk."

"Yes, but don't you think it's a risk we should take, if he actually is the reincarnation of Sheli?" said his sister in an eager voice. "Then he could help us vanquish the Dracones once and for all and return the Upper Mountains to our people, to whom it rightfully belongs."

Keo found that an odd thing to say. The Dracones had not mentioned anyone else living in the Upper Mountains when they first arrived here after King Murza started killing them off. He wondered why that was.

The young man looked between his sister and Keo for a couple of seconds before sighing, lowering his bow, and saying, "All right, sister. You win. We'll take this young man and his friends to the village and let the elders decide if he is the reincarnated Sheli. If he isn't, then we can simply send him and his friends on their way. But if he is … then perhaps we will finally be able to end this war between our people and the Dracones once and for all."

The young man looked at Keo and his friends. "Do you wish to come with us to the village?"

"Of course," said Dlaine, before any of the others could speak. "Just show us the way and we will follow."

The young man nodded as he slung his bow over his shoulder. "Then follow closely. The path to the village is difficult to traverse and hard to find if you don't know the Mountains very well. The Great Mountain Man is never kind to unprepared travelers."

# Chapter Ten

THE PATH TO THE village was indeed treacherous and difficult to traverse on foot. They had to travel across rocky, uneven ground, cling to the sides of cliffs that dropped a hundred or more feet down, and climb up unforgiving mountainsides with powerful wind that threatened to knock them off at every gust. It got to the point where Keo was starting to regret agreeing to go to the siblings' village, especially because he didn't see how this was possibly related to their mission to reunite the Kingdom.

The brother and sister duo identified themselves as Rackan and Nobia, with Rackan being the older brother and Nobia the younger sister. According to Rackan—who, despite his distrusting attitude, was far more talkative than Nobia—they were members of a group of people known as the Horanians who had lived in the Upper Mountains for centuries before the arrival of the Dracones some seventy years ago. Rackan claimed that the Dracones had largely wiped out their people, leaving only one village left, which was always on the verge of being destroyed due to the presence of the Dracones. Rackan also claimed that the only reason the Dracones had yet to completely wipe them out was because the Horanians were dragon hunters and had grown increasingly effective at taking down beasts five times their size in battle over the years.

That certainly explained the unusually strong arrows that Rackan and Nobia used, but it didn't explain where the Horanians had come from or why Keo and the others hadn't even known about them until about an hour ago. Rackan told Keo that he could ask the elders about their past once they arrived at the village, because the elders knew the history of the Horanian people better than he or Nobia did. Even so, Keo interpreted that as Rackan wanting to limit his interaction with Keo as much as possible due to the fact that he clearly didn't trust Keo or his friends at all.

The entire trip to the village didn't take much longer than a couple of hours or so, by which time the sun had risen high enough to warm up the area more and give them more light to see by. They had to climb one last cliff—a particularly steep one this time—before they came upon the village itself, which, like the Nest, was nestled between two large mountains.

The village that spread out before them was much smaller than the Nest, though that was most likely due to the fact that its human inhabitants were smaller than the Dracones. There were about two or three dozen stone huts and slightly less other buildings of varying sizes scattered all around, although Keo noticed that they were not scattered too widely. They reminded Keo of the burned and blackened stone ruins that he and the others had seen on their way up the Upper Mountains a few days ago, which made him wonder if those ruins had been what was left of the other Horanian villages that had been destroyed by the Dracones.

"Is that your village?" said Dlaine, panting as he put his hands on his knees and looked at the small village below. "It sure is small."

"It's all that's left after decades of war against the Dracones," said Rackan. "We can't afford to make it any bigger, not when we don't have the numbers to sustain it."

Rackan sounded bitter about that, like he wished for the village to be bigger, but knew that it was an impossible dream at the moment. It made Keo feel a little sorry for him, even though he was still annoyed at how Rackan had implied that he was a serial killer just waiting to happen.

"Again, follow us," said Rackan, gesturing for Keo and the others to follow Nobia and him. "But carefully, quietly, and politely. The Village Guard have orders to shoot anyone approaching the village they don't recognize. If they see me and Nobia, however, they'll hold their fire until we tell them that you are our guests."

"And you definitely don't want to anger the Guard," Nobia added, speaking up for the first time since they had left the camp area. "They are the best of the best. Once, they killed a fully-grown male Dracone who attacked the village with only four arrows."

"Only four?" said Keo in disbelief. "How can you kill a fully-grown male Dracone with only four arrows?"

"It's not about how many arrows you have, but rather, how you use them and were you put them," said Rackan. "As I said, our people have been fighting the Dracones for decades. We know all of their weak points and the best ways to kill them, even when they are in their dragon forms."

"In any case, that's why you want to be careful around the Guard," said Nobia, her tone far too cheerful for the grim subject. "Otherwise ... well, you know."

With that, Rackan and Nobia made their way down the slopes to the village below. Keo exchanged worried looks with his friends, because he was starting to fear that this might just be a trap laid out for them by the siblings. Still, Keo and his friends followed them anyway, because they had come too far to simply turn around and leave now.

As they walked down the slopes, Keo caught hints of red in the rocks and cliffs around them. He only ever saw them out of the corner of his eye, but he believed that the flashes of red belonged to the Village Guard, who were obviously following them as they drew nearer to the village. No arrows flying yet, but as always whenever Keo found himself in an uncertain situation, he rested a hand on Gildshine's hilt, ready to draw it at a moment's notice. Thankfully, Easan also seemed to be aware that they were being followed, because he walked with his hand on the hilt of Shadowbane as well.

Neither Rackan nor Nobia seemed to be afraid of the men in red hoods above, but that made sense, because they were native of the village and so were probably safe from being shot at. Keo guessed that the only reason that his friends and he weren't currently full of arrows was because of the siblings' presence, which likely caused the Village Guard to wait and see if they were a threat. Even so, Keo kept expecting to hear the *twang* of bows and the sound of arrows flying through the air toward them at any moment.

But they entered the village completely unharmed, which

would have made Keo relax, but he now noticed scared or distrusting faces peeking out from the windows or doorways of the huts in the village. Most of the faces vanished whenever he or his friends tried to look at them, as if they were afraid of being seen by the strangers, but a few stayed still. Yet none of them came out of the huts, even though Rackan and Nobia were walking with Keo and his friends unharmed.

Then, without warning, a man dashed out of one of the huts and came to a halt in front of Keo and the others, halting their progress into the village. The man looked older than Rackan and Nobia, perhaps in his thirties or so, with a short, scruffy beard and a red hood similar to what the siblings wore. Like the siblings, he also carried a bow and a quiver of arrows, in addition to the ax tied to his waist, probably for close combat, although considering how the Horanians spent most of their time fighting the Dracones, Keo wondered how useful an ax would be against the Dracones' thick and nearly impenetrable scales.

"Rackan? Nobia?" said the man, whose voice was surprisingly deep for a man his age. He had an accent like Rackan's, except even thicker. "Who are these strangers? Did they force you to bring them here?"

"No, Captain, we brought them here on our own free will," said Rackan, shaking his head. He gestured at Nobia. "Sister Nobia insisted that we take them to the village because she believes that the young man with the burning sword is the reincarnation of Sheli, the Great Mountain Man's son."

The man known as the Captain looked between Keo and Easan, a frown on his face. "Which one does Nobia think is the reincarnation of Sheli?"

"That one," said Nobia, pointing at Keo. "He says he's the *shelmai*, though I don't know what that is. But it sounds like Sheli to me, so I think that means that he might be the reincarnation."

The Captain looked at Keo with a critical, questioning gaze. Keo noticed that the Captain had an arrow loaded in his bow, probably ready to fire it if Keo and the others proved dangerous.

"He does not look like Sheli, but then, I suppose that the legends don't say that Sheli would have to look like himself upon reincarnation," the Captain said. "But I still am not sure that this man and his friends should be allowed in the village. You remember the story about the old man and the stranger, don't you, Nobia?"

"I do," said Nobia, nodding, "but I think we can trust these people. I don't think they're bad, but if they do turn out to be a threat, we shouldn't have any trouble killing them."

Keo bit his lower lip, but he said nothing because he didn't want to mess up whatever Dlaine's plan was, even though as far as he could tell Dlaine had no plan at all. He noticed that Easan looked annoyed, perhaps at the implication that Nobia considered him and the others easy to kill, although it was sometimes hard to tell what Easan was annoyed about, considering how he seemed to have a permanently angry or annoyed look on his face at all times.

"Are you going to see the elders?" said the Captain.

"Yes," said Nobia, nodding. "The elders are supposed to be able to tell if someone is the reincarnation of Sheli, so I thought we'd bring this man to see them."

"Armed?" the Captain questioned.

"We'll ask them to give up their weapons before we enter the

Temple," said Nobia.

The Captain, however, shook his head. "No. I must ask that this man and his friends hand over all weapons to me. As Captain of the Village Guard, it is my duty to ensure the protection of the people of this village. I don't want a bunch of possibly dangerous strangers running around the village with swords like those."

The Captain gestured at Keo and Easan's swords, which were still sheathed at their sides. Even so, Keo and Easan both took a step back, but then Keo heard the pulling back of a bow and, looking over his shoulder, saw three men in red hoods standing behind them, with their arrows aimed at Easan and him. Keo hadn't heard those members of the Village Guard sneak up on them, which made him understand why Nobia was so confident that they could take care of him and his friends if they tried to cause any trouble. Easan also looked surprised, as did Maryal and Dlaine, but none of them said anything, probably because the Village Guard looked they just needed one excuse to shoot them and they didn't want to give it to them.

"Okay," said Nobia. She looked at Keo and his friends. "Keo, will you and your friends please give your weapons over to Captain Salme? It won't be forever. Just until you either leave the village or are no longer deemed a threat."

"Give up our weapons?" Easan said in an offended voice. "To strangers like you? Why, that has to be the—"

"We'll do it," Keo interrupted Easan. "That's fair. We know that you Horanians don't know us, so, of course, you can't trust us just yet. That's fine."

Easan looked at Keo like Keo had just suggested that they murder his firstborn son. "Keo, what are you thinking? Didn't you just hear what I said?"

"I did, but it's fine," said Keo. "These people aren't our enemies. And like Nobia said, it won't be for long. I imagine we'll get our weapons back before the day is over."

Easan looked like he was about to ignore Keo's orders and simply start fighting the Village Guard, but he thankfully seemed to understand why Keo was doing this, because he removed his hand from Shadowbane's hilt and said, "All right. But if anything goes wrong, I'm blaming you."

Keo nodded, but said nothing in response. He and Easan removed their swords from their belts and handed them to Captain Salme, who took the swords with as much care as if they were made out of glass. Because those were the only weapons they actually carried with them, none of the others had to give up anything to Captain Salme or the other members of the Village Guard, although they did take away Dlaine's cutting knife, even though it wasn't a weapon, because it could be used as one. Dlaine let them take the knife, but he did so while grumbling about how that was his favorite knife and that he hoped that the Village Guard didn't damage it while they kept it with the other weapons.

After that, Captain Salme allowed them to continue to advance deeper into the village, but not without the three members of the Village Guard from before following them. Even though Keo and the others were unarmed and clearly no threat to the Horanians, Captain Salme apparently believed that they still posed a threat to the people, otherwise he wouldn't have ordered the Village Guard to follow them. Sure, Keo didn't hear Captain Salme order the Village Guard to follow, but he also didn't think that the Village Guard were following them of their own free will. Neither Rackan nor Nobia seemed to notice or care if they did, but then, the Village Guard were on their side, so of course they didn't worry about the tough-looking men in red hoods armed with huge bows and thick arrows that could pierce dragon hide.

Thankfully, it wasn't long before they came upon the Temple that Nobia had mentioned earlier. It was easily the largest building in the village, though that wasn't saying much, considering how small the rest of the buildings were. It was as tall as three huts stacked on top of each other and had an elaborate steeple that appeared to be burnt black. There were two windows on the highest floor, two on the second highest floor, and two on the entry level, with an open doorway that lacked a door. The Temple looked even older than the rest of the village, which made Keo assume that the Temple was the first building to have been built here.

Upon entering the Temple, Keo and his friends found themselves standing in a fairly wide-open room. The room felt ancient, particularly with the carvings on the walls that appeared to depict a man carrying a mountain on his back. A set of ancient stone steps led up to the upper floors, but they did not go up the steps.

Instead, Nobia turned to face Keo and his friends and said, "Please wait here a moment while I get the elders. They're on the upper floor and don't know that you are here yet. Don't worry; I won't be gone long." She looked at Rackan. "Brother, can you keep an eye on them while I get the elders? Just to be safe."

"Of course, sister," said Rackan, glancing at Keo and the others as if they were a bunch of no-good thieves who couldn't be trusted with even one lem.

Nobia nodded and then dashed up the stairs and was gone in an instant, leaving Keo and the others standing in the Temple room with Rackan and the three silent but threatening-looking members of the Village Guard.

As soon as Nobia left, Keo looked at Rackan and asked, "What is this Temple for?"

Rackan, who looked surprised at Keo's question, nonetheless answered, "It was built ages ago by our forefathers, before the Dracones came and slaughtered our grandparents. It was built to be a place of worship, where we would go to give thanks and sacrifices to the Great Mountain Man, who had built our home for us and had protected and provided for our people for as long as we can remember."

"I see," said Keo. He glanced at the carvings of the man carrying the mountain on his back. "And is that a carving of the Great Mountain Man himself?"

"It is," said Rackan, nodding. "It depicts the creation of the Upper Mountains. After the Great Mountain Man laid the foundations of this place, he went to the Great Northern Sea to retrieve the Upper Mountains from its depths. He pulled the entire mountain range from the sea floor and brought it here in a day, although he had to rest for a week afterward due to the sheer weight of the Mountains on his back wearing him down."

"The Great Northern Sea?" Maryal said as she brushed back some of her hair. "Do you mean the Frozen Ocean to the north?"

Rackan shrugged. "I don't know. I have never been that far north before. All I know is what the elders and my parents have told me, which is that there is a sea to the far north that is completely frozen for all but a few months of the year. Have you seen it before?"

Maryal shook her head. "No, I haven't, but I read about it in a book once and had a teacher who said he visited it in his youth, prior to the fall of the Kingdom of Lamaira."

A confused frown appeared across Rackan's lips as he folded his arms over his chest. "I still don't know what this 'Kingdom of Lamaira' is."

"We'll tell you about it later," said Dlaine. "After, of course, we meet with the elders."

"Very well," said Rackan. "I am not sure that you are telling the truth about this 'Kingdom of Lamaira,' but maybe the elders will be able to confirm its existence for us. They know far more about the Upper Mountains and the outside world than anyone in this village."

"Really?" said Maryal. "How many elders are there?"

"Four," said Rackan. "And they are all very intelligent and wise, much wiser than me, at any rate."

"Speaking of the elders, what's taking 'em so long to get down here?" said Easan, looking up at the ceiling of the Temple. "Nobia's been gone for a while."

"The elders spend hours every day locked up in their rooms, where they meditate on the best ways to lead our people and protect us from the Dracones," said Rackan. "And they dislike being interrupted unless it is something truly important that can't be put off for very long, like the possible identification of the reincarnation of Sheli."

"How long will we have to wait, then?" said Easan in annoyance.

"Not much longer, my impatient friend," said an aged but vaguely familiar-sounding voice above. "Or not at all, I should say."

Keo and the others looked up the stairs, which was where the voice had come from. Nobia came rushing down the stairs, like she was in a hurry, and then stopped next to Rackan just as the feet of the first of the elders appeared at the top of the stairs. As the elders made their way down the stairs, Rackan, Nobia, and the three members of the Village Guard who had come with them all knelt, though neither Keo nor his friends followed their example.

Keo watched as the three elders came down the steps one by one. The first was an elderly woman, tall and thin, with a claw-shaped scar on her right cheek, the second was a short man who looked like he must have been strong in his youth, and the third was another woman, but much smaller and bent over than any of them. All three of them wore dark gray and brown robes, which contrasted sharply with the bright red hoods of the Village Guard and Rackan and Nobia.

The first elder, the tall and thin woman, pointed at Keo with her staff and said, "Are you the one that young Nobia told us about? The possible reincarnation of Sheli?"

"Yes," said Keo, nodding. "My name is Keo of the Sword, but where is the fourth elder? We were told that there are four of you."

"Ah," said the first elder, glancing up at the ceiling. "Brother Zamel was napping when young Nobia came up to tell us about what she and her brother found, but he should be here soon."

*Zamel?* Keo thought, tilting his head to the side. *Now where have I heard that name before? I know I heard it somewhere recently, but where?*

Then the sound of wood hitting against stone echoed down from the staircase. It sounded like someone was using a walking stick for help.

The first elder looked up and said, "Ah, that must be him. Brother Zamel has been dealing with a terrible limp recently, so he has had to lean on his walking stick for help."

Then another set of feet appeared at the top of the steps. As the feet of the last elder made their way down the steps, Keo continued to puzzle over the name Zamel. It sounded so familiar, yet every time he searched his memories for anyone with that name, they came up completely blank. Yet he was absolutely certain that he had heard it somewhere before, even if he could not currently place it.

The three elders turned to look up at the last elder, who was now almost completely down. The last elder, Brother Zamel, had a more muscular-looking body than his fellow elders, although he was clearly past his prime. Like the others, he wore dark gray and brown robes and used a staff for support, but he had a strange-looking black ring on his finger that the other elders lacked.

But it wasn't until Keo saw Zamel's face that he suddenly remembered where he had heard that name before. It had been back in Tain, when he had been listening to the Keepers telling Easan and him about the last duel for the Throne of Lamaira. The name had been mentioned offhandedly, which was probably why Keo did not remember it until now, but when Brother Zamel finally reached the bottom of the steps to join the rest of his fellow elders, Keo could not believe his eyes.

He was looking at the aged face of his father, King Riuno, son of King Murza and the last King of Lamaira.

# Chapter Eleven

**B**ROTHER ZAMEL," SAID THE first elder as Zamel stood beside the other elders, "how was your nap? Did it help the pain in your back?"

Zamel grunted and rubbed his back, a scowl on his aged but still handsome features. "Not really. This old body is having a harder and harder time recovering from pain, unlike in my youth, when I could wrestle a mountain bear and take only a day to recover, if even that."

"Old age affects us all," said the first elder, nodding in agreement. "Anyway, brother, this is the man that Nobia told us about, the one known as Keo of the Sword."

Zamel turned his attention to Keo, a curious look on his face. But when his eyes rested on Keo, a brief look of shock appeared on his face, as if he had just seen a ghost.

But then the look of shock went away, replaced by the solemn look of curiosity on his features from before. No one else seemed to have noticed Zamel's brief shock, but Keo was certain that he had not imagined it. Zamel had recognized Keo because, Keo knew, Zamel was his uncle.

Many years ago, after Keo's grandfather had died, the Throne of Lamaira had been left vacant, with Murza's two children, the brothers Riuno and Zamel, the only two eligible heirs to succeed Murza. But Murza had not left any instructions stating definitively who was to succeed him as King of Lamaira, so the next King was decided via duel between Riuno and Zamel. Riuno had been victorious and then crowned the King of Lamaira afterward, while Zamel had lived as a minor noble in Castle Lamaira until he disappeared in the chaos that had enveloped the Kingdom after Riuno's death. That was the story that the Keepers had told Keo, although he had not thought about the story at all until just recently and was, in fact, surprised by how clearly he remembered it.

In any case, that meant that this 'Brother Zamel' was likely the same Zamel who had been Riuno's brother, the one who had disappeared after Riuno's death and whose fate had been a mystery to everyone. Zamel certainly looked old enough to be Riuno's brother and bore a striking resemblance to him, despite looking much older than any of the statues of Riuno that Keo had seen.

The only question now was, what was Zamel doing here and should Keo bring this up to everyone? He didn't see any real harm in it, but what if Zamel ordered the Village Guard to kill him and his friends for revealing his true identity to everyone? It seemed better to play along with 'Brother' Zamel until he had a better understanding of what was going on here. As unlikely as it was, he *supposed* that this Zamel could be unrelated to him and he didn't want to say anything foolish without more evidence.

"Are you from beyond the Mountains, then?" said Zamel. He had that same accent as the other Horanians had, which almost made Keo doubt his original hypothesis until he realized that it didn't sound quite as natural as the other Horanians' accents.

Keo simply nodded and said, "Yes. Not all of us hail from the same country, but all of us are from the ruins of what was once of the Kingdom of Lamaira. Have you heard of it?"

"We have heard of a powerful kingdom that once covered the lands from the foot of the Upper Mountains to the forests far to the south of this place," said the first elder. "But we have never actually met anyone from there, nor did we know that it is now little more than a ruin."

"That's what we're trying to fix," said Keo. He put a hand on his chest. "You see, I am also the son of the last King of Lamaira, a man known as Riuno. Have you heard of him?"

None of the elders seemed to recognize the name, except for Zamel. Another brief look of surprise appeared on his face, but it was only there for an even briefer moment than his other look. That confirmed it for Keo, but he still did not openly identify Zamel just yet.

"Nay, we have not," said the first elder, shaking her head. "Our people have spent their whole lives in these Mountains, away from your kingdom, so we know very little about what has happened beyond our home"

"Nor do we care to know," said Zamel, speaking a little too hurried for Keo's tastes. "We only came down because young Nobia said that she thinks that you are the reincarnation of Sheli, the Great Mountain Man's son."

"Ah, yes," said the first elder. "I almost forgot about that. We came down to see if there is any truth to that claim"

"That's great and all, but we have a few questions that need to be answered first," said Dlaine, drawing the elders' attention to him. He gestured at the Temple they stood in. "For example, who are you people? Where did you even come from? We didn't even know that there were people living in the Upper Mountains. We thought that only Dracones lived here."

All four elders scowled at the mention of the Dracones, which made them all look fiercer than they normally did. The Village Guard also moved slightly, as if responding to a threat, while Rackan and Nobia exchanged surprised but angry looks with each other, as if Dlaine had just said something offensive.

"You mean that you outsiders truly did not know that the Upper Mountains have been the home of the Horanian people for centuries?" said the first elder.

"We didn't even know you guys existed at all," said Dlaine. "Mind giving us a history lesson?"

The first elder stroked her long chin. "Well, I suppose we can. Afterward, we can perform the test to confirm—or deny—Keo's identity as Sheli."

Then the first elder gestured at the three members of the Village Guard, who were still kneeling. "Please leave. Your presence is no longer needed here. Go back to Captain Salme and rejoin the rest of your brothers in protecting the village."

Without a word, the three members of the Village Guard stood up, bowed at the elders, and left through the open doorway of the Temple and were gone before Keo even realized it.

"There," said the first elder before she looked at Keo and the others again. "I sent them away because their presence made the situation far more tense than it ought to be. It will be easier for you to listen if you are not afraid of being shot with an arrow."

Keo raised an eyebrow. "You mean you aren't afraid of us

possibly hurting you? Not that we are, but I thought that you Horanians didn't trust outsiders so easily."

"When did we say that we trusted you?" said the first elder. "It is simply clear to me that you are not a bad man, though if I'm wrong, we can deal with you and your friends easily."

Keo wondered why she thought it would be 'easy' to deal with Keo and his friends without the Village Guard nearby to fight, but he decided not to ask about it. He did, however, make a note not to act in any way that might arouse the suspicions of the elders or the siblings, because he had a feeling that at least some of them were looking for an excuse to harm him and his friends, particularly Zamel, who was stroking his beard in a way that suggested that he was uncomfortable with the presence of Keo, although again no one else except for Keo seemed to notice.

"Anyway," said the first elder, pointing at herself, "allow me to introduce us first. My name is Osina and this is Shinisa and Hanoc. You have already heard Zamel's name."

Shinisa was the other female elder, while Hanoc was the male one. Both nodded at Keo when Osina said their names, while Zamel continued to look uncomfortable while trying not to look uncomfortable, although Keo didn't think he was succeeding very well in that regard.

"What are your names?" said Osina.

"I'm Keo, and this is Dlaine, Maryal, Easan, and Jola," said Keo. He paused. "You can't see Jola because she's invisible, but she's somewhere nearby, I'm sure."

"You're sure?" said Osina, exchanging doubtful looks with her fellow elders. "How do we know she hasn't sneaked off to do some mischief?"

"Because that's not how she works," said Dlaine, folding his arms across his chest. But then he patted something at his knees that Keo could not see and said, "But if you need the reassurance, she's right here by my side. See? I'm even patting her."

The way Dlaine patted Jola looked awkward and Keo couldn't imagine that Jola actually enjoyed it, but he did not hear Jola's voice in his head, so he assumed that she did not mind it too much. The elders, thankfully, no longer looked as panicked as they had just a few seconds ago, although Zamel now appeared to be trying to think of a way to get out of this situation without anyone noticing him leave.

"All right, then," said Osina. "Now, where are all of you from again?"

"We come from beyond the Upper Mountains," said Keo. He pointed at himself. "From the remains of the Kingdom of Lamaira. I am the son of the last king of Lamaira, who died two decades ago, and I am on a mission to reunite the three warring factions that took over the remains of the Kingdom after my father's death."

Keo glanced at Zamel when he said that, but only very briefly so that no one would notice. The look of recognition and fear on Zamel's face confirmed that he was indeed the brother of Riuno, although that still left many unanswered questions that Keo would have to seek the answers for later.

"Interesting," said Osina, resting both hands on the top of her staff. "If you are trying to reunite the warring factions in your home, then why did you come so far north? The Horanians have certainly never been a part of this 'Kingdom of Lamaira' you speak of."

"Because they were trying to form an alliance with the Dracones, elder," said Rackan, speaking up so suddenly that Keo looked at him in surprise. He pointed at Keo and his friends. "That is what they told us when we first met them."

The elders exchanged shocked and puzzled looks, while Keo held up his hands and said, "It's not as bad as he makes it out to be. We did indeed come north to try to form an alliance with the Dracones, but that is because there is a great threat to both humanity and the Dracones that is about to rise and we need the combined effort of both species to stop it."

"And what is this threat you claim is coming, Keo?" said Osina, though she was now looking at Keo more carefully, as if she trusted him even less now than she had before. "An enemy nation from the south?"

Keo shook his head. "It isn't human. We are trying to prepare for the rise of the demons of old. If we don't stop them, then they'll kill all of us, human and Dracone alike."

"The demons of old?" said Osina. "We have never heard of these demons before. Where are they going to come from?"

"We don't know, but we've faced several demons along our journey already and will likely face many more before we stop them for good," said Keo. "But how can you not know about the demons? Back in Lamaira, everyone knows about them, even if not everyone believes that they actually exist."

"Because we Horanians do not have 'demons' in our legends," said Osina. Then she looked at Rackan and Nobia. "Children, did either of you see any of these 'demons' nearby when you first met Keo and his friends?"

"No, elder, we did not," said Rackan, shaking his head. "But I believe that these strangers are lying, because this is the first time I've heard of these so-called 'demons' myself."

"Lying?" said Easan, glaring at Rackan. "Why would we lie?"

"To hide your real intentions for forming an alliance with the Dracones," said Rackan, who didn't back down at Easan's glare at all. "And those intentions are the same as the intentions that all traitors to our people have had: To ensure your own survival when the Dracones inevitably come after your people."

"What the hell?" said Easan. "We're not looking out for our own well-being. We're—"

Dlaine rested a hand on Easan's shoulder, causing Easan to look at him and say, "What?"

"I just wanted to make sure we're all keeping cool heads here," said Dlaine in his most diplomatic tone. "It's pretty clear to me that there is a lot of misconceptions on both sides about who we all are. Why don't we calm down and listen to each other's stories first before we start making assumptions and jumping to conclusions about each other based on nothing more than our own preconceptions?"

Easan looked like he was going to disagree, but he must have thought better of it, because he just shrugged Dlaine's hand off his shoulder and said, "Fine. But they go first."

"Exactly," said Dlaine. He looked at Osina. "Forgive Easan. He's a little hot-headed."

"Of course he is," said Osina, nodding wisely. "Youth is always more passionate than old age. Anyway, we told you that we would tell you about our history, so let us start. Rackan, Nobia, I want both of you to be quiet unless you have something important to add or someone asks you a question."

To Keo's surprise, Rackan and Nobia nodded, although Rackan looked just as unhappy as Easan about not being allowed to speak his mind.

Osina then turned and started walking toward the back of the Temple, gesturing for Keo and the others to follow. Curious, Keo and his friends followed Osina and the elders, with Rackan and Nobia taking up the rear. He glanced over his shoulder at them, but neither sibling seemed likely to attack him or his friends, although he was all too aware of how willing they were to attack if they felt that they or the elders were threatened by Keo and his friends. Keo also noticed Zamel pointedly avoiding looking at them, which meant Keo needed to keep a closer eye on him.

"Our history stretches back many thousands of years," said Osina as they walked. "The Horanians originally lived far, far to the north, on the shores of the Great Northern Sea, where our ancestors carved out a tiny civilization in the middle of the ice and snow. The old stories say that our ancestors ate fish and hunted seals, but they also worshiped the ice gods that dwelt in the frost."

Keo nodded. "Why did they move?"

"Because the Great Northern Sea became inhospitable to human life," said Osina, shaking her head. "The winters became harsher and harsher and strange beasts made of ice started to attack the people, creatures that the legends call the Ice Men. These new enemies forced our ancestors to head south until they reached the Upper Mountains some five hundred years ago, and we have lived here ever since."

They stopped at the back of the Temple, which had a simple, ancient-looking painting on it. The painting looked like a map, but it was unlike any map of Lamaira Keo had ever seen. It showed a series of mountains at the bottom, along with a vast, untamed wilderness to the north of it that had strange cat-like creatures drawn on it, and then a massive frozen sea north of that. There were words on it in a language that Keo couldn't read, though the words were quite faded, which would have made it hard to read even if Keo could read it.

Osina gestured at the map. "This is an ancient map, drawn by the founders of this village shortly after they reached these mountains, that depicts the area north of these mountains, as well as the route they took to get here. As you can tell, it was quite the journey."

"And you've had no contact with the outside world at all during that time?" said Keo.

"Some of our ancestors did attempt to go farther south, but they ran into violent and dangerous people who slaughtered them without mercy," said Osina. She glanced at Keo and the others and frowned. "I presume those were your ancestors."

Keo scratched the back of his head. "Well, I certainly don't remember hearing about my ancestors killing your ancestors, but maybe they did."

"I wasn't attempting to start an argument, but was merely making an observation," said Osina. "In any case, our ancestors decided to carve out a life among the mountains, which were created by the Great Mountain Man long ago."

"But just who is the Great Mountain Man?" said Maryal. "We've never heard of him."

"The Great Mountain Man is the man who created these Mountains," said Osina, gesturing at the floor, although she was probably gesturing at the Mountains that they stood upon. "He is as old as the earth and wiser than the mountain owls. Where he came from, we do not know, but our ancestors met him when they first came here and he promised to protect our people in exchange for worship and honor from us."

"Where is the Great Mountain Man now?" said Maryal, looking around the Temple as if she expected to see him standing in a corner waiting to be introduced.

"Among the Mountains, most likely," said Osina. "He has not been seen for centuries, but we know that he is here and that he hears and answers our prayers, because he rules over the Upper Mountains in the same way that a landowner rules over his land."

"I saw him once," said Nobia, speaking up suddenly and causing everyone to look at her. She didn't look at all afraid of so many people looking at her at once, which made Keo wonder if she wasn't quite as shy as he thought. "Once, a long time ago, when I was just a little girl, I saw him walking among the Mountains."

"Nobia," said Rackan in a reprimanding tone, grabbing her arm and causing her to look at him. "Weren't you listening to Elder Osina when she said that we are not to interrupt unless it is important?"

"I know," said Nobia, "but—"

"Listen to your older brother, Nobia," said Osina. "I know that you claim to have seen the Great Mountain Man, but that is not relevant at the moment, especially because you don't have any proof to back up your story."

"But I *did* see him," Nobia insisted. "And he told me that his son was about to be reincarnated soon and I think that—"

"Nobia!" said Rackan, his tone reproachful. "If you don't stop interrupting, I will drag you out of here myself."

That must have been a more serious threat than Keo thought, because Nobia did indeed shut up. Or maybe Nobia did not want to miss out on listening to Keo and his friends, though Keo did wonder why Rackan acted more like her father than her brother. Now that he thought about it, though, Keo did not remember seeing either of the siblings' parents, which made him wonder where they were at the moment.

"I apologize for the interruption," said Osina to Keo and the others. "Young Nobia here claims to have seen the Great Mountain Man once, but we've never been able to verify that claim. She is always eager to share her story, but we do not want to fool you into believing that you might see him when most people never will."

"I understand," said Keo, nodding, although that earned him a glare from Nobia, though he didn't look at her as he spoke. "Please continue where you left off."

"Very well," said Osina. "Under the Great Mountain Man's rule, we Horanians created a new country and home for us in these mountains. The legends state that it was never easy, that our ancestors fought wildlife and weather and all kinds of obstacles as they built towns and villages in these mountains, but eventually they succeeded and we lived on that success for centuries until seventy years ago."

"What happened seventy years ago?" said Keo, although he had a feeling that he already knew.

"The Dracones arrived," said Osina. Her tone became grim. "They came as suddenly and swiftly as a thunderstorm in the middle of a bright summer's day. In the initial attacks, they completely overwhelmed us with their superior brute strength, flight, and fire breath, even though we outnumbered them. Village after village was burned to the ground and many who avoided being cooked alive often ended up as meals for the Dracones' children, who would hunt them down as they fled deeper into the Mountains."

Osina spoke bitterly of that, as if she had witnessed it herself. Considering how old Osina apparently was, Keo figured that she probably had indeed seen some of it herself. The other elders, including Zamel, looked just as bitter as Osina, like they, too, were remembering those days.

"Why?" said Maryal, who sounded horrified by Osina's tale. "Why did the Dracones attack you like that?"

"Because they wanted to make the mountains into *their* territory, of course," said Osina. "And they would have succeeded in slaughtering us all if not for the ingenuity of the people. The survivors rallied together and, using a mixture of the knowledge passed down by our ancestors along with some new techniques we found effective against the Dracones' monstrous forms, we managed to defend this village from them."

"You mean this is the only Horanian settlement in the Mountains?" said Maryal.

"Correct," said Osina without a hint of happiness in her voice. "There were two others, but they were quickly overwhelmed and destroyed, though we managed to save a few survivors. Even then, we were ourselves nearly overwhelmed until the Dracones finally decided to leave us alone, although we continue to keep an eye out for them anyway in case they decide to attack again."

"That's what the situation has been like for seventy years now?" said Keo.

"Indeed," said Osina. "And it is unlikely to change anytime soon. The Dracones have created a nest for themselves higher up in the mountains, which we cannot enter due to their powerful guards."

"So there is a stalemate between you and the Dracones, then," said Dlaine.

"In a way, you could describe it that way, but it is a little bit different than that," said Osina. "We believe that the Dracones could come down and destroy us any time of their choosing, but they have, for some reason, decided to spare us. I think they simply do not view us as a threat to their safety anymore, so they have no reason to spend time and effort killing us off."

"That, and we always make sure to hit them hard whenever they *do* try to hunt us like deer," said Hanoc, a smirk on his face. "Hit 'em with more arrows than they can count."

"Yes, that's true," said Osina, "we do make sure to give them hell whenever they attempt to give us trouble, although we have not had to fight back against them recently due to their leaving us alone."

Keo stroked his chin. "So you are not related to the humans who live beyond the Mountains at all, then."

Keo said that while keeping an eye on Zamel, who had been very quiet during this entire exchange. Zamel's expression was hard to read, mostly because the elder was not looking at Keo directly. He seemed to be trying to avoid looking at Keo in the face, perhaps because Keo reminded him of his brother Riuno. But again, Keo did not share his suspicions aloud, because he wasn't confident yet that his conclusions were sound and didn't want to distract from the current discussion at the moment.

"We are completely unrelated to them," said Osina. "As I said, your ancestors likely killed off some of my ancestors, forcing us to stay here in the safety of these Mountains rather than travel any further south."

"That explains why you've never heard of Lamaira, then, or the demons," said Keo. "Because you aren't even from Lamaira at all."

*Except for Zamel,* Keo wanted to add, but again he held back because he didn't want to speak that particular truth just yet, though again he noticed Zamel was trying not to draw any attention to himself.

"Yes," said Osina. "We've been too busy living and surviving in these mountains to care about what is happening beyond them, though it sounds like quite a bit has happened recently."

"Much has," said Keo. "And much will, unless we stop the demons before they rise again."

"Why don't you tell us about these demons?" said Osina. "We have never heard of them before, but they sound quite serious and dangerous."

Keo nodded and then told them all about what he and his friends had done ever since Keo met that first demon back in the Low Woods. The elders and the siblings were good listeners, although Zamel looked uncomfortable again. That made Keo wonder for the nth time already what Zamel was even doing here and why none of the elders or siblings had bothered to explain that, either.

When Keo finished, both the elders and the siblings appeared troubled by his story.

"If what you say is true, then that is a serious problem indeed," said Osina. "These demons sound like a threat to every living being in the world."

"They are," Keo insisted. "That's why we went to the Dracones. We need their power to stop them once and for all, even though the Dracones rejected our offers to form an alliance with them."

"I still see no proof of these demons," said Rackan, folding his arms over his chest. "And even if they do exist, they have clearly not gotten this far north, so why should we worry about them?"

"Young Rackan has a point," said Zamel, who spoke rather quickly. "These demons may be dangerous, but it sounds to me like they simply want to destroy Lamaira. I doubt they will try to come here."

Keo found it suspicious that Zamel agreed with Rackan, but he simply said, "You're both wrong. The demons are not the kind of beings to be content with one target. If they succeed in completely destroying Lamaira, they will no doubt attempt to conquer the lands around it, including these Mountains. And trust me when I say that the demons are infinitely worse than the Dracones."

"I find that hard to believe, considering how monstrous the Dracones are," said Osina. "But I will take your word for it, although like Zamel and Rackan, I doubt they will come here, and even if they did, we could fight them off with our strong young men and women."

"Not unless you happen to have magical weaponry," said Keo. "The demons can't be harmed by conventional weapons. You need to have magically-enhanced weapons to stand a chance of even hurting them, or know how to cast spells at least."

"Well, we have none," said Rackan, "and we don't need any. We've survived against the Dracones for decades without anything more than our bows and arrows and creativity. I think that will be more than enough to handle these demons, should they decide to come after us."

Keo was going to say that Rackan really didn't grasp the naivete of what he just said, but then Osina waved a hand and said, "We are getting off-topic. Whether or not these demons exist or whether they will attack us and if we will be able to defend ourselves from them should they choose to attack, is irrelevant. We must instead focus on discovering whether Keo is in fact the reincarnation of Sheli or not."

Keo had almost forgotten all about that until Osina mentioned it just now. He glanced at Nobia, who looked happy that they were finally going to go forward with the test, whatever it was.

Looking at the elders again, Keo said, "What is this 'test' that you have to put me through?"

"We will show you," said Osina. "Just follow me to the—"

Osina was interrupted by the roar of some massive creature from outside the Temple, followed by the sound of fire burning through stone and then the cries of pain and fear from the people. Through the open doorway of the Temple, Keo caught a glimpse of a burning building before one of the members of the Village Guard burst through the doorway, panting hard as he rested his hands on his knees.

"What is the problem, archer?" said Osina to the Guardsman, who was still catching his breath. "What was that roar we just heard?"

Panting hard, the Guardsman looked up from under his red hood and said, "A large Dracone has appeared out of nowhere and is attacking the village. And even worse, our arrows are having no effect on it at all."

# Chapter Twelve

A DRACONE?" SAID OSINA, after another roar from outside nearly deafened Keo. "Where did it come from?"

"We don't know," the Guardsman admitted. "It appeared from the clouds out of nowhere just a few minutes ago. The rest of the Guard is attempting to stop it, but it's faster and more ferocious than past Dracones have been. We've already lost a few Guardsman plus a few villagers."

"Are the villagers being evacuated underground to the shelters?" Osina demanded.

"Yes," said the Guardsman, nodding. "Captain Salme has already issued an order to the whole village telling everyone to escape to the catacombs until the Dracone threat is dealt with. He sent me to escort you and the other elders to the Temple's basement until the Dracone has been killed or driven off."

"I understand," said Osina. She looked at Keo and the others with a serious expression on her face. "Will you be joining us underneath the village? We have room in our own shelter for you five if you wish to join us."

"You have underground shelters?" said Keo.

"Yes," said Osina, nodding. "We built them to allow the villagers to hide underground during a Dracone attack, because the Dracones prefer to attack from the air. Every house and building in the village is connected to the bunkers so everyone can reach safety."

"I think that sounds like a great idea," said Dlaine, putting his hands on his hips and looking at the others. "Not like there's much we can do against a Dracone, right?"

"I think that Dlaine has a good point," said Maryal, wrapping her arms around her body and glancing at the exit. "Better to wait out the attack until it's over."

Although Keo hated hiding, he had to admit that Dlaine and Maryal had a point. There was no way that he could or the others could beat a fully-grown Dracone, even if Keo had had Gildshine with him.

So Keo was just about to say that they should go into the underground shelters with the elders and siblings when Easan said, "No. I'm going to go fight it, but after I retrieve Shadowbane."

"What?" said Keo, looking at Easan in surprise, ignoring another roar from outside. "Why?"

"Because unlike the rest of you, I'm not a coward," said Easan. He looked at the Village Guardsman who had entered and said, "Guardsman, where are visitors' weapons kept?"

"In the guard tower," said the Guardsman, pointing to the left, though he was likely pointing at a building outside of the Temple. "It is right next door to the Temple, but I don't think it is wise for an outsider like you to join the—"

The Guardsman was interrupted when Easan dashed out the entrance without hesitation, leaving everyone else standing there in surprise.

"What the hell?" said Dlaine, looking after Easan with shock and anger. "What's that kid thinking? He's going to get himself killed."

"I don't know," said Keo, shaking his head in frustration. "But I'm going to have to go get him. The rest of you should go into the bunker with the elders."

"But what if you get killed?" said Maryal. "You know how powerful those Dracones are."

"Easan will most definitely get killed if we do nothing to help him," said Keo. "So unless you want Easan to die, I have to help him. Don't worry, though, because I won't be long. I'll be back with him before you know it."

"We are coming as well," said Rackan, who had already drawn an arrow from his quiver, as had Nobia, who managed to look quite fierce despite her short stature. "We're also members of the Village Guard, so protecting the village is part of our duty."

"You mean you don't object to me going with you?" said Keo, looking at Rackan in surprise.

"If you are only going to make sure that your friend doesn't get killed, then I see no reason you can't come with us," said Rackan. "As long as you and your friend don't get in the way of our assault, it shouldn't be a problem."

Keo nodded. "Okay. But first, I need to get Gildshine, just in case the Dracone attacks me and I need to defend myself."

Retrieving Gildshine from the guard tower was easy enough, because the Guardsman in the tower gave it to Keo as soon as Rackan ordered him to. The Guardsman claimed that Easan had been by just a few minutes ago to retrieve his own sword, which the Guardsman had given him without question after Easan had said that he was working with the Village Guard to stop the Dracone attacking the village. That was a big fat lie, but apparently Easan had been quite persuasive about it. The Guardsman had also said that Easan ran off toward the smoking buildings near the village's entrance, where the Dracone was last spotted.

As Keo, Rackan, Nobia, and the first Guardsman from before ran through the streets, Keo smelled smoke in the air and saw thick columns of the stuff rising from the buildings near the village's entrance. The twanging of bows and flying arrows could be heard, punctuated every now and then by the roars or flames of the Dracone, but he did not see the Dracone itself until they dashed out into an open area of the village where the fighting was taking place

At least a dozen Village Guardsman, all wearing the red hoods that signified their job, stood on the ground or on top of nearby buildings, shooting arrow after arrow at the Dracone. Keo at first thought that the Dracone was Tananeen, because its scales were just as black as hers.

But this Dracone was much larger than Tananeen, almost as large as a fully-grown male Dracone. Its wings were wide as the town square, while its muscular legs looked strong enough to shatter stone. Its thick claws left gouge marks wherever it stepped and its red eyes—which seemed familiar to Keo, although he could not recall where he may have seen them before—glared as hotly as fire. Its long tail whipped through the air behind it, while a handful of smoking black buildings nearby showed that the creature had already caused quite a bit of damage. The sudden appearance of the Village Guard, however, had clearly distracted it from destroying any more buildings. Keo did not see any corpses nearby, but that hardly comforted him, because this Dracone was clearly trying to kill the annoying humans that were attacking it.

Not that the Village Guard's attacks were doing much good. Their arrows bounced off its hide and wings, like it was wearing a suit of armor, although the multiple attacks from a variety of angles seemed to be confusing the Dracone to the point where it wasn't sure who it should attack first.

"Do you know this Dracone?" Rackan asked as he took aim with his bow.

Keo shook his head. "No. I've never seen it before." He looked around and frowned. "But where's Easan?"

"No idea," said Rackan. "Doesn't matter. We're going to attack and kill that thing, so just stay out of the way and—"

He was interrupted by a blast of golden flame shooting out from between two nearby buildings and striking the Dracone in the side. The Dracone let out a roar of pain, while at the same time Easan dashed out from between the two buildings with Shadowbane in his hands. The Village Guard stopped shooting at the Dracone and watched in surprised as Easan ran over to meet the Dracone head on.

"There he is," said Nobia, without a hint of sarcasm. "Looks like he's about to fight the Dracone."

"The idiot," said Keo, shaking his head. Nonetheless, he hefted Gildshine on his shoulder and said, "You guys cover me while I go and get him. He's going to get himself killed if he keeps this up."

Without watching for a response from Rackan or Nobia, Keo ran toward the scene of the battle. The Dracone, which was no longer roaring in pain, was now eying Easan angrily, as if it was offended that a human like him had actually managed to harm it. To his credit, Easan didn't seem to be afraid of the Dracone, but that didn't mean that he was behaving rationally.

"Come on, now!" Easan shouted at the Dracone, waving Shadowbane at it. "Come at me! You don't scare me, you big, dumb, overgrown winged lizard!"

The Dracone snorted pitch-black smoke from its nostrils and suddenly lashed out at Easan with its front claws. It moved too fast for Easan to dodge, but Keo tackled Easan to the street, causing the Dracone's claws to miss.

Keo and Easan rolled across the street before untangling. Easan immediately got back up and did not offer to help Keo back to his feet, although Keo didn't have any trouble standing back up again, although he had scraped his arms when they had rolled across the street.

"Keo?" said Easan in annoyance. "What was that for? I was doing just fine!"

"You were about to get sliced in half," Keo said. He pointed at the Dracone, which looked a little confused at their sudden disappearance. "Where did you get the stupid idea to fight that thing on your own?"

"It wasn't stupid and I wasn't even on my own," Easan insisted, gesturing at the various Village Guardsmen, who had resumed firing arrows at the Dracone, though they were just as ineffective as ever. "They were helping. And anyway, did you notice how none of their arrows even tickled the creature, while my fire blast did?"

"Yeah, but fighting a Dracone head on like that by yourself is still stupid," Keo argued. "It just needed one blow to take you out or cripple you for life. Besides, we already are on shaky terms with the Dracones and I don't want you to make it worse by attacking one of their own."

"The Dracones have already made it clear that there's nothing we can do to convince them to become our allies," said Easan. "So who cares if we attack one of their own? Don't you care about the innocent people of this village?" He lowered his voice, which made it hard to hear above the twanging of bows and the growls and snarls of the Dracone. "Or are you more loyal to your other heritage than you are to humanity?"

Keo opened his mouth to say that that was ridiculous, but then Rackan shouted, "Keo! Fire!" and Keo looked and saw that the Dracone was aiming its open, smoking mouth at him and Easan, completely ignoring the arrows from the Village Guard that bounced uselessly off its hide.

The Dracone unleashed a long stream of fire at Keo and Easan, but it wasn't the normal orange-red fire of the other Dracones. Instead, it was black and red, although it burned just as hotly as the rest.

Keo and Easan separated, causing the stream of black and red fire to strike the portion of the street where they had been standing previously. Easan immediately responded by firing golden flame back at the Dracone, which struck the Dracone again, while Keo moved as far away from the Dracone's flame as he could. He still didn't want to fight the Dracone right away, because he was absolutely certain that this would be a mistake, but then the Dracone looked at him and started approaching him, moving rapidly on its claws.

Alarmed, Keo drew upon the fire deep in his body, causing Gildshine to burst into golden flame. He hurled a blast of golden fire at the Dracone, hitting it square in the face, forcing it to stop and roar in pain.

Then Easan appeared by the Dracone's side and stabbed it in the flank with Shadowbane. The sword sank into the Dracone's thigh, causing it to roar in pain again and kick Easan instinctively. The blow sent Easan flying, with Shadowbane still in his hands due to having been yanked out of the Dracone's leg when it hit him. Easan crashed on the street, where he lay with a stunned look on his face.

"Easan!" Keo cried, but he had no time to worry about Easan, because the Dracone came at him again.

Once it was upon Keo, the Dracone raised its claw and swiped at him. Keo ducked, successfully dodging the claw and then slashed at the Dracone's arm, his sword cutting through its flesh. The Dracone roared in pain again as black blood bled from the wound, which made Keo stare in shock at it for a moment. He also noticed black blood leaking out from the Dracone's leg, where Easan had stabbed it.

"Black blood?" said Keo. "What the—"

He was interrupted by the sound of flame and looked up in time to see the Dracone charging a stream of fire in its mouth. He was still too shocked by the implications of the Dracone's black blood to dodge, but he didn't have to, because at the last moment Nobia tackled him out of the path of the fire.

In the next instant, a blast of black and red flame exploded from the Dracone's mouth and struck the part of the street where Keo had been standing mere moments before. Because Keo and Nobia hadn't rolled very far, Keo felt the intense heat of the Dracone's fire as it blasted the street. It was like standing in front of a burning furnace, although it lasted only for a couple of seconds before the flame died out. The Dracone looked over at Keo and Nobia with pure and unmistakable hatred in its eyes.

"Thanks for the save," said Keo as he got back up and helped Nobia to her feet. "Thought I was going to die there."

Nobia nodded, but before she could say anything, Keo pointed Gildshine at the Dracone's face and unleashed another burst of golden fire. The burst struck the Dracone in the face, but this time, rather than enraging it to attack further, the Dracone staggered backwards, which made Keo think at first that he might actually be able to kill it after all.

But then the Dracone spread its wings and, with a mighty flap, soared high into the sky. The Village Guard's arrows flew after it, but all of the arrows missed as the Dracone flew out of their range.

The Dracone flew higher and higher until it vanished in the clouds above, though not without letting loose a final roar that sent chills down Keo's spine. He watched the sky, expecting the Dracone to return at any second, but it soon became clear that the Dracone had indeed fled.

As Gildshine's golden flames went out, Keo ran over to Easan, who was sitting up and rubbing his head. Even though Easan had been knocked back hard by the Dracone, he didn't look badly wounded.

"Hey, Easan, how do you feel?" said Keo as he stopped beside

Easan, looking down at him with a worried look. "Can you walk?"

Easan winced said, "No broken bones, I think, but walking will be a pain. But I still must stand up."

Keo held out a hand toward him. "Then let me help you up."

Easan batted Keo's hand away, however, and he said, "I can stand up on my own, thanks. I don't need your help."

Easan tried to stand up, but then grabbed his stomach where the Dracone had hit him and winced at the pain. Then he took a deep breath and rose slowly to his feet, although it was very clear that he was still in great pain from the Dracone's attack. He didn't complain about it, however, probably because he didn't want to show any weakness to Keo or the Village Guard.

Speaking of the Village Guard, Keo looked around to see them now converging on the scene of the battle. Most of them went over to the smoking buildings that the Dracone had destroyed, perhaps to inspect the extent of the damage, while Rackan and Nobia walked over to Keo and Easan with grim expressions on their faces.

"How are you?" said Rackan, looking from Keo to Easan and back again like he was searching for injuries. "Either of you suffer any serious injuries?"

Easan tried to shake his head, but winced again and said, "Just a little bruised is all. I'll be fine."

"I'm fine," said Keo, wiping sweat off his brow. "Just tired from the battle."

"That's good to hear," said Nobia with a sigh. "I was a little worried because I thought that the Dracone was going to kill you."

"It would have if you hadn't saved me from its fire breath," said Keo. He glanced at the sky again, at the clouds that the Dracone had fled into. "I doubt this is the last we'll see of it, though. I do wonder why it ran, though."

"Probably because you and your friend had hurt it more than it expected," said Rackan with a snort. "One thing we've learned about fighting the Dracones is that they don't like prey that fights back. Especially if that prey can hurt them. But yes, I agree, it will probably be back at some point, because Dracones also hold grudges for a long time."

*You can say that again,* Keo thought, thinking of Queen Sayot and her refusal to help humanity due to what Keo's grandfather had done to the Dracones decades ago, but aloud he said, "I just hope that it doesn't bring any friends with it. We barely managed to beat back one. If it had had allies, none of us would have survived."

"You are probably right," said Rackan. He frowned and glanced at the sky. "I'll have to speak with Captain Salme about setting up more guards. I just wonder why our lookouts didn't see the Dracone until it attacked."

Keo also glanced at the sky, but unlike Rackan, he already had a theory about the true nature of the Dracone that may have explained why the lookouts hadn't seen or noticed its approach. He did not, however, want to dwell on it, because if it was true, then the situation was going to be far more complicated than he first thought:

That Dracone was actually a demon.

# Chapter Thirteen

ACCORDING TO CAPTAIN SALME, there were no casualties during the Dracone/demon's attack. Some of the Village Guard had received bad burns and there was a lot of property damage, but it was not nearly as bad as it could have been, largely due to the quick response of the Village Guard and Keo and Easan. Some of the Village Guardsmen even thanked Keo and Easan for their help, because Keo and Easan's distraction had been the main reason that the Dracone demon had failed to kill any of the Guardsmen. Captain Salme told them that they usually lost two or three men in every Dracone attack, so for everyone to survive like they did this time was seen as something like a miracle by the Village Guard and many of the villagers themselves. That a few buildings had been burned out did not dampen the miraculousness of this event, mostly because it seemed like the villagers were used to having to do major repairs after a Dracone attack.

Because Keo and Easan did not suffer any severe injuries, they went back to the Temple. Rackan and Nobia had already gone ahead of them to tell the elders and Keo's other friends that the Dracone was gone and that it was safe to come out now, which meant that Keo and Easan had to walk back by themselves.

As they walked through the streets of the village, Keo looked at Easan. Easan, as usual, was scowling, which may have been because of the pain from the blow he had taken from the Dracone, but Keo figured that it was probably something else.

Easan must have noticed Keo staring, because he said, without looking, "You're going to trip if you don't watch where you're going."

"You still realize that what you did was foolish, right?" said Keo, although he glanced at their path just to make sure there was nothing in the street that could trip him anyway. "Even though you didn't die or suffer any crippling injuries."

"I know what you think about it, but that doesn't mean that I agree," said Easan, shaking his head. "And besides, it worked out in the end. We stopped that Dracone from destroying the entire village, which I'm absolutely certain it would have done if we had not intervened."

"I know, but it was still a foolish and unnecessary risk," said Keo. "The Village Guard could have handled it without us."

Easan looked at Keo with disbelief. "Could they?"

Keo was about to say yes, but then he understood what Easan was actually asking. "So you suspect that that thing was a demon, too."

"Of course it was a demon," said Easan, rolling his eyes as they walked past a couple of children who were running in the direction they came, probably to go see the damage from the Dracone's attack. "Red eyes, black blood, complete immunity to the Guards' arrows, only hurt by our golden fire ... you'd have to be blind or stupid not to see it for what it was."

"I didn't know that demons could look like Dracones,

though," said Keo. "I wonder if that was its true form or if it took on that shape for some reason."

"I bet that that demon was trying to frame the Dracones," said Easan. "For some reason it was trying to provoke a conflict between the Horanians and the Dracones. I just know it."

"Why, though?" said Keo. "What do the demons have to gain from that?"

"Isn't it obvious?" said Easan as they turned a corner. "If Queen Sayot was telling the truth earlier, then the Dracones could easily crush the demons, and the demons know that. But if the Dracones are too busy fighting the Horanians, then that makes it easier for the demons to do whatever it is that they want to do here without having to worry about the Dracones coming after them."

Keo stroked his chin, thinking about Easan's theory. "That makes a lot of sense. It fits with the subtle and deceptive behavior of the demons. The only question is, will the Horanians believe us if we tell them that it was not actually a Dracone that attacked them?"

"Doubt it," said Easan. "You heard how much the Horanians hate the Dracones. We don't even have proof to back up our own theories, even if they are true. Besides, as foreigners, they probably trust us even less than the Dracones."

"Then what should we do?" said Keo. "Hunt down the Dracone demon and kill it and show them the corpse?"

"I don't know," said Easan. "Maybe, but by the time we do that, the Dracones and Horanians might be too busy killing each other to notice or care. I think we should just keep going south to Western Lamaira."

"You suddenly seem a lot less gung ho about going after that demon," Keo observed. "Didn't you say that you're *not* a coward?"

Easan glared at Keo. "There's a difference between responding to an attack in your home and going out into the streets looking for a fight. Besides, we don't know the Upper Mountains well enough to even begin to guess where it might be hiding, so it would be a waste of time to try to hunt down."

To Keo, these sounded like convenient excuses so that Easan wouldn't have to do anything hard, prompting him to say, "Easan, what is your *real* reason for wanting to fight the demon? It isn't just because you wanted to show that you are braver than the rest of us, is it?"

Easan looked away from Keo, focusing on the street upon which they walked, like he was not going to say anything else. That made Keo realize that he had hit a sore point, which made him doubt that Easan would talk.

Then Easan said, still without looking at Keo, "I don't need to tell you that. Besides, the Temple is coming up, so I think you should get ready for your test to see if there is yet another thing that is special about you."

Keo looked ahead and saw that they were almost at the Temple now. He considered briefly asking Easan again about his motivation for that reckless act earlier, but Easan's tone and demeanor likely meant that he was in no mood to answer any of Keo's questions. He would ask Easan about it later, after all of this was over.

The two of them entered the Temple, where they found the elders and everyone else standing where they had been earlier, prior to the Dracone attack. Thankfully, none of them looked hurt, which made sense, seeing as the Dracone had not gotten very far into the village, although the elders looked disturbed anyway, as did Dlaine and Maryal. Jola, as always, was invisible, but Keo had no doubt that she was just as disturbed by this sudden attack as everyone else.

"Keo, Easan, are you two okay?" said Maryal, looking at them as they approached everyone else. "Did either of you get hurt?"

"Easan got kicked by the dragon, but he's going to be all right," said Keo, nodding at Easan, who seemed uninterested in talking to anyone at the moment. "Rackan and Nobia told you all what happened, right?"

"Yes," said Osina, who was now leaning on her staff with a troubled expression on her face. "While I am glad to hear that no one was killed or seriously wounded, that Dracone's attack was too sudden for my liking. It's even stranger that the Dracone landed in the village, because we usually spot them far enough ahead to be able to prevent them from entering."

"I agree, elder," said Rackan, nodding. "Regardless, this attack should not be tolerated. I say we should send a hunting team into the Mountains to find and kill the beast before it returns to finish what it started. We need to send a signal to the Dracones that we will not tolerate that kind of nonsense from them, even if they didn't actually kill anyone."

"Are you sure that it was actually a Dracone, though?" said Keo, after exchanging looks with Easan. "What if it was something else?"

"What else *could* it have been?" said Rackan in annoyance. He gestured to the open doorway. "It looked like every other

Dracone I've seen in my life. I don't see how it could possibly be anything else."

"Because it actually looked and acted a fair bit different from other Dracones," said Keo, folding his arms across his chest. "Easan and I think that it wasn't a Dracone at all, but a demon that took on the form of a Dracone in order to fool us into believing that the Dracones attacked."

The elders and the siblings exchanged skeptical glances with each other, except for Zamel, who almost looked like his worst fears had come true. Again, Keo was tempted to out Zamel here and now, but he refrained from doing so, if only because he didn't want to cause even more stress for everyone and distract them from the main point he was trying to make.

"That is an ... interesting theory," said Osina. "But I don't see any proof that this is anything other than yet another attack from our sworn enemies."

"The Dracone had the red eyes and black blood of a demon," said Keo. He looked at Dlaine and Maryal in the hope that they would back him up. "You guys have seen demons before. Doesn't that sound exactly like a demon?"

"Yeah," said Dlaine, "but the only problem is that we didn't get to see it. But we'll accept your theory anyway, because that sounds just like something that the demons would do."

"Well, of course your friends would agree with you," said Rackan, rolling his eyes. "But that proves nothing except that you have friends who, like all friends, are willing to stand up for you no matter what."

"Aye, Rackan speaks the truth," said Osina. "Regardless of the Dracone's true nature, we must first perform the test to find out if you are the reincarnation of Sheli, as Nobia says. We can talk more about this Dracone later, after the test is finished."

Keo wanted to keep arguing the point, because the presence of demons in the Upper Mountains meant that things were about to get very bad, but he could tell that neither the elders nor the siblings wanted to talk about this point at the moment, and that any further attempts by Keo to broach the issue would likely make them like him and his friends even less than they did now. It was frustrating, because that meant that it would take them much longer to figure out how to deal with the demon than it otherwise would, but Keo decided to accept this for now and make sure that they talked about it as soon as the test was done. He did not know for certain why this demon was in the Upper Mountains, but he doubted that it was for any pure or noble reasons.

"All right," said Keo. "Then what is the test? And why is it so important that you find out if I am the reincarnation of Sheli or not?"

"Because we believe that Sheli will lead us to drive the Dracones out of the Upper Mountains and restore these lands to us," said Osina simply. "Sheli was said to be a great warrior and an even better leader during his short time on this world, so we believe that his reincarnation could be just as good as him. What do you say? Do you think you will be able to lead us, if you are indeed the reincarnation of Sheli?"

Keo sincerely doubted that he would lead the Horanians to drive out the Dracones, even if he did somehow turn out to be the reincarnation of this Sheli person. He was, after all, part Dracone himself, and he had no interest in fueling the continuing war between the Dracones and Horanians.

He was just about to say so when Dlaine nudged him in the ribs, causing Keo to look at him and whisper, "What?"

"Can we talk for a minute?" said Dlaine. He nodded at the others. "In private?"

Sensing that Dlaine had something important to talk about, Keo nodded and said, "Sure. What is it?"

"I'll tell you after we get a private space," said Dlaine. He looked at the elders. "Can you excuse us for a bit so we can talk? It'll only be for a minute. After that, we'll be right back and we can get that test started right away."

Osina and the other elders didn't look happy about yet another delay, but Osina said, "Very well. But please do not spend too much time talking, because we would prefer to get confirmation or denial of Keo's identity as quickly as possible."

Both Keo and Dlaine nodded to show understanding and then retreated to one of the corners of the room farthest away from the others. Once they were far away enough that the others could not hear them if they whispered, Keo said to Dlaine, keeping his voice low, "What did you want to talk about?"

"What will happen after you complete the test and it turns out you are the reincarnation of this Sheli guy," said Dlaine, his voice as low as Keo's, rubbing his hands together eagerly. "It ties into why I agreed to let those two siblings take us to their village in the first place, even though I consider it to be a diversion from our main quest."

"Yeah, I was wondering about that earlier," said Keo. "Why?"

Dlaine glanced at the elders and siblings—who were now talking to Easan, who seemed to be telling them about the Dracone attack in greater detail—and looked at Keo again.

"Remember how Queen Sayot rejected our offer of a human/Dracone alliance to stand against the demons?"

Keo scowled at the memory. "How can I not? She was very rude about it."

"I think that a part of her hostility had to do with the Horanians," said Dlaine, gesturing at the elders and siblings. "The two sides have been fighting each other for decades, so there's a lot of bad blood between them. Queen Sayot probably thinks that the rest of Lamaira is like the Horanians, which is why she doesn't want to risk the safety of her people by allying with us."

Keo frowned. "Yes, but Sayot started hating humans because of what my grandfather, who was not a Horanian, did to her and her people. I don't see where you're going with this."

"It's simple," said Dlaine. He put one hand on Keo's shoulder and looked him straight in the eye. "You need to prove that you are the reincarnation of Sheli and then, as the new Horanian leader, create a peace treaty between the Dracones and Horanians. End the conflict between the two sides for good, in other words."

"How am I supposed to do that?" said Keo in annoyance. "The Dracones have already made it clear that they don't want to work with any humans. The only reason they tolerated us was because Tananeen protected us and because we saved their eggs from the Brothers White Blood. If I become the leader of their hated enemy, that will just confirm all their worst fears about us and make them even less likely to listen to me."

"Not necessarily," said Dlaine, shaking his head. "If that Dracone that attacked was indeed a demon, like you and Easan think it is, then there's a good chance that it is going to attack the Dracones, too, if it hasn't already. You can then use that as an opening in which to convince the Dracones and Horanians to work together to stop the demons, which are a much bigger threat to them than they are to each other."

Keo scratched the side of his head. "I still don't quite get what you're trying to say here."

"It's simple," said Dlaine, who sounded like a teacher trying to be patient with a particularly slow student. "By proving to the Dracones and the Horanians that the demons exist and are a threat to them, not only will you get two new allies, but you will also be that much closer to reuniting the Kingdom and stopping the demons once and for all."

"Okay," said Keo, "but I don't understand how I am supposed to use this to our advantage. Even if I can unite the Dracones and Horanians on this one issue, that doesn't mean they will agree to help us defeat the demons outside of the Mountains. If we drive the demons out of the Mountains, what's to stop the Dracones and Horanians from resuming their current conflict?"

"Offer the Dracones land in the Kingdom of Lamaira after the demons have been defeated and you are crowned King of Lamaira," said Dlaine. "Tell them that you will let them live peacefully in Lamaira with everyone else and that you will keep other humans from attacking or disturbing them. The Dracones clearly don't like the Upper Mountains, so I imagine they would be more than happy to accept your offer, while the Horanians would not object because they consider the Mountains to be theirs anyway, so they aren't going to try to stop the Dracones from leaving for greener pastures." He smiled. "It's a win-win no matter how you look at it."

"Is that why you wanted to go with them?" said Keo. He was

amazed at how quickly Dlaine had thought up all of this. "How did you even know that this could work?"

"I didn't," said Dlaine, shaking his head. "I was working mostly on instinct and guesswork for a while there, until Osina told us the history of the Horanians. Then it all clicked and I realized that my instinct was right, as it usually is."

"It sounds good, but I'm worried that it might not work out the way you described," said Keo. "What if it turns out that I'm not the reincarnation of Sheli at all?"

"If you're not the reincarnation of Sheli, that will make things harder," said Dlaine, "but that won't change the fact that the demons exist and present a clear threat to both sides. Therefore, we'd only need to alter the plan just a little bit to accommodate that bit of information. Otherwise, there's no reason it shouldn't work out as long as we are smart about it."

Dlaine certainly sounded confident about his plan, so confident that even Keo had a hard time disagreeing with it, whatever its flaws may be. Even so, deep down, Keo had a feeling that they were overlooking some important detail that would completely derail their plan no matter how it worked out. But he couldn't think of what this detail was or why it was so important, so he just ignored it for now and decided to think about it later.

"Now that we're both on the same page here, let's go back to the elders and get that test underway," said Dlaine with a grin on his face, patting Keo on the shoulder. "Don't want to mess up this perfect opportunity, right?"

"Right," said Keo, but he still found it hard to ignore his doubts, no matter how confident Dlaine was about the plan.

# Chapter Fourteen

THE TEST TOOK PLACE outside of the Temple, in a small courtyard that was connected to the back of the Temple. According to Osina, the small courtyard was usually where the elders went out to perform their daily prayers to the Great Mountain Man, because it was believed that the Great Mountain Man slept in the morning at the bottom of the dry well in the center of the courtyard. The elders would often go to the dry well early in the morning, often before the first rays of the sun peeked over the mountain peaks, and pray into the well for guidance and help from the Great Mountain Man. The Great Mountain Man was said to have spoken from the dry well in the old days, but had gone silent ever since the arrival of the Dracones seventy years ago, although the elders continued their morning prayers because of tradition.

Keo stood in front of the dry well. He looked down the well and smelled nothing but dirt and dried mud. He tried to see the bottom, but it was completely black down there, and according to the elders, the dry well went down deep into the earth, even underneath the foundations of the Upper Mountains themselves. Nobia had even told Keo that you could toss even a large, heavy rock down there and you would never hear it hit the bottom no matter how long or patiently you waited, although no one ever threw anything into the well because that was considered disrespectful to the Great Mountain Man.

Then Keo looked around at their surroundings. Dozens of people from the village—who, unlike the Village Guard, wore mostly plain brown or gray wool clothes, though a handful of women had pretty pink flowers in their hair, which Keo recognized as a species of mountain flower he had once seen when he and his friends had climbed up the Upper Mountains several days ago—stood outside of the courtyard walls, which went up to about their waists, watching the test with curious eyes. The people had started coming to the Temple only a few minutes ago, because the news had gotten out that the reincarnation of Sheli had been found and no one wanted to miss it. There were even a few members of the Village Guard nearby, although they appeared to be here more for security reasons than anything.

Although none of the Horanians looked threatening, Keo didn't feel comfortable with all of them staring at him like that. He suspected most of them were grateful that he and Easan had driven off that demon, but he saw more than a few suspicious eyes watching him among the people. No doubt most of them saw him and his friends as strange foreigners who were not to be trusted, even if they had just helped the Horanians survive an encounter with a powerful demon.

*Maybe they heard that we were trying to form an alliance with the Dracones,* Keo thought, shivering when a cold wind blew through the courtyard. *That would certainly make us look a little less respectable in their eyes, for sure.*

Dlaine, Maryal, Jola, and Easan stood at the other end of the courtyard, behind Keo. They were supposed to be silent during the test, although the elders had given them permission to stand in the courtyard itself anyway because they were his friends. Easan looked like he thought this whole thing was a huge waste of time, while Dlaine nodded encouragingly at Keo and Maryal gave him the thumbs up. He couldn't see Jola, as usual, but he knew that she was probably there supporting him anyway, because that was what friends do.

Rackan and Nobia stood on the other side of the courtyard walls, near an older couple who appeared to be their grandparents. Keo still did not see their actual parents anywhere, but he decided not to worry about that. Nobia smiled at Keo when he caught her eye, while Rackan looked a bit like Easan in that he clearly didn't think that Keo was the reincarnation of Sheli and that this whole thing was a pointless waste of time that could be better spent tracking down the demon that had attacked earlier.

As for the elders, they stood on the other side of the well directly opposite Keo. All four of them were now wearing heavy wool coats, probably to keep themselves warm in the cold mountain air, and were talking quietly among themselves in a language that Keo couldn't understand. Osina had told Keo that the elders needed to take a few minutes among themselves to talk about the test, although Keo didn't see what there was to talk about. Maybe they were discussing the details of the test to make sure they all knew it.

In any case, it made Keo impatient and a bit nervous. He kept glancing at the sky, expecting the demon Dracone to swoop down from the clouds or the surrounding peaks and attack everyone, but the thick gray clouds and the lonely peaks seemed as demon-free as ever. It made Keo wonder if there were any other demons in the Upper Mountains or if this particular demon was working alone.

He stopped thinking about this, however, when the elders finished speaking among each other and looked at Keo. Osina stepped forward, a serious expression on her face, an expression shared with the other two elders Shinisa and Hanoc, although Zamel, as usual, looked a bit worried, but he hid it well under his serious frown. Still, Zamel looked like he wanted to be anywhere but here at the moment, which made Keo wonder exactly what Zamel expected to happen that made him so nervous about the situation.

"Now, Keo," said Osina, her old voice snapping Keo's attention back to her, "are you ready for the test that will prove whether you are the reincarnation of Sheli, the only son of the Great Mountain Man himself?"

Still not knowing what the test was, Keo nonetheless nodded and said, "I'm ready."

"Good," said Osina. She then looked at the dozens of Horanians standing outside of the courtyard, watching the people inside the courtyard silently. "My fellow Horanians, I am pleased to see that so many of you are here to watch this ceremony, especially with that recent Dracone attack less than an hour ago. Although no lives were lost in that attack, it is a clear example of the dangers that we face in our homelands from the invaders who do not care about or respect our history and culture. Our gathering here today to test this foreigner, who may be the reincarnation of Sheli that we have been waiting for, is a testament to the enduring strength of the Horanian people."

That speech seemed awfully grand for such a small gathering of people, more like a speech that a king might give to a nation than a village elder might give to her villagers. The Horanians did not react with jubilation or anything, but the Horanians seemed like a fairly reserved people to Keo anyway, so it was probably less due to their depression and more due to the fact that they did not like to celebrate loudly and brightly even if one of their leaders praised their strengths.

Then Osina gestured at Keo. "This man is known as Keo of the Sword, a man who comes from the southern Kingdom of Lamaira, well beyond these Mountains. He has not known the Great Mountain Man or us, but we believe that he may be the reincarnation of Sheli. If he is, then he will lead us to drive out the Dracones and restore the Upper Mountains to our rightful ownership; if he is not, then we will simply send him and his friends on their way and focus instead on responding to the earlier Dracone attack."

Keo had been wondering what they were going to do to him and the others if he turned out not to be the reincarnation of Sheli. A part of him had worried that they might even kill his friends and him, although now that he thought about it, that was a ridiculous worry to have, seeing as the Horanians had already shown themselves to be far less hostile to him and his friends than the Dracones had. He decided not to worry about it.

Osina looked at Keo again and said, "Keo of the Sword, we will now begin the test. Allow me to explain it to you briefly."

Osina rested a hand on the lip of the dry well between them. "As I have told you, we believe that the Great Mountain Man rests at the bottom of this well whenever he is not walking among the Mountains. Our legends say that this well was built by Sheli, who would come here every day to speak with his father about the state of the Upper Mountains before his untimely death."

Keo had not heard that part of the story before, but he nodded in understanding anyway.

"The test, then, is simple," said Osina. "You must speak into the well, asking the Great Mountain Man to identify you. If you are indeed the reincarnation of Sheli, then all of us will hear the Great Mountain Man speak. But if you are not, then the well will be as silent as it has been for centuries and we will send you and your friends on your way to wherever it is that you wish to go."

Keo nodded again, trying not to show his nervousness because he had a feeling that it would not make him look good to the Horanians. Besides, speaking into a well wasn't the most difficult thing in the world anyway, so he didn't have any reason to be nervous, especially if, as he suspected, he wasn't actually the reincarnation of Sheli at all.

So Keo leaned over the well, looked directly down into it, smelling the old rock smell within it, and said, as clearly as he could, "Great Mountain Man of the Upper Mountains, I am Keo of the Sword and I am speaking to you today in order to find out if I am the reincarnation of your son, Sheli. If I am, please respond with confirmation; if I am not, then don't."

Then Keo stopped speaking. He wasn't sure if that was all he should say or not, but seeing as the elders did not ask him to keep speaking, he assumed that he had said all that he was supposed to say.

Pulling back, Keo glanced up at the elders. They were now staring at the dry well as intently as if they were awaiting the explosion of a volcano. A quick glance around the courtyard showed Keo that everyone else was staring just as intently as them, if not more so, including Keo's friends.

A long silence hung over the area as everyone waited for a response from the Great Mountain Man. Keo had no idea how long they were supposed to wait for the Great Mountain Man to respond, but he figured that it wouldn't be that long. Yet he did not say anything about it because he was afraid that he might mess something up if he did.

As the minutes dragged by and the silence continued to flow unabated, it became increasingly clearer to Keo that he was not the reincarnation of Sheli at all. That didn't surprise him in the least, seeing as he had suspected that right from the start. But it did mean that they would have to change their plan to unite the Dracones and Horanians against the demons, although Keo figured that Dlaine was already altering the plan to accommodate this turn of events.

Finally, Osina and the other elders looked up from the dry well at Keo. There was disappointment clear on their faces, except for Zamel, who looked more like he was trying to pretend to be disappointed. He actually seemed relieved, which made Keo highly suspicious.

"It appears that Keo of the Sword is not, in fact, the reincarnation of Sheli," said Osina, raising her voice to be heard by everyone watching the ceremony. "If the Great Mountain Man will not respond, then it is obvious that our wait for Sheli's reincarnation must resume."

Looks of disappointment appeared on the faces of the people in the crowd waiting the test, although a handful, like Rackan,

184 | TIMOTHY L. CEREPAKA

looked pleased about it, like they were happy that a foreigner like Keo was not the reincarnation they had been waiting for. A quick glance over his shoulder at his friends showed Keo that his friends looked a little disappointed as well, except for Easan, who was smirking like he had known this was going to be the result from the start.

"Thank you, Keo, for taking the time to do this," said Osina as Keo looked at her again. "Even though you are not the reincarnation of Sheli, we still appreciate the work that you and your friends have done to protect us from the Dracone that attacked us earlier. You may stay in the village as long as you need before you leave."

Keo smiled. "You're welcome, elder. We will accept your generous offer to stay in the village until we are ready to—"

A sudden tremor in the ground interrupted Keo. Keo looked down at the earth, wondering if this was an earthquake, but the ground was not cracked under his feet. He looked up at the elders, who were staring at the earth with as much surprise as he felt. A cursory look at the crowd watching the ceremony showed that they also had felt the tremor, but that did not explain where the tremor had come from or what it meant.

"Did you feel that?" said Keo to the elders. "That tremor? Is that normal?"

"No, it's not," said Osina, shaking her head. She looked up at Keo in astonishment. "The Upper Mountains never suffer from tremors or earthquakes. But the legends do say that—"

Another tremor—this one stronger than the last—cut off Osina, because it nearly knocked her off her feet, although her fellow elders managed to catch her before she fell. It also almost knocked Keo down, but he leaned against the lip of the well to avoid falling over.

That was when Keo realized that the tremor was coming from the well. He looked down the well, but again saw nothing due to the darkness of its depths. Yet he was certain that he heard something down there, a deep, booming noise that was too ominous for his tastes. It sounded like a huge avalanche, but also like a voice, and it spoke in a language that Keo could not understand. The words sounded nothing like Lamairan or any other language that Keo had heard before.

Looking up at the elders, Keo saw understanding dawning on their faces, who seemed to understand what the voice in the well was saying. Even Zamel seemed to understand it, although unlike the others, horror was mixed with shock in his eyes.

The voice continued to speak for a couple of seconds before it gradually faded away. The ground ceased shaking under their feet and soon all was back to what it had been mere moments before, only this time there was a different feeling in the air, like a momentous event had just happened and no one was quite sure what to make of it.

Keo looked around again. The people outside of the courtyard had been stunned into silence, including Rackan and Nobia. Keo's friends looked a little less stunned, but they still appeared to have lost the ability to speak themselves.

It was the elders who appeared most stunned of all, particularly Osina, who looked like she had just seen a ghost. Zamel even looked a little sick, but Keo didn't pay attention to him.

Instead, Keo said to Osina, "What was that?"

Osina snapped out of her shock and looked up at Keo with wide, frightened-looking eyes. She looked down at the dry well briefly before looking up at Keo again, as if she was unsure what to say.

"That was the Great Mountain Man," said Osina. Her voice was softer than usual, forcing Keo to strain his ears to hear her. "That is the first time that I—or anyone else—have ever heard him speak."

"And what did he say?" said Keo.

Osina closed her mouth and pursed her lips. She seemed to be trying to understand what she had just heard, which made Keo feel more than a little apprehensive.

"He said ..." Osina's voice trailed off. "He said ..."

Annoyed, Keo said, "What did he say?"

Keo's annoyed tone seemed to have touched Osina the wrong way, because her shocked expression turned into an angry scowl and she pointed at Keo with her staff. Anger blazed in her eyes, anger that made Keo step back in surprise.

"He said that you are a liar and a deceiver," said Osina, her voice full of wrath, "and that you and your friends must be put to death ... immediately!"

# Chapter Fifteen

OSINA'S WORDS WERE BARELY out of her mouth before Keo heard the *twang* of a bow from his right and saw an arrow flying straight through the air toward him. He ducked, narrowly avoiding the arrow as it soared overhead.

Meanwhile, the elders were moving away from him as fast as they could while Osina yelled, "He is not Sheli's reincarnation! The foreigner and his friends are not to be trusted! Kill them all before they escape! The Great Mountain Man demands it!"

The members of the Village Guard who had been present for the ceremony immediately raised their bows and started firing arrow after arrow at Keo and his friends. Keo drew Gildshine from its sheath at his side as he dodged another arrow and fired two bursts of flame at the Guardsmen as the crowd of onlookers scattered to avoid getting caught in the crossfire. Still, the Guardsmen did not run; instead, they dodged Keo's flames and continued to shot arrows at him.

But Keo's flames had given him enough time to run over to his friends, who were also dodging arrows and fighting back against the Guardsmen who attacked from a distance. Maryal used her wind magic to knock arrows out of the air, while those few arrows that managed to avoid her wind spells bounced harmlessly off the invisible shield that Jola had summoned. Easan had drawn Shadowbane at some point and was firing off his own blasts of golden flame at the enemies, but his aim was off and he kept missing the Guardsmen and hitting the streets or nearby buildings instead.

As for Dlaine, he was just standing between Maryal and Easan, looking worried and astonished by this unexpected turn of events. Keo ran up to him, again narrowly avoiding an arrow on his way there, and stopped in front of Dlaine, panting and wiping away the sweat from his brow.

"What the hell is going on here?" said Dlaine, his hands on his head as he looked at the various Guardsmen who were attacking them. "Why are they suddenly attacking us?"

"The Great Mountain Man told the elders we were liars and deceivers, apparently," said Keo, wincing when he heard one of the arrows bounce off of the barrier around them, even though it had not come near him. "And now they're dealing with us the same way that they apparently deal with all of the liars and deceivers they run across."

"By killing us?" said Dlaine in shock. "This doesn't make any sense. What have we lied to or deceived them about? We're not their enemies. What is going on?"

"I don't know, but I do know that we have to get out of here before they overwhelm us," said Keo, looking at the Guardsmen, who were now making their way into the courtyard where they stood. He also spotted more red-hooded men with bows coming from the streets and buildings to join them. "I don't know how long Jola will be able to hold them back with her barrier."

*Not long,* came Jola's response in his head. *Their arrows aren't much, but I'm getting tired from the events of the day and their arrows just keep coming.*

"Then we need to get out of here quickly," said Keo. "There's no way we can fight them all, at least not here."

"But how?" said Dlaine. He gestured around them. "They've got the area surrounded. See?"

Dlaine had a point. No matter where Keo looked, he saw nothing but red-hooded men with loaded bows at every corner. They stood in the streets, on top of nearby buildings, just beyond the walls of the courtyard, and everywhere else they could stand. Keo was surprised at how large their force was, seeing as the Horanians were not a large people, but regardless of how many there were, it looked like the Village Guard had blocked off every possible escape route. That meant they were trapped.

But Keo would never admit that aloud. He looked this way and that, searching for any way out that he might have overlooked, but with all of the Village Guard constantly firing arrows at them, it was impossible to find any possible routes if they even existed. He wondered just how much longer they had until Jola's barrier broke and they all became corpses filled with arrows.

Then an idea occurred to Keo and he looked down at where he assumed Jola was standing. "Jola, you can teleport, right?"

*Yes, I can,* said Jola. *And I know what your idea is. You want me to teleport all of us out of here, right?*

"Right," said Keo, nodding. "Can you do that while also ensuring that the Guardsmen don't get us?"

*It will be difficult to teleport so many people at once, especially under pressure like this,* said Jola. *But this seems to be our only way to escape, so I'll do it. Just make sure that everyone is holding hands and that at least one of you guys is touching me.*

"Okay," said Keo. He looked at Dlaine, Maryal, and Easan, who were now looking at him for orders as arrows bounced off Jola's shield. "All right. Everyone, hold hands, because Jola is going to try to teleport us out of here and we need to be in contact with her to make sure we all come with her."

"We're running?" said Easan. "Like cowards?"

"We're not cowards," said Keo, shaking his head. "But there's just no way we can beat all of these archers, at least right now. So, unless you want to find out what it feels like to get hit with a dozen arrows specifically designed to kill a Dracone, hold hands and get ready to teleport."

Easan looked like he was going to ignore Keo's orders and resume his fighting against the Guardsmen, but then he shut off Shadowbane's power and sheathed his sword. He grabbed Maryal's hand, who then grabbed Keo's hand, who in turn grabbed Dlaine's hand, and Dlaine rested one hand on Jola. The arrows still struck against the barrier, but none of them had yet to make it through.

"All right," said Keo. "We're ready when you are, Jola."

*Okay,* said Jola. *Here we go!*

Without warning, the area around them vanished and was immediately replaced by a familiar-looking place: The clearing where they had first met Rackan and Nobia. The remains of the fire they had made this morning was still there, still slightly warm, but the clearing itself was completely devoid of any other people or creatures.

Keo and his friends immediately let go of their hands. As soon as they did that, Easan staggered forward and threw up. That sudden action on his part made Keo and the others start, but they could do nothing for him until Easan finished. Once he did, Easan stood up and turned around to face the others, his face paler and sicker than before.

"Oh …" said Easan, grabbing his stomach. "That … was … awful …"

"Side effect of teleportation," said Dlaine, folding his arms over his chest. "If you aren't used to it, it can make you throw up your supper. How do you feel now?"

"Bad," said Easan. He shuddered. "Very bad, but I think I will recover."

"Good," said Keo. He looked around at the cliffs and boulders surrounding the clearing, but did not see any Village Guardsmen anywhere. "Jola, why'd you teleport us back here? We're not that far from the village."

*It was the farthest I could teleport without killing myself,* said Jola, who sounded tired. *I would have teleported us farther, but I didn't have the energy to do it.*

"What if the Guardsmen come after us?" said Maryal, rubbing her hands together anxiously. "They know where this place is, or at least Rackan and Nobia do. There's nothing to stop them from coming after us again."

"But they don't know where we went," Dlaine pointed out. "For all they know, we might not even be in the Upper Mountains anymore. But I agree that we should get going. They might very well decide to hunt us down and right now we have a huge head start on them that we could lose very easily if we waste too much time here."

Keo stroked his chin, thinking. "I'm not sure we should run."

"You're right," said Dlaine, rubbing the back of his head. He glanced at Easan and then at an empty spot near his feet, probably where Jola was. "Easan and Jola need to rest and get their strength up again. Doubt they could go very far in their current conditions."

"That's not exactly what I meant," said Keo, shaking his head. "I think that we shouldn't leave the Upper Mountains just yet, even after Easan and Jola recover."

"What?" said Dlaine, staring at Keo in astonishment. "Keo, are you listening to yourself? What reason could we have for staying here when everyone and their dog hates us? The Dracones hate us, the Horanians hate us, and that Mountain Man guy hates us, too, apparently."

"Dlaine's right," said Maryal, nodding. "Somehow we really messed up here. Better to head south to the Divinians, who might be more willing to listen to us than the Dracones or Horanians were."

"You guys have good points, but you don't understand why I think we should stay," said Keo. He looked up at the clouds, remembering the demon/Dracone from before. "That demon is still here and it will probably continue to attack both sides if we don't stop it."

"Why don't we just let the Dracones deal with it?" said Dlaine. "The Dracones are supposed to be able to kill demons, right? They can probably deal with it on their own."

"Perhaps, but the fact is that this demon is unusually strong," said Keo. "Easan and I both hurt it pretty badly, but we couldn't kill it. We need to find it before it can cause anymore harm."

"How are we supposed to do that?" said Dlaine, putting his hands on his hips. "In case you hadn't noticed, the Upper Mountains are enormous. That thing could be hiding anywhere. How are we supposed to find it?"

"I don't know, but I'm sure we'll figure something out," said Keo. "The demons are never shy about letting us know when they're around. I bet that demon will come after me at some point, though when, I don't know."

Maryal gulped and looked up at the sky as if she expected to see the demon swoop down suddenly and pluck them off the ground. "Oh, I hope not. I'd rather not fight a demon that looks like a fully-grown Dracone. That wouldn't be very fun."

"I agree, but we've made it our mission to kill all demons no matter how strong they are," said Keo. "Besides, I'm interested in finding out what it's even doing here. It might have just been following us, but I think that the demon has another reason for being here, even though I don't know what that reason is."

"Who cares why it's here?" said Dlaine, throwing his hands into the air in exasperation. "There's no way I'm going to fight it. If you're trying to save the Dracones and Horanians, well, that's silly, seeing as they both hate us."

"Even if they hate us, we have to help them anyway," said Keo. "You remember what Queen Sayot told us, about how humans and Dracones used to work together. The Dracones may never accept us, but maybe if we kill this demon for them, they will at least be aware of the seriousness of the threat that the demons pose to the world, even if they won't work with us."

Dlaine shook his head. "I still think it's silly, but I guess there's no convincing you otherwise, is there?"

"No, there isn't," said Keo. "But I have other reasons for wanting to stay as well."

"Such as?" said Maryal.

Keo looked over his shoulder in the direction that the Horanian village lay, although he could not see it due to the cliffs and boulders behind him. "Do you remember the Horanian elder named Zamel? The fourth one who was the last to meet us?"

"Yes, what about him?" said Maryal.

Keo folded his arms over his chest and said, "I think that Zamel is my uncle."

Dlaine and Maryal looked at Keo in surprise. Easan, on the other hand, just sat on the ground and continued to look miserable, although he had brought out his flask full of water and was taking sips from it, probably to calm down his upset stomach.

"Your uncle?" said Dlaine. "What in the world are you talking about? Are you part Horanian too or something?"

"Nothing like that," said Keo. "You see, back in Tain, I was told that my father had a brother named Zamel. After my grandfather's death, Zamel and my father dueled over who would win the throne and become the next King of Lamaira. My father won and became King, while Zamel stayed in the castle as a minor noble until my father's death, at which point he vanished during the chaos that enveloped the Kingdom afterward."

"Does anyone know what happened to him?" said Maryal.

"The Keepers told me that no one does, although most believe that he died," said Keo. "But I think that Zamel somehow survived and then made his way here to the Upper Mountains, where he somehow became a Horanian elder and remained hidden from the rest of the Kingdom until we saw him."

"Now that you mention it, I did think that Zamel bore a resemblance to you," said Maryal, stroking her hair. "Nothing obvious, but the shape of his face was similar to yours. I just dismissed it as coincidence, though perhaps I should have realized that it was, in fact, destiny."

"What is your uncle doing here, then?" said Dlaine. "How did a foreigner like him become an elder? And how come he hasn't even bothered to return to the Kingdom and try to reunite it himself, if he really is Riuno's brother?"

"I asked myself those same questions," said Keo, "but I don't have the answers to them. That is why I want to stay here in the Mountains. I want to find out why he's here and what he's planning, if anything."

"If he went into hiding, I doubt it's anything good," said Dlaine, shaking his head. "But even if he's up to no good, I don't understand how you are going to find out what he's doing. If we try to go back to the Horanian village, we'll be filled with more holes than a beggar's shirt."

"That's why I said we need to find and kill the demon," said Keo. "If we can do that, we can prove to the Horanians that we're not evil. Then they might let us back into the village, where we'll be able to find out just what my uncle is doing here."

"I get it now," said Dlaine. "I'm still worried, though, because now we will have to actually *find* the demon and that might take a long time, considering how huge these Mountains are. There are probably a ton of places where that demon could be hiding, so we could spend months, I'm sure, searching for it without any success."

"Yes, we probably could, if we were going to search for it

ourselves," said Keo, "but like I said before, the demon has shown that it is interested in me. Therefore, we merely need to lure it out into the open, where we can fight it ourselves."

"Can we really beat it, though?" said Maryal. "You said that you and Easan had a hard time killing it, after all. You guys managed to wound it, but it survived and probably will be even harder to kill now that it knows what to expect from you in a fight."

Keo considered Maryal's concerns. While Keo had slain plenty of demons in the past, he had to admit that this particular demon seemed different. It seemed bigger and stronger than most, able to handle both him and Easan as well as the entirety of the Village Guard with relative ease. If they fought it again, then they might not be strong enough to beat it even if Keo and Easan went all out.

"We need to get stronger," said Keo, stroking his chin in thought. "Or at least I do. If we run into that demon again, I don't think that it will be quite as easy to beat. The only question is, how?"

"I can help," said a familiar female voice from behind one of the nearby boulders.

Tananeen stepped out from behind the boulder. She looked the same as she had a couple of days ago, only now there was a long, thick scar running down the left side of her face, which marred her face.

"Tananeen?" said Dlaine, starting when he saw her. "Where the hell did you come from? Have you been following us this whole time?"

Tananeen shook her head. "No. I just tracked you down a few

minutes ago, although I overheard your entire conversation."

"So you know that we've been with the Horanians and about the demon, then," said Keo. He folded his arms across his chest. "Tell me, did your people really kill off the Horanians when you first arrived here?"

Tananeen didn't look at Keo as she said, "Yes. My mother led the charge because she and the others were angry at all humans at the time, including humans like the Horanians who aren't related to the Lamairans. I wasn't born at the time, so I did not participate in it, but the Horanians hate me just as much as if I had."

"Why didn't you tell us about them back in the Nest?" said Dlaine. "Sure would have been nice to know about this band of mountain people who worship a giant that they think pulled these mountains out of the sea like a rock and placed it here before we ran into them."

"I didn't think you'd run into them, because the Horanians typically don't interact with visitors to the Mountains," said Tananeen. "I apologize for that. I should have warned you, but I didn't, and it sounds to me like you were nearly killed."

"That we were," said Dlaine, nodding in annoyance. "Their god told them to kill us because he said we're 'liars and deceivers.' Can you believe that?"

"I have never understood their god, so I cannot say what he was thinking when he said that," said Tananeen with a shrug. "All I can guess is that the Great Mountain Man dislikes foreigners just as much as his followers do."

"Right," said Keo. "But regardless, why did you come search for us? I thought that you wanted to stay with your people."

Keo didn't bother to hide the bitterness in his voice. Tananeen seemed to hear it quite well, because she still didn't look at him. Instead, she rubbed her ugly scar, like it was a habit she had developed recently.

"A day after you and your friends left, we were attacked," said Tananeen. "A man in black, with red eyes, attacked the Nest without warning. He crushed many eggs and killed several of our younglings and wounded quite a few mothers before we drove him off, which is how I got this scar, because I helped drive him off and he attacked me for it. My mother and the others believe that the man was a Horanian, but I knew he was a demon because of his red eyes. No one would listen to me, however, and now my mother has started to make plans to retaliate against the Horanians, intending to finish them off once and for all."

"Oh," said Keo. "That's bad."

"Even worse, my mother has somehow fooled herself into believing that you and your friends are working with the Horanians," said Tananeen. She shook her head. "I don't know why she thinks that, but regardless, she's assembled a small team of hunters to track and kill you and your friends. They haven't yet left the Nest because my mother wanted to make sure that everyone knows the plan of attack on the Horanian village, but they will soon and once they do they will not waste any time in killing all of you."

"Oh," said Keo, glancing up at the sky, which was currently empty of dragons. "That's even worse."

"So I went to find you to inform you of this so you and your friends could be prepared," said Tananeen. "That, and I also wanted to make sure that you were aware of the demon, in case it tried to come after you."

"A bit late there, lady," said Dlaine, glancing at Easan, who still looked a bit pale but seemed to be recovering. "We were attacked by a demon that looked like a Dracone in its dragon form back in the Horanian village. Think it was probably the same demon as the one that attacked the Nest."

"A demon that can take on the form of a human and a dragon?" said Tananeen in astonishment. "I have never heard of such a creature before."

"Yeah, neither have we, but it tried to destroy the village and only ran away because Keo and Easan hurt it," said Dlaine, shaking his head. "The Horanians think that it was one of your people and so they're getting ready to strike back against you, though don't know when."

"I see now," said Tananeen. "The demon is trying to instigate war between the Horanians and my people. A brilliant move on its part, because the demons must remember how we Dracones helped humanity defeat them the first time a thousand years ago. If humanity and the Dracones are too busy fighting each other, then it will be easier for the demons to rise again."

"That's what we're thinking," said Keo, nodding. "The only question is, how do we stop the Dracones and Horanians from wiping each other out?"

"We gotta find and kill the demon," said Dlaine. "Duh. We need to find proof that the demons are playing both sides and the only way to do that is to find the demon and show it to the Dracones and Horanians."

"But we've already established that we can't beat it on our own," said Keo. "Even if I and Easan were at full strength, that thing is just too big and powerful for us to fight."

"That is why I said I could help," said Tananeen, drawing everyone's attention to her again.

Keo looked at her skeptically. "Do you mean that you are going to help us kill the demon?"

"Yes, but I want to do more than that," said Tananeen. She pointed at Keo. "I want to train you to learn how to use your Dracone powers. I believe that if you can do that, then you will be able to defeat this demon with no problem."

Keo looked down at his hands, remembering how they had caught fire during his battle with the Brothers White Blood a few days ago, as well as the surge of strength that had accompanied the fire. He had liked that feeling well enough, but it had also been accompanied by a savageness deep within him that he hadn't even known was there and would have preferred to forget. It was an animalistic savagery that felt as alien to him as air did to fish.

He looked back up at Tananeen, uncertainty on his face. "Why do I need to learn how to use those powers?"

"Because I believe that it is part of your destiny," said Tananeen. "I believe that you must master your human and Dracone abilities in order to fight the demons. The demons are getting stronger and stronger and your human form by itself will not be enough to stand against them in the coming months. You will need the full power of your abilities to defeat them, because the demons will use their full power to defeat you."

Tananeen sounded all but certain of that, which made it hard to doubt her. And Keo didn't really want to, because he liked the idea of being more powerful than he currently was, because even though he had handled the demons they had fought so far pretty well, he was also worried that he was starting to stagnate in his training. Besides, he had seen firsthand just how powerful the Dracones were and so knew that if he could access even a tenth of that power that it would be all worth it.

But again, Keo remembered how utterly savage he had behaved toward the Brothers a few days ago. It had felt like a monster lying deep within his chest had awakened, a monster he wasn't sure he wanted anything to do with. It may have helped him save Jola from the Brothers, but he was worried that he had simply gotten lucky there and that if he accessed it again, he might hurt more than just his enemies.

"I know I cannot force you to train under me, Keo, but I believe it would help you if you did," said Tananeen. "Now, will you or will you not accept my offer?"

Although Keo still felt hesitant about it, he looked Tananeen straight in the eye and said, "I accept it. My only question is, will we have enough time to train before the demon strikes again or the Dracones and Horanians fight each other?"

"I won't be able to give you the in-depth training that we normally give our younglings as they grow due to a lack of time, but I will be able to help you learn the basics at least," said Tananeen.

"Okay," said Keo, nodding. "Where will we train? Here?"

"This place is too open and easy to find," said Tananeen. "But I know of a better place not far from here where we can train without being easily found by either Dracone or Horanian. Follow me."

# Chapter Sixteen

**T**HE PLACE TO WHICH Tananeen took Keo and his friends was another clearing similar to the first, except wider and hidden by the tall peaks on all sides. It took them only half an hour to reach the place, but Tananeen assured them that the clearing's isolation, along with a Dracone spell of her own devising, would make it difficult, if not impossible, for anyone— human, Dracone, or demon—to find them without their knowledge.

That made Keo feel safer, until he saw the clearing itself. Large Dracone skeletons—most in their dragon forms—were scattered here and there. Some of them were quite large, almost as large as Queen Sayot, while others were smaller, including a few that appeared to have died as younglings. There were about a dozen skeletal remains of Dracones, with some being nearly complete skeletons, while others were merely a claw or a foot or a head or jawbone. Some looked like they had died sleeping, while others had holes where they had been stabbed or perhaps bitten.

All in all, the clearing looked like a graveyard. Keo hated graveyards, always had, but there was something about this graveyard that made him want to leave. It was more than just his normal revulsion toward skeletons and tombstones, but a more primal disgust, as if his body knew that bad things had happened here and that he should leave right away if he did not want bad things to happen to him.

"What is this place?" said Keo, looking around as they walked into the area, which was very quiet aside from the wind blowing through it.

"A cemetaria," said Tananeen, gesturing at the various skeletons scattered about. She seemed very tense, however, as if she was just as repulsed by this place as Keo was. "A Dracone cemetery. It is where we put our dead. There are a dozen scattered all around the Upper Mountains, some easier for humans to reach than others."

"It's creepy," said Maryal with a shudder. "Why don't you bury your dead?"

"Because we Dracones don't believe in that," said Tananeen, shaking her head. "It's why we make our burial places far from the Nest. That way, we don't have to smell the decaying bodies of our dead or deal with contracting illnesses from the rotting corpses."

"Did we have to come and train *here*?" said Keo. "Isn't there somewhere else we could train instead?"

"What, afraid of the dead?" said Easan with a smirk. He no longer looked as pale and sick as he did earlier, though he didn't look perfectly healthy, either. "I didn't know you were superstitious, Keo."

"He's not," said Tananeen, shaking her head. "We Dracones have a natural aversion to the sites of our dead. Granted, most living beings dislike being around their dead, but we Dracones are actively repelled by our dead. It is taking all of my willpower just to stay here, rather than run away to somewhere safer."

"Safer?" said Easan. He looked at the inanimate bones and frowned. "These bones don't look dangerous to me. Well, maybe if they fell on you while you're standing under them, but if not, then I don't see what's so unsafe about them."

"I cannot explain it, mostly because I believe it isn't a rational aversion on our part," said Tananeen. She pressed one hand against her chest. "It's an instinctive aversion to our dead that flows through our blood and is built into our bones. We can fight it, but it is hard to do so."

"Well, I still think it is silly," said Easan, shaking his head.

"But I see why you chose to train Keo in this place," said Dlaine. He gestured at the nearby skeleton of a Dracone. "If your species has a natural aversion to your own graveyards, then that means it is unlikely that any of those hunters you mentioned will come looking for us here."

"Exactly," said Tananeen, nodding. "It will, however, make it harder for both of us to concentrate, although we will hopefully not have to stay for long. Just long enough to teach Keo the basics."

Keo nodded, but he still wondered if there really wasn't a better place to train. He now understood that he was likely feeling the Dracones' natural aversion to their own dead, but that didn't make it any easier to handle. If anything, that made it harder, because he now had the excuse that it was only 'natural' to run, even though he rationally knew that there really wasn't anywhere safer in the Mountains than this place at the moment.

"And it isn't just the Dracones who will avoid this place," said

Tananeen. She pointed in the general direction that the Horanian village lay in. "The Horanians tend to avoid our graveyards as a rule as well. I do not know why, but I think that they believe that the graveyards of us Dracones are haunted by spirits of our deceased."

"There *aren't* any Dracone ghosts around here, right?" said Dlaine, looking around in alarm. "That's just a superstition of theirs, right?"

"Yes, but it's not one we've ever bothered to correct, seeing as it keeps them from desecrating the graves of our dead, which I am sure they would do if given the chance," said Tananeen. "It is sad, but the Horanians well and truly do hate us because of what my people did to theirs seventy years ago."

All of this talk about the Horanians suddenly made Keo remember something. He said to Tananeen, "Tananeen, have you ever seen the elders of the Horanians?"

Tananeen looked over her shoulder at Keo as they entered the graveyard, a frown on her face. "No. I rarely go near their village and their elders never leave it. All I know from what other Dracones have told me is that they have four elders, two men and two women."

"That much is true, but you don't know the identity of one of the men," said Keo. "It's Zamel, the brother of my father. You know, the one who went missing after my father's death?"

Tananeen suddenly stopped, staring at Keo in shock and forcing Keo to stop as well so he wouldn't walk into her. "Zamel? Impossible. He died during the chaos after your father's death."

"I don't think he did," said Keo, shaking his head. "One of the elders of the Horanians is a man named Zamel. He looks just like my father, except older, like how my father would look if he had managed to live to his seventies. I'm sure he recognized me, especially after I told the elders who I was."

"You mean you didn't know that the brother of your husband was in the same Mountains as you?" said Dlaine, who had stopped along with Maryal, Easan, and Jola. He tilted his head to the side. "I thought you knew more about these place than we do."

"Like I said, I have never actually seen the elders and don't know their names," said Tananeen. She ran a finger down her scar in thought. "But if Zamel truly is one of them, then that is news indeed. And not good news, either."

"Why?" said Keo. "I didn't get a chance to confirm his identity, but if he really is the same Zamel that we know of, then maybe he could help us."

"Considering he didn't try to 'help us' when Osina ordered those damn archers to use us as target practice, I doubt he cares much for us," said Dlaine, folding his arms across his chest and shaking his head.

"That's a good point, Dlaine, but there is another reason why Zamel's presence in the Upper Mountains is not good," said Tananeen. "You see, Zamel was more like his father than Riuno was. He hated Dracones, absolutely despised us. I met him a few times during my courtship of Riuno, but it seemed like any time I was in the castle, he was out. Once he even insulted my looks, which earned him a beating from Riuno."

"He knew you were a Dracone?" said Keo.

"No, I don't think so," said Tananeen. "I think he suspected it, but as I told you before, we kept my true nature a secret from everyone except for a few loyal servants. I think he just didn't think I'd make good queenly material or perhaps was still jealous at his brother for winning the crown. Zamel was always jealous of your father, even before Riuno became King."

"I see why he decided to take up residence with the Horanians, then," said Dlaine, shaking his head. "They also hate your people, so I bet he feels right at home among them."

"That he does, but it still doesn't explain why or how he got here," said Tananeen. She looked in the direction of the Horanian village, like she could somehow see it through all of the mountains and cliffs and boulders around them. "Like everyone else, I thought he had been killed during the chaos of the fall of the Kingdom. Almost every other minor noble who didn't defect to one of the three factions that arose from the Kingdom's ashes died, and neither the Magicians nor the Divinians or the Restorationists ever claimed to have Zamel among them."

"Very strange," said Dlaine, stroking his chin. "What do you think that means?"

"I have no idea," said Tananeen. "Aside from his blatant and obvious jealousy of Riuno, Zamel was always hard for me to read. Perhaps he had some political enemies who he was afraid would kill him after Riuno died, because I know for a fact that Zamel constantly got into trouble in the capital and that more than one of the other minor nobles wanted him dead."

"How come no one killed him, then?" said Keo.

"Because your father always protected him," said Tananeen. "Even though Zamel was always jealous of him, your father never hated him, not even once. I never understood it, because as a Dracone my natural reaction to a jealous sibling would be to leave him to defend himself from his own enemies, but it was well-known among the nobles that your father would unleash his wrath on anyone who harmed his younger brother. And your father could get very angry when he wants."

"If Zamel is still alive, why didn't he take the Throne after Riuno's death?" said Maryal. "The Throne has been empty for over two decades. What's to stop him from taking it?"

"That's another question I don't have the answer to," said Tananeen. "My guess is that Zamel was probably too cowardly to take the Throne and enforce order on the Kingdom, so he ran all the way out here where no one could find him. Zamel was never as good at inspiring loyalty among the people as your father was."

"But he ran to the home of the Dracones, the people he hated?" said Keo. "Doesn't make a lot of sense."

"It does if you consider the fact that literally none of his enemies would think to look for him here," said Maryal. "In fact, even we wouldn't have come here if your mother hadn't met us at Tain and asked us to come."

"The Upper Mountains are indeed a very good place for a Lamairan to hide if they need to, because none of the three factions consider this part of their territory," said Tananeen. "Of course, that doesn't mean it is an easy to place to hide in, when you consider that both we Dracones and the Horanians tend to be intolerant of outsiders."

"This is just one big mystery after mystery," said Keo, shaking his head. "We're missing something, but I don't know what."

"We will have to find out later," said Tananeen. She resumed walking into the graveyard, gesturing for Keo and his friends to continue to follow her. "Come. Your training must still be done, regardless of whatever Zamel is planning. Remember, the demon is still the immediate threat, so we must get you ready to fight it."

Keo and his friends followed Tananeen until they reached the graveyard itself, at which point Tananeen gestured for Keo's friends to stand under the shadow of one of the Dracone skeletons. None of Keo's friends looked thrilled about having to stand so close to one of the dead Dracones, but they did it anyway, because Tananeen explained that she and Keo would need a lot of room if they were going to train and that she did not want any of them getting in the way and possibly hurting themselves in the process.

After Keo's friends stood where they were supposed to, Keo and Tananeen took a spot in the center of the graveyard, standing several feet opposite one another. The air was still cold and the clouds above were still gray, but Keo tried to focus on his mother anyway, despite the chill of the mountain wind that blew through at that moment.

"All right, Keo, are you ready to start the training?" said Tananeen.

Keo nodded. "Yes. What are we going to focus on first?"

"Transformation, of course," said Tananeen.

"Transformation?" said Keo in surprise. "Do you mean changing from human to Dragon?"

"Yes," said Tananeen. "That is what we will practice. We have to do that because the ability to transform from human to dragon at will is one of the most important—and useful—abilities that we Dracones have."

Keo looked down at his body, which looked and felt as human

as ever. "How do I know if I can transform or not? I'm not a pure-blood Dracone, after all. I'm only half-Dracone."

"Perhaps that is true, but I suspect that you can transform anyway," said Tananeen. She gestured at Gildshine. "Your golden flames show that you can at least generate fire from within yourself."

"Can all Dracones in human form do that?" said Keo.

"Most can," said Tananeen. She snapped her fingers and a blue fireball appeared in her hand, small but bright. "But we usually prefer to breathe it in dragon form because it is much stronger that way."

"I see," said Keo. "All I've ever been able to do is summon it over my sword or, in some cases, on my hands. I've never been able to shoot it from my mouth."

"That's because it is impossible to breathe fire through your mouth as a human," said Tananeen. She gestured at her own mouth and throat. "The human form is incapable of breathing fire. Even if you could, I wouldn't recommend it, because the intense dragon fire would burn you up from the inside and kill you."

Keo shuddered at the thought. "Okay, but how, exactly, *do* I transform? How do I even know I can?"

"The fact that you can summon fire is a good sign that you can, in fact, transform into a dragon," said Tananeen. "But you are a special case. The vast majority of Dracones are born in their dragon forms and learn how to transform into their human forms at a later date. You, on the other hand, were born human and are now trying to learn how to transform into your dragon form."

"Does that mean it will be difficult for me to learn?" said Keo.

"It may," said Tananeen. "But you are actually at the right age to learn how to transform. Most Dracones don't succeed in mastering transformation until they reach young adulthood, close to your age, sometimes sooner, sometimes later. Many will try before then, but often they end up getting stuck between forms, which can be uncomfortable and even painful depending on how it is done. So most Dracones wait until their bodies have fully matured before they attempt to master the transformation process."

Keo felt along his back, where he imagined large dragon wings sprouting forth. "But you've never trained a half-Dracone like me."

"True," said Tananeen. "To my knowledge, you are the only half-Dracone in existence. Still, I've noticed that you have many Dracone traits, so I believe that with the right training you should be able to transform into a dragon and back just like any other Dracone your age."

"Then let's do it," said Keo. "I'm ready when you are."

"All right," said Tananeen. She held up one finger. "First, you must imagine what your dragon form will look like. You must visualize it."

Keo frowned. "How am I supposed to do that when I have never transformed and don't know what my dragon form will even look like?"

"It isn't necessary that you know how your dragon form looks like right away," said Tananeen. "You can imagine it however you want. Your actual dragon form will probably look different than what you imagine, but the one in your imagination is merely supposed to be a base for you start from, not the final form you will actually take."

Keo folded his arms over his chest and glanced at his friends, who were watching quietly, saved for Maryal and Easan, who seemed to be talking to each other about something. "Should I warn my friends?"

"No," said Tananeen, shaking her head. "Your transformation shouldn't affect them. Now just close your eyes and focus, focus hard, on what you believe your dragon form will look like. Imagine it in as much detail as possible."

As skeptical as Keo was, he decided to listen to Tananeen about this. She seemed to know what she was doing. Besides, he saw no harm in visualizing what his dragon form might look like.

So Keo closed his eyes and focused as hard as he could on visualizing what he might look like as a dragon. Because he had no idea what he might actually look like, Keo used Tananeen's own dragon form as a base.

He imagined that he would be much larger than Tananeen, seeing as he was male and most male Dracones seemed to be larger than their female counterparts (with the exception of Queen Sayot, of course). He imagined that his wings would be huge, perhaps as wide as the clearing where they had met Rackan and Nobia, and that his scales and skin would be silver. He had no reason for believing that they would look silver. He just liked the color.

He imagined that his dragon form would have a series of long spikes running down its back, the spikes growing progressively larger until the one right at the base of his neck was about half as tall as himself. His eyes would be colored golden brown, while his claws would be as sharp as Gildshine, if not sharper. He would have a long tail, like a whip, except as thick as a tree, with more spikes on it.

Keo kept adding more and more detail to the imagery, until soon he saw a perfectly detailed dragon in his mind's eye. Feeling that he had added enough detail, Keo stood there, waiting to feel his human body transforming into something close to what he imagined, but the longer he stood there, the longer he felt as normal and human as ever.

Frustrated, Keo said, without opening his eyes, "Tananeen, am I transforming yet? I don't feel any different."

"Have you visualized your dragon form in sufficient detail?" said Tananeen.

"Yes," said Keo, nodding. "It's so detailed that I could touch it if it actually existed."

"Then you need to imagine your human self transforming into that form," said Tananeen. "Now focus again on your mental image. Don't allow anything else to distract you."

Keo wasn't sure how focusing on his mental image was supposed to help him transform, but seeing as Tananeen was the teacher here and he was not, he decided to listen to her advice.

So Keo focused again on the mental image of his dragon form that he had come up with earlier. This time, he imagined himself in his human form in its place and tried to imagine his human form changing into his dragon form. As before, he used Tananeen's own shape shifting as the basis for his, seeing as that that was what he was most familiar with.

Watching in his mind as his human form transformed into his dragon form, Keo noticed that it looked very painful. It hadn't look painful when he had seen the other Dracones transform before, but then, Keo realized that those Dracones had had far more experience in transforming than he had. Even so, just the thought that it was painful made him feel even more nervous about the transformation than normal, if only because he didn't want to feel the pain.

Still, Keo watched the transformation over and over, focusing on the ways in which his body grew and his face lengthened and large wings sprang from his back. He kept expecting to feel the transformation in real life at any moment, but it seemed like no matter how long he waited, he felt nothing. This just made his frustration grow, until his eyes snapped open and he looked at Tananeen in annoyance.

"Have I transformed yet?" said Keo, feeling along his body with his hands, although it all felt and looked normal to him.

"No, but that doesn't mean you should give up," said Tananeen. "Transforming is a difficult technique to master even if you, like most of our younglings, have been raised among adult Dracones who can transform at will. That you have been raised among humans who don't know anything about transformation means that learning this technique may take much longer to learn than it ordinarily would."

"But I don't have time for that," said Keo. "Somewhere out there is a demon that is trying to kill us, not to mention both the Dracones and Horanians are still after us. And with the demons about to rise again in two months, I really don't have all of the time in the world to spend learning this or any other technique."

"I'm sorry, but there is no way to speed up the learning process unless you put your mind to it and stop complaining," said Tananeen. "Complaining to me accomplishes nothing, seeing as I can't control how quickly you can learn how to transform."

"I know, but are you sure there isn't some way to speed up the process?" said Keo. "Like some kind of Dracone spell or ritual that could make it easier?"

"Not that I know of," said Tananeen. "You will simply have to achieve transformation through hard work and effort. Otherwise, you will never learn it at all."

"Maybe I *can't* learn it," said Keo. He glanced at his normal human hands. "Maybe that's not the half I got when I was born. Maybe I'm more human than Dracone, in more ways than one."

"Well, I see no reason to think that until you've tried your hardest and still haven't succeeded," said Tananeen, shaking her head. "And you clearly have not tried your hardest."

"How would *you* know that?" said Keo, putting his hands on his hips. "It's not like you know me all that well, considering how we were separated from each other for almost my entire life."

"Because you are very much like your father," said Tananeen. "And he always became frustrated whenever things did not come easy to him. Although he never gave up quite *that* easily."

Keo didn't like Tananeen's tone at all and he said, "Are you saying I'm less patient than my own father?"

"Yes, but I attribute that mostly to your age," said Tananeen. "You are still quite young, both in human and Dracone years. You haven't yet built up that perseverance that comes with age."

"I've persevered through a lot already," Keo said. "Traveled through two different countries, across hundreds of miles worth of land, fought and killed half a dozen demons, traveled up these Mountains … frankly, I'd say I've done more stuff than most men twice my age."

"Then you should understand already that learning a new skill like transforming is not easy or quick," said Tananeen. "And that there is no short cut to learning it except through hard work and effort."

"Then why are you even teaching it to me at all?" said Keo. "If it's such a time-consuming task to learn, then why not teach me something easier and quicker to learn?"

"Because it does not need to take tons of time," said Tananeen. "Like any other skill, different people take different amounts of time to learn it. Some Dracones catch on quickly, others take longer. In either case, both have learned the technique by never giving up and practicing every day."

Keo scowled. "Well, maybe it's harder for me because I'm half-Dracone, rather than a full-blooded one. That ever occur to you?"

"It has, but I think that the opposite is more likely," said Tananeen. "I believe that there is something special about you, a specialness you can only unlock if you work for it. Now, are you done complaining or are you going to keep whining to me about how hard this all is?"

Keo wanted to keep arguing the point, but then he realized that the others were still watching and he realized how foolish he was making himself look. He still wasn't happy about how difficult learning this technique was going to be, but he decided that Tananeen was right and that complaining wasn't going to be helpful.

So Keo nodded grudgingly and said, "All right. Let's continue. I'll try not to complain too much."

# Chapter Seventeen

THE NEXT FEW HOURS were mostly full of Keo trying to transform. He stood there across from his mother, imagining his human self transforming into his dragon self again and again. Every time he did it, he expected his physical body to suddenly transform and for him to tower above everyone else, but he did not feel even one part of his body change. The entire exercise was starting to feel increasingly useless and even counterproductive, although Tananeen insisted that this was the only way for a new Dracone to learn how to transform.

Once, Keo did feel his arms become a little bulkier, which excited him enough to open his eyes and look at them just to see if they looked dragon-like. Unfortunately, that caused his concentration to snap and his arms lost what little extra bulk they had gained. That earned him a scolding from Tananeen, who told him that you didn't open your eyes even if you felt your body transforming, because when you were learning how to transform you needed to be fully concentrating on your mental image at all times, regardless of what you felt in your body.

That annoyed Keo, but when he remembered that he had vowed not to complain, he simply resumed his mental training.

Even so, Keo found it hard to focus on his mental image of his human form transforming into his dragon form, because he was so annoyed with his own lack of progress that he focused more on that than on the image in his mind.

Eventually, Tananeen called for a break, at which point Keo and she went over to the others and joined them for lunch, which Dlaine was setting up using the supplies they carried in their packs. The others were already eating by the time Keo and Tananeen joined them, but Easan looked up from his bowl of stew as they approached.

"How did your training go?" said Easan as Keo sat down between him and Maryal. "It looked boring."

Keo looked at Easan in annoyance. "It *was* boring. And I didn't transform even a little."

"That's because you got distracted," said Tananeen, who sat on the other side of the small fire, next to Dlaine, who was too busy eating his own stew to speak. "After we finish lunch, we can get back to the training. You will have an easier time focusing if your stomach is full."

Keo supposed that Tananeen was right, but he didn't feel very happy about his progress. He just took a bowl of stew that Maryal offered him and started eating, although he hadn't even realized until that moment how hungry he was. Then again, he hadn't eaten since breakfast this morning, because the Horanians had not provided him or his friends with any meals back in their village.

As they sat there eating, Keo looked up at the sky again. He realized that it had become a habit of his ever since he and his friends entered the Upper Mountains nearly a week ago now. Probably because quite a few dangerous things hid in the sky of the Upper Mountains, such as human-hating Dracones and demons. In any case, the sky was, as usual, covered in thick gray clouds, so Keo returned his attention to the meal he was eating with the others.

*Better not worry about that right now,* Keo thought. *Just eat.*

Still, Keo could not help but find it strange how the demon, at least, had not found them yet. The Dracones avoided this graveyard (and for good reason, Keo thought) and the Horanians didn't even know where Keo and his friends had teleported to, but the demon should have been able to find them easily. That Keo had not seen it at all since they left the village made him worry that things were going a little too easily for them right now. He fully expected the demon to attack at any moment, and based on the way that Tananeen and Dlaine occasionally looked around, he wasn't the only one expecting an attack like that.

But the meal went by peacefully enough, with not even one hint of the demon anywhere. When Keo and Tananeen finished, they returned to their spot in the center of the graveyard and resumed training.

More hours went by as Keo continued to try to transform. He made certain this time to avoid being distracted by the cold, his friends, Tananeen, the clouds, the sense of dread he felt in the graveyard, or anything else in the area. He replayed the mental image in his head of him transforming into a dragon as quickly and clearly as he could.

Despite his hard work, Keo saw no progress whatsoever, save for a brief stirring in his chest that almost shattered his concentration. But Keo remembered what happened the last time he let his excitement over his growth affect him and so he ignored it in favor of focusing on his mental image. Unfortunately, that stirring soon went away and Keo once more found himself mentally repeating the same image in his head time and again fruitlessly.

By the time Tananeen called for another break, the sun had nearly set and Keo felt exhausted, even though he hadn't done much more other than stand there and imagine things. He supposed it was probably to do with the fact that he had done many things that day, including fighting that demon and narrowly escaping death at the hands of the Horanians. Regardless, all Keo wanted to do was rest. He was still frustrated and disappointed by his own lack of progress, even after Tananeen reassured him yet again that it was nothing unusual and that they would try again tomorrow, but he was too tired from the events of the day to argue with her or anyone else.

Because the graveyard was still the safest place to sleep, Keo and his friends, along with Tananeen, chose to sleep in the graveyard for the night. While Dlaine, Maryal, and Easan managed to go to sleep without any difficulty, Keo found it almost impossible to sleep because of his instinctive Dracone dislike of sleeping near their dead. Tananeen didn't seem to have any trouble sleeping, however, which made Keo feel a little jealous, even though he understood that she probably simply had more experience than he did in ignoring her instincts.

# Chapter Eighteen

**K**EO HARDLY GOT MUCH sleep that night. It was mostly due to his instinctive aversion to the Dracone skeletons, but he also worried that they might be attacked in the night by the demon. True, Jola stayed up to keep watch, but Keo still found it hard to relax long enough to get more than a couple of hours of sleep.

In the morning, after breakfast, Keo and Tananeen returned to their spot in the center of the graveyard to continue practicing Keo's transformation, while Keo's friends stayed on the margins where they promised to keep a look out for anyone—Horanian, Dracone, or demon—that might be coming to the graveyard. Keo was tired and sleepy, even with the cold air nipping at his ears.

Tananeen must have noticed, because she said, "Keo? You seem distracted by something. Are you all right?"

Keo shook his head to snap himself out of his thoughts and looked up at Tananeen. Unlike him, she seemed far more well-rested, far more alert and ready to practice. She had probably gotten more sleep than him, though that did not make him feel any better about his own lack of sleep.

"I'm all right," said Keo with a yawn. "I just didn't get as much sleep last night as I wanted. It was hard to ignore the skeletons."

Tananeen nodded in understanding. "Yes, most Dracones cannot sleep at all near their dead. I only managed it because I have a strong will and can override my own instincts to an extent, but it is still far from easy and I didn't sleep quite as well last night as I normally do."

"Oh," said Keo. He yawned again. "So what are we going to do today? Just the same thing as yesterday?"

"Essentially, but I want to try something a bit different," said Tananeen. "I took into account your complaints and difficulties from yesterday, when you said you were having a hard time focusing on your mental image."

Keo perked up when Tananeen mentioned that. "Do you mean that you really *do* know a shortcut for learning how to transform?"

"No," said Tananeen, shaking her head. "But just because there isn't a shortcut to success doesn't mean that there are not shorter paths to it."

Keo rubbed his hands together eagerly. "Then hit me with it. I'm listening."

"All right," said Tananeen. She tapped her forehead. "One thing that differentiates us Dracones from humans is that we can mentally connect with one another. It's a very limited, basic sort of telepathy, which we can't force on anyone and doesn't let us read other peoples' minds very deeply unless they give us their consent."

"Really?" said Keo curiously. "Why do we have that?"

"It's normally meant to be used by groups of Dracones during hunting," said Tananeen. "It allows small groups of Dracones to coordinate their attacks far more easily than talking aloud. Thoughts move faster than lightning bolts, so if a bunch of Dracones got together to hunt, they can connect their minds for easy communication."

"Interesting," said Keo. "Can it be used during war, too? It sounds to me like it would be useful in battle."

"It can be, but usually isn't," said Tananeen. "While having this sort of limited telepathy is helpful when hunting for your next meal, in war it is very different, because in war you are usually fighting dozens if not hundreds of people at once and that sort of chaos requires a lot more independence than our limited telepathy allows. Our limited telepathy can turn a group of Dracones into a hive mind if they're not careful, which ironically enough actually takes away all of the benefits of this linked telepathy."

"Okay, but I don't see how this will help me learn how to transform," said Keo, scratching an itch behind his ear. "Unless you're going to suggest that I give up my individuality, that is."

"I would never suggest such a thing," said Tananeen. She tapped her forehead again and then pointed at Keo's forehead. "Instead, I am going to link our minds together for a moment so I can see if there is some sort of mental block preventing you from focusing as easily as you should."

Keo put a hand on his forehead. "How much access will this give you to my mind?"

"Only as much as you allow," said Tananeen. "I won't be able to see your deepest memories or thoughts, but your surface level ones will be as easy for me to read as a book."

"Will I be able to read your thoughts?" said Keo.

"Yes, because our connection will be two-way, although you

still will not be able to read as much as I can of yours," said Tananeen.

"Okay, but why do you think that my mind has some kind of mental block?" said Keo. "Are you saying that I shouldn't be struggling so hard to learn this technique as I am?"

"It's not that, necessarily," said Tananeen, shaking her head. "I simply want to confirm that you can, in fact, transform. Transformation is just as much mental as it is physical. By searching your mind, I should be able to determine whether you inherited that technique from me or whether your Dracone half lacks that power."

Keo rubbed his forehead. "Why didn't you do this to me yesterday? Wouldn't we have saved a lot of time that way?"

"We would have, but I was simply confident that you could do it, seeing as you can summon dragon flames with your sword and hands," said Tananeen. "But since you are obviously struggling hard here, that made me think that you might not have the ability at all. I came up with this idea last night as I drifted off to sleep in order to make sure that you can in fact transform."

Keo gulped. "If we do it, will it hurt?"

"It shouldn't, seeing as you are half-Dracone," said Tananeen. "The process of linking minds is not painful, although it can take some getting used to, seeing as most people go their whole lives without ever feeling another mind inside their head that is not theirs."

Keo glanced over at the edges of the graveyard, where he saw his friends walking and talking. "Could you link my friends' minds to mine?"

"No," said Tananeen. "The mind linking process can only

work between two or more Dracones. Because you are half-Dracone, it should work, but your friends are all pure humans, so we couldn't link their minds to ours even if we wanted."

"Including Jola?" said Keo.

Tananeen frowned. "Your friend is unique, but I don't think she will be able to join us. She is still human, as far as I know, so I don't think that she can join us, despite her obvious skill in telepathy."

There was something about the way Tananeen frowned when Keo mentioned Jola that made him wonder if he had said the wrong thing. Or maybe there was something about Jola that Tananeen didn't like. Keo understood, because Jola, for all her helpfulness, was still quite strange even to him and he really didn't know too much about her past, aside from the fact that she had escaped from the infamous Dark Prison once and had known Dlaine for years.

"Okay," said Keo, nodding. "I just wanted to make sure."

"All right," said Tananeen. "Now I believe that you understand the process. Do you want to start?"

Keo didn't like the idea of having another mind inside his, even if it was his own mother's. He valued the privacy of his thoughts too much to simply let Tananeen in heedlessly. On the other hand, if this would help speed up the transformation learning process, then Keo would be a complete and utter fool to reject it in order to take the harder path. Besides, Tananeen probably would not do anything malicious with whatever thoughts of his that she might find in his head. She was his mother, after all, although that didn't mean much to Keo, because he still thought of her as abandoning him years ago when he was a baby.

Nonetheless, Keo gave Tananeen the thumbs up and said, "Yes, I'd like to start right away. I want to be able to transform into my dragon form as quickly as possible."

"Very well, then," said Tananeen. "But I must warn you that the mind linking process might feel strange at first. I presume you have never done it before, at least with a Dracone like myself. So try not to react negatively to whatever you feel. I promise that it is feels worse than it actually is."

Keo nodded. "I understand. Let's get started. I can handle whatever you throw at me."

Tananeen actually smiled when he said that, even though Keo wasn't trying to joke around. "Just like your father, always ready for anything. All right. Here we go."

Tananeen pressed the three middle fingers of her right hand against her forehead and closed her eyes. Keo stared at her for a couple of seconds, wondering when he'd feel anything out of the ordinary, when suddenly he felt an uncomfortable presence in his mind that was certainly not his own.

It was an odd feeling. It felt like someone was literally walking around the inside his brain, poking and prodding and peeking underneath the gray matter at whatever was underneath. Like Tananeen had said, it wasn't painful, but it was a disorienting feeling nonetheless, causing Keo's focus to become weaker and scattered. He grabbed his head, but otherwise could do nothing to make that odd feeling go away.

Then he heard Tananeen's voice in his head say, *Keo, can you hear me? Are we connected?*

Keo looked at Tananeen. She was standing as still as a statue now, with her head inclined slightly downwards, her eyes closed, and her fingers on her forehead. *Yes, I can hear you.*

*Then the connection was a success,* said Tananeen, who sounded quite pleased. *Now I will need to access a bit deeper into your mind to help you. Will you grant me that access?*

Keo hesitated. *How deep, exactly, are we talking about here?*

*Deep enough so I can access your imagination, which is where your mental transformation must first start,* said Tananeen. *Once I have access to your imagination, I should be able to confirm whether or not you can actually transform.*

It all sounded esoteric to Keo, but he decided that he could trust Tananeen with access to his imagination, so he said, *All right. You can check it out. But please don't be in there too long. I don't like the feeling of someone else's mind in my own.*

*I will be in there only as long as I need to be,* said Tananeen.

With that, Keo felt Tananeen's mind moving through his, going deeper and deeper into his thoughts. It felt strange to him, so strange that a part of him was tempted to just kick Tananeen out entirely so that he would have his mind to himself again, but he tried not to behave in any negative way. He knew that Tananeen was trying to help and was going to let her do what she needed to do even if it felt a little bit uncomfortable to him.

A few seconds later, Keo heard Tananeen say, *I'm in your imagination,* but that was all he heard from her. He did, however, feel her even deeper into his mind now, but now he felt part of her own worry, like she had found something that shouldn't be there. But since she hadn't actually said anything yet, Keo figured that it was probably nothing too serious.

That was when Keo remembered that Tananeen had said that

he had access to her mind in the same way she had access to his. The idea of poking around in someone else's mind made him feel a little uncomfortable, but since he was getting bored standing around waiting for Tananeen to find and remove the mental block that she was looking for, he decided to see if he could access her mind.

But before Keo could get very far, he blinked and suddenly found himself standing back in the Dracone graveyard opposite Tananeen. Tananeen herself had lowered her hand from her forehead and opened her eyes again, but now they looked worried. It took Keo a moment to realize that she had broken off the connection between them, although he wasn't sure why. He was, however, grateful that she was no longer in his head, because her presence had been one of the most uncomfortable experiences in his life and was one that he did not wish to repeat again.

"Tananeen?" said Keo, looking at her cautiously. "What happened? Did you find the mental block that's keeping me from transforming?"

Tananeen rubbed her forehead like Keo had just punched her there. "I didn't find any mental block, which I suppose means that you can transform with the right training."

Keo's face broke into a wide grin that he didn't even bother to try to hide. "Really? That's great. But you don't sound very happy about it."

"Because your transformation seems a bit … different," said Tananeen. She frowned again, a larger frown than before. "It isn't quite the same as the transformation for most Dracones."

"How does it differ?" said Keo. He looked down at his body and patted his chest. "Is it something to do with my body?"

"That's not it, exactly," said Tananeen. "It's hard to describe, but in your mind, I saw something that didn't quite make sense to me. It looked like you, but not the same."

Keo rubbed his forehead again, which still felt a little strange even without Tananeen in there anymore. "Me, but not the same? That's helpful."

"As I said, it is hard to describe," said Tananeen. "I believe what I saw was your transformation, but it looked unlike any transformation I had ever seen. That may mean that your transformation will be different from the transformation of every other Dracone I know of."

"Is that why I'm having such a hard time achieving it?" said Keo. "Is it because it's different?"

"In all probability, yes," said Tananeen. "I think it is very likely that you may need different training than what most younglings receive, although I don't know what, exactly. I think a lot of the traditional training techniques will still help, but you may need more than just that in order to achieve transformation."

"Is my form better or worse than what most Dracones get?" said Keo.

"I don't know, seeing as you have yet to achieve transformation, but I do know that it is different," said Tananeen. "Now I did run into a few mental blocks in there that I did away with, which should make it easier for you to transform, but you will still need to put in the work."

Keo nodded. "Sounds good to me. At least I know that I can transform now. I think that will make it easier for me to practice, knowing that it isn't a complete waste of time after all."

"That's good to hear," said Tananeen. "Now, I—"

"Keo, Tananeen!" cried Maryal. "Wait!"

Keo and Tananeen looked to Keo's left. Maryal, Easan, and Dlaine were running toward them as fast as they could, almost like they were being chased by something, although Keo did not see anything pursuing them from behind. His friends stopped several feet from him and his mother, Dlaine putting his hands on his knees as he panted, while Maryal brushed some of her hair out of her eyes, a look of worry on her face.

"What's the problem?" said Keo, turning to face his friends. "Did you guys see something?"

"Jola said that she saw several members of the Horanian Village Guard sneaking among the peaks nearby," said Dlaine, gesturing to the east. "She said there were about a dozen of them, each armed with a bow and a sword, and they don't seem to be hunting dinner."

Keo stared at Dlaine in shock. "How did they find us? I thought that the Horanians avoided Dracone graveyards."

"No idea," said Dlaine with a shrug. "Jola just said that they were nearby and seemed to be heading this way. That means we don't have much time left to stand here and be shocked about this."

"All right," said Keo, albeit reluctantly. "We should leave, then." He looked at Tananeen. "Any idea of where we should go?"

Tananeen stroked her chin in thought. "I believe there is a cave nearby that we could hide in for a while. It is difficult for humans to get to, but—"

Tananeen was interrupted by the roar of a dragon somewhere in the distance, although it sounded closer than Keo was comfortable with. Keo looked to the west, in the direction where the roar had come from, and caught a glimpse of a red dragon flying among the peaks before it vanished from view.

"Uh oh," said Dlaine, who seemed to have also seen it. "Please don't tell me that I saw a dragon flying over there."

"You did," said Keo. "And it was a red one, too."

"Probably Veta," said Tananeen. "And I doubt he's alone. If so, then that means that escape will be even trickier. We Dracones are savage hunters and never give up once we pick a target."

"Great," said Keo, shaking his head in frustration. "We've got both the Village Guard *and* the Dracones coming here? How did the Dracones even know where to find us? I thought that the graveyard was supposed to repeal them."

"Just because we have an instinctive dislike of graveyards doesn't mean that we can *never* set foot in them, as you and I have already shown," said Tananeen. "As for how they found us, we Dracones do have a strong sense of smell. I think it is likely that they tracked us down via smell."

"That's probably it, then," said Keo. "All right. We can't beat both the Village Guard and the Dracones by ourselves. We need to leave right away. We should go to that cave that Tananeen mentioned."

"I am having second thoughts about that," said Tananeen as she looked to the west and then to the east. "While the Village Guard will probably be unable to follow us there, the Dracones will have no trouble reaching its peaks; then we'd be boxed in and have no way to escape."

"What do we do, then?" said Easan in annoyance. "Just stand here and wait for the Horanians and Dracones to come and divide us between them? Because that would be so much better than running, of course."

Keo scowled, not at Easan's sarcasm, but at the toughness of the situation. Even with Tananeen on their side, Keo doubted that they would be able to last long against the combined force of the Dracones and the Village Guard. He suspected that the Dracones and the Village Guard might fight each other once they got here, but considering how both groups were looking for him and his friends, he certainly couldn't expect the enmity between the two peoples to save them.

*Come on, Keo, think of a plan,* Keo thought as he looked around the area, searching for anything that might spark a plan in his mind. *Anything at all that might help you and your friends escape.*

But it was pretty obvious to Keo that they could not escape, nor could they fight. Although Keo and his friends were strong, he had seen firsthand just how powerful and vicious both the Dracones and the Horanians could be. If they fought, it would likely end in bloody deaths for all of them except maybe Tananeen, but even Tananeen might not survive, because he had a feeling that the Dracones would probably think of her as a traitor and try to kill her as well.

But then Keo realized that he was looking at this situation entirely wrong. He looked at the others, who all expressed varying degrees of worry on their faces, and said, "Guys, I have an idea about how we can survive this. But I'll need all of your help to do it. Come over here quickly; we don't have much time before the Dracones and Horanians get here."

# Chapter Nineteen

TEN MINUTES LATER, KEO, Tananeen, and his friends all stood in the very center of the Dracone graveyard. Keo and Easan had drawn their swords, while Maryal and Jola were ready to cast spells, and Dlaine had his fists at the ready. As for Tananeen, she had no weapons to speak of, but had assured Keo that she was ready to transform into her dragon form at a moment's notice. Keo hoped that she would not need to, but it was nice to know that he could count on her to do that if necessary.

As the sun in the sky rose overhead, Keo looked to the east and to the west. He did not yet see either the Village Guard or the Dracones, but he knew that he would soon. Jola had informed him less than a minute ago that both groups would reach the graveyard at roughly the same time, which was good because Keo wanted and needed them both here at the same time in order for his plan to work.

The others looked nervous, even though Keo had explained his plan as thoroughly to them as he could. Easan had been the one to voice his objections most stridently, but when Keo had asked Easan if he had any alternatives, he had fallen silent, probably because they had no real, workable alternatives at this point. Of course, there was no guarantee that Keo's plan would work, either, but because it was all they had at the moment, Keo hoped it would.

A couple of minutes later, Keo saw the members of the Village Guard enter the graveyard from the eastern side, with their bows already drawn with arrows. As Jola had said, there were about a dozen of them, although from a distance it was impossible to identify any of them. Keo wondered if Rackan and Nobia were among the Village Guard or if they had stayed behind at the Horanian village. In all likelihood, Rackan was probably among them, seeing as he hated Keo and seemed like the sort of guy to look for any opportunity to strike at him. Nobia had seemed to genuinely like Keo, so he doubted she was among them, although considering how much she respected the Great Mountain Man, Keo wouldn't have been surprised if she was among that group of hunters.

But the Village Guard did not get an opportunity to unleash their arrows at Keo and the others, because exactly two seconds after they entered the graveyard, four large dragons flew over the nearby mountain peaks and landed on the floor of the graveyard. The lead dragon—who had red scales—was definitely Veta, but Keo did not recognize the other three, which were blue, beige, and gray, respectively. Not that it mattered, because assuming everything went according to plan, Keo would not need to know their names.

As soon as the Dracones landed, the members of the Village Guard immediately aimed their bows at them, as if they had forgotten all about Keo and the others. The Dracones, too, immediately took notice of the Village Guard and all four of them growled deeply, particularly Veta, who stepped forward like he was going to wipe out the entirety of the Village Guard himself.

Seeing as having the two fighting each other would mess up Keo's plan, Keo nodded at Easan and the two raised their swords and fired bursts of golden flame at both sides. Their aim was intentionally off, because they were aiming more to draw the attention of the Dracones and Village Guard rather than hurt them.

It worked. The Village Guard and the Dracones dodged the fireballs and looked over at Keo and the others. Although the Village Guard and the Dracones clearly did not trust each other, they seemed to be willing to put aside their enmity for the moment to destroy Keo and his friends, because they started walking toward him and the others with frightening speed. The Dracones didn't even seem to notice Tananeen; and if they did, they didn't seem to care.

But before either the Dracones or the Village Guard could get very close, they hit an invisible barrier that Jola had created and was maintaining around Keo and his friends. The Village Guard futilely shot arrows at the barrier before stopping quickly, because it soon became obvious that their arrows were not going to break through the barriers. The Dracones tried to claw their way through the barrier, but like the Village Guard, their efforts failed and they stopped trying to break through.

Seeing an opportunity, Keo stepped forward and, raising his free hand, said, "As you both can no doubt tell, we are safely behind this magical barrier. Even if you combined all of your might, you won't be able to get us, so I suggest that you stop wasting your time and energy and listen to what we have to say."

"What you have to say?" said Rackan, who Keo now noticed was indeed a part of the Village Guard, although Nobia was nowhere to be seen among them. He punched the barrier, but it did nothing. "Why should we listen to you taunt us? We were given a mission to kill you and your friends, per the orders of the elders."

Veta snarled a deep, throaty snarl as he said, in a monstrous voice, "For once, I agree with the human. Did you put up this barrier to *taunt* us? It would have been wiser for you to flee while you still had a chance, because we Dracones will break through eventually and kill you all, including the traitor Princess Tananeen."

Tananeen stiffened. "Wait … are you saying that my mother gave you orders to kill me?"

"Yes," said Veta, nodding. "She is getting tired of your sympathy and love for humans. But we're perfectly willing to spare you if you would step aside and let us kill the humans."

Tananeen looked briefly shocked, but then she shook her head and, resting one hand on Keo's shoulder, said, "No. I will not let you kill my son or his friends."

Now that surprised Keo, who had not been expecting her to say that. But he didn't look up at her, because he needed to focus on the Horanians and the Dracones in order for his plan to work.

"Your son?" Rackan repeated. He pointed at Keo in disgust. "Hold on. Are you telling me that Keo is not merely a *friend* of the Dracones, but one himself?"

"I am half-Dracone," said Keo, before Tananeen or Veta could speak. "My father was human, but my parentage doesn't matter. What matters is that you are both wrong for thinking that I only wish to taunt you. I don't. Instead, I want to talk to you and convince you that trying to kill me and my friends is a big mistake."

"How is killing a liar and Dracone lover like yourself a mistake?" said Rackan. "You deceived us all with your talk about trying to save your land from these so-called 'demons.' Why should we listen to you?"

"I feel the same way," said Veta. He bared his teeth, as did the other Dracones standing behind him. "We were given the task of killing you by the Queen, whose authority must never be questioned. Even if you saved some of our unborn, the fact is that many of our brethren have been killed and it is all your fault."

"Both of you are wrong," said Keo, shaking his head. "You are angry for understandable reasons, but you are still wrong. My friends and I are not your enemies. That Dracone that attacked the village and that human who attacked the nest are."

"What Dracone?" said Veta, scowling. "I don't remember hearing the Queen order any of us to attack the Horanian village recently."

Rackan glared at Veta from the other side of the barrier. "Liar! We were attacked yesterday by one of your brothers. Don't try to pretend like that didn't happen."

"Whether it did or did not, we are not responsible for it, tiny human," said Veta. "On the other hand, the human who attacked us looked like one of your own. Was it you, perhaps?"

"I have no idea what you're talking about," said Rackan. "The elders have not ordered anyone to attack your little Nest recently. Stop trying to make yourselves look like victims."

"We Dracones never victimize ourselves, though I'm afraid I

can't say the same for you humans," said Veta. He snorted, causing smoke to rise from his nostrils. "Because we are not weak."

Rackan opened his mouth to argue some more, but Keo raised his hand again and said, "Hold on. You're both right, but also wrong. The human that attacked the Nest and the Dracone that attacked the Horanian village are one and the same."

"One and the same?" said Veta. "How so?"

"It's obvious," said Rackan, shaking his head. "What Keo is saying is that the person we are talking about is a normal Dracone who can transform between human and dragon form. Like most Dracones, this person is clearly a liar and a deceiver."

That earned him a death glare from Veta and the other dragons that probably would have resulted in an all-out fight between the two sides if Keo had not quickly said, "Rackan is wrong. The person we're talking about is neither human nor Dracone. He may look like one or the other at times, but it's just a disguise to mask his true identity."

"Then what *is* he?" said Rackan. "If he isn't human or Dracone, then what does that make him?"

"A demon," said Keo. "A powerful one, too. He's been changing between human and Dracone forms in order to frame both sides and incite violence between your peoples."

"Oh, there's that 'demon' talk again," said Rackan. "Tell me, liar, where is your proof that these so-called 'demons' even exist? Or that this one in particular exists and is behind both attacks?"

"Keo is correct that demons exist, but he's obviously wrong that there is one in the Upper Mountains that is attempting to manipulate both sides against each other," said Veta. "If there was one running around, we Dracones would know about it."

"Demons aren't so easily found," Keo said. "They are crafty and subtle creatures, perfectly capable of hiding themselves from non-demons. They rarely attack head-on or take responsibility for their actions unless they are backed into a corner and have no other options on the table."

"Even so, you still haven't offered any proof that this demon exists, much less that it is manipulating us," said Veta. He clawed at the barrier, but his massive claws were unable to penetrate it. "Now, lower your barrier so we can do to you what we have done to humans throughout the last seven decades."

"I can back up Keo's claim," said Tananeen. "I have seen demons before and the human that attacked the Nest looked far more demonic than human."

"Same with the Dracone that attacked the Horanian village," said Easan, nodding. "It was no Dracone, even though it looked just like one. That much I could tell."

"All you are offering is hearsay from a human and a traitor," said Veta. "That's not enough proof. In fact, that isn't proof at all. If you are a liar, as the other humans say, then you are a terrible one for sure."

"Listen, I don't have much proof to back up my claims, but you have to believe me," said Keo. "This is exactly the sort of thing that demons do. They hide in the shadows, manipulating events from the distance, and don't show themselves until circumstances force them to or they choose to. You have to believe me."

"Why should we believe you when you yourself admitted that you don't have any proof to back up your assertions?" said

Rackan. "We're not idiots, you know."

"And if you have no proof to back up your theory, then we have even less reason to listen to your obvious lie designed to save you and your friends from both of us," said Veta. "While I ordinarily would never even think to work with the Horanians, the fact is that at the moment I believe that you and your friends are a bigger threat to the Dracones than they are. So once we get this barrier down, we'll focus on killing you and then see what we'll do about the Horanians after that."

"We Horanians will do the same," said Rackan. "Our hatred for the Dracones runs deep, but I'd much rather kill you and your band of liars than waste time fighting them."

Easan looked at Keo with an annoyed look on his face. "Was this how your plan was supposed to unite the Horanians and Dracones? Because if so, this is the worst plan ever."

Keo glared at Easan briefly before looking back at the Horanians and the Dracones. He stepped forward, making himself look as urgent as he could, as he said, "You're both going to make a terrible mistake if you try to kill us and then fight each other. You are playing directly into the demon's hands. Even if you don't kill each other, you will be killed by the demons once they rise again."

"Unsubstantiated threats don't scare us," said Rackan, gesturing at his fellow Guardsmen. "For that matter, they don't seem to scare the Dracones, either."

Keo bit his lower lip. He had suspected that this plan might not work. He had hoped that maybe the Horanians and Dracones would realize how suspicious this entire set up was and would have agreed to at least search for the demon, but now it was pretty clear that both sides were even more set in their own beliefs than they had been even just a few minutes ago. Jola's barrier would probably continue to hold up even if both sides attacked with everything they had, but sooner or later the Horanians and the Dracones would break through and then Keo and his friends would be in for the fight of their lives.

"Got any other ideas?" Dlaine murmured as the Horanians stepped backwards to give them room to fire their bows and smoke started rising dangerously from the nostrils of the Dracones. "Any at all?"

Keo shook his head and murmured back, "That was my only plan. I thought they would listen."

"Well, I now see why you're our leader," said Easan, rolling his eyes. "Because trying to overcome decades-long hatred between two peoples by blaming their problems on something you can't even prove exists is certainly what a wise leader would do."

"Your comments are really not helping right now," said Keo, who was doing his best to resist the urge to stab Easan in the face with Gildshine. "Everyone, get ready, because once this barrier goes down, we're going to have to fight for our—"

Keo was interrupted by a loud, earsplitting roar that made everyone, including the Dracones, wince. Keo initially thought that the roar had come from one of the Dracones on the other side of the barrier, but when he saw them cringing from the loud roar, he suddenly understood where it was coming from.

Just as that realization dawned on Keo, one of the Guardsmen pointed up at the sky and shouted, "Another Dracone!"

Everyone looked up just in time to see a massive black

Dracone hurtling through the air toward them. It landed with a crash hundreds of feet away from the barrier, the impact sending up a massive dust cloud that obscured the black Dracone from view.

Immediately, the Village Guard and the Dracones turned to face it. The Village Guard aimed their bows at the beast, while the Dracones snorted more smoke and looked ready to let loose a combined stream of flame, but no one attacked yet because of the dust cloud obscuring their view of the creature.

A second later, a loud *whomp* echoed through the air as the black Dracone's wings blew away the dust cloud surrounding it. The black Dracone—no, the demon—rose to its full height, but it looked much bigger than it had the day before. It towered over not only the humans, but the Dracones as well, and its wingspan was wider, too, perhaps wide enough to wrap around the full-grown Dracones if it cared to try.

The demon's red eyes glowed dangerously as it looked down upon the humans and the Dracones. It bared its teeth, which were a sickening yellow color now, but they also looked even sharper than ever. It appeared that the demon had somehow gotten stronger since Keo last saw it, which didn't make him feel any better about their survival chances.

"That's the Dracone from yesterday," said Rackan in disbelief. "The same one that tried to destroy our village. But it's bigger."

Veta let out a deep growl. "That is no Dracone that I know of. It is a demon."

"See?" said Keo, pointing at the demon. "Now do you guys believe that there is a demon trying to manipulate your peoples to fight each other?"

"But what is it doing here?" said Rackan. "Why did it show itself now? Isn't it ruining its own plan by revealing to us?"

"You are assuming that I plan to let any of you live long enough to warn your friends about my plan," said a familiar high, manic voice that seemed to come from the demon itself, even though it had not opened its mouth. "Too bad that I am not going to let anyone in this graveyard escape alive today."

Before the startled eyes of everyone in the graveyard, something rose from the back of the demon's neck. At first, it looked like some sort of weird tumor, like a big black bubble that grew larger and larger, until soon it melted away, revealing a familiar white-lipped and crazy face that Keo had not seen in a while.

Ankem, the surviving member of the Brothers White Blood, smiled down at the humans and the Dracones, with no fear anywhere in his eyes. "Surprised to see me? That's good, because I would have been disappointed with myself if you hadn't. It would have meant that I had slipped up, but I can see that I am still as clever as ever. Too bad the same can't be said about you."

# Chapter Twenty

ANKEM LOOKED MUCH WORSE than he had the last time Keo saw him. He no longer wore his white and red robes. Ankem was completely shirtless, his pale upper chest pulsating with some kind of dark light just beneath his skin. His eyes had a deep reddish hue, similar to the demon's, while his legs were sunk completely inside the demon's neck, leaving only his arms, head, and upper torso exposed. His veins were black against his skin, which made him look both terribly ill but also deadly and threatening.

"Ankem," said Keo, not hiding the disgust in his voice. He gripped Gildshine with both hands and held it before him in defense. "I was wondering when we'd see you again."

Ankem's smirk looked far more monstrous than before. "And I was wondering when I would get a chance to avenge my brothers, who you brutally slaughtered like lambs."

"Who is Ankem?" said Rackan, who, despite aiming his bow at the demon, sounded slightly terrified. "I have never heard of him."

"He is the man who kidnapped seven of our unborn a few days ago," said Veta, a snarl coloring his words. "It was only thanks to Keo and one of his friends that they managed to rescue them, except for one. I had thought that the kidnapper had fled the Mountains for good."

"I did, but I didn't leave entirely," said Ankem, shaking his head. He rested one hand on the back of the demon's neck, which looked less like flesh and more like some kind of strange black liquid given solid form. "As one of the Brothers White Blood—the only surviving member, as of recently—I can never give up on a mission I am given. My family's entire reputation would be ruined if I were to go back home after failing to kill my target. That I cannot allow, because that would dishonor the memory of my brothers and our ancestors."

"So now you decided to show yourself?" said Veta. He stepped forward, as did the other three Dracones by his side. "Then tell us the location of the last egg, the one you stole. If you don't, we will rip you out of your demon and make you tell us by force."

Ankem patted the back of the neck of the demon that he was fused to, his smirk as wide as ever. "I thought you would have realized it by now, but I guess you Dracones really aren't much better than mindless beasts."

"What are you talking about?" said Veta. "All I see is a demon serving you."

"Then you are blind," said Ankem. "Because this is not a mere demon. This is the unborn Dracone that I stole, but it is no longer a mere Dracone. It has been infused with the power of the demons that will rise again soon and drown all of Lamaira in darkness and death."

Everyone stared at the demon, stunned by this revelation. Even Tananeen looked surprised by this, while Keo actually lowered Gildshine he was so surprised.

"What?" said Veta, who seemed to be the only person capable of speaking at the moment. He pulled his head back and squinted his eyes, as if viewing the demon from a distance. "That is not one of ours. That is a demon that merely *looks* like one of us."

"It does look a little different from a normal Dracone, but I can assure you that its body is the host of the demon," said Ankem. "When I fled the cave where my deceased brothers and I held the eggs, I originally took one of the eggs with me with the intent of bringing it back to the Magical Council and giving it to them if I failed to kill Keo. I thought that giving the Magical Council their very own Dracone might convince them to pay me anyway even if I failed at the mission I was supposed to do."

"But you obviously didn't," said Veta. He growled and clawed at the earth. "What did you do instead?"

"I was contacted by the King of Demons, Aknar Roba, himself," said Ankem, his voice becoming higher and crazier as he spoke. He put both of his hands on his head, his smirk looking utterly insane. "He told me that he would help me accomplish my mission, avenge my brothers, and maintain the reputation of my family by giving me the power of the demons. I accepted the offer, thinking that it was better than returning home a failure, and then … it happened."

Keo stepped forward and said, "What happened?"

"The power of the King of Demons did," said Ankem. He stroked the back of the demon's neck. "I cracked open the egg and allowed the King of Demons to pour some of his power into it. As a result, the creature that emerged from the egg was no longer a pure Dracone, but a demon with all of the power that a fully-grown Dracone commands."

"How did it grow so fast?" said Veta. "You only stole it a few days ago. Most Dracones take at least a century to reach their full growth, sometimes longer."

"The power of the demons is beyond mortal comprehension," said Ankem, his eyes wide and crazy. "The power accelerated the Dracone's growth, meaning that it leaped a century in less than a day. And now, it is stronger than any Dracone."

"I doubt that," said Veta, shaking his head. "The demons of old fell before the might of our people."

"Exactly why the King of Demons decided to use your own power against you," said Ankem. "But anyway, the accelerated growth of the Dracone was not the only thing that the King did. He also used his dark power to fuse me with the demon, to make us one. I still retain my original personality and memories, but now, I am far more powerful than I could ever be on my own."

"Are you saying that the King of Demons has risen?" said Keo, looking around just to make sure that the King was not nearby.

"No," said Ankem. "The King of Demons, along with his most powerful minions, are still trapped in the seal that that has restricted their freedom for a thousand years. But it has grown exponentially weaker over the past seventy years, to the point where the King of Demons can now contact people and offer us but a mere taste of his true, unstoppable power even if he is unable to free himself."

"If this is an example of the King of Demons' power at its weakest, then I don't want to see it at its full power," said Dlaine with a shudder.

"But soon, everyone will see it," said Ankem. "The demons are far closer to rising again than even you realize. The Days of Darkness are upon us, and only those who have allied with the demons will survive."

"You're a fool, Ankem," said Keo, shaking his head. "The demons don't care about any humans, even humans who help them. You let your guard down, they will destroy you without even thinking about it."

Ankem put his hands on his chest. "Do you think such lies can convince me? If so, you are extremely misguided. I have witnessed the true power of the demons and know that they will not only spare me, but also give me back my brothers, because the King of Demons can reverse death."

"Reverse death?" Keo repeated. "I've never heard that the King of Demons can do that."

"Because he can't," said Tananeen. "None of the legends mention anything about the demons' leader having that ability."

"You are naïve if you believe all of those biased legends about the demons, most of which were created by the demons' sworn enemy, the so-called 'Good' King," said Ankem with a sneer. "But who cares? What matter is that I am going to destroy you all now and prevent the Dracones and Horanians from knowing that I've been playing both sides against each other."

"I knew it," said Keo. He looked from Veta to Rackan, although the two of them were focused more on Ankem and the demon than on Keo. "Do you see? I was right. Your real enemy is him, not me or the others."

"But why show yourself now?" said Dlaine. He gestured at the Dracones and Horanians. "They were already about to kill us on their own. Your plan wouldn't have been ruined."

"Because the King of Demons commands it," said Ankem. "He told me to ensure that you were eliminated. I could not be sure that the Dracones and Horanians would actually finish you off themselves, so I decided to step in and ensure your deaths personally."

"Will you eliminate us, also?" said Rackan, gesturing at himself, his fellow Horanians, and the Dracones.

"Of course," said Ankem. "I cannot risk you returning to your respective people and informing them of my existence. Besides, I think your deaths would only add fuel to the fire of hatred between your peoples, because both sides will blame your deaths on the other, never suspecting that they are being played by someone far cleverer than themselves."

"Not unless we kill you first," said Rackan. "While I normally hate the Dracones with every fiber of my being, I am willing to put aside that hatred for now if it will ensure the survival of my friends and I."

"Same here," said Veta, nodding. "Now that we know who the true enemy is, we need not waste time fighting the wrong battles."

Ankem chuckled. "So you think I am the *true* enemy ... how silly. You don't even realize who the real enemy is."

"Are you going to tell us or are you just going to treat us with condescension?" said Tananeen.

"Why would I reveal that last secret to any of you?" said Ankem. "Knowledge is power, after all, although even power is useless if you cannot live long enough to use it."

"It doesn't matter who this 'real' enemy is," said Veta with a snarl. "What matters is that even a demon like yourself cannot stand against our combined might. A dozen Horanian archers, five Dracones, a halfbreed, and his four friends is not quite the Queen's Legion, but it is more than enough to destroy a demon and an arrogant human like yourself."

"Arrogant? You're one to talk," said Ankem. "Only a fool like yourself would ever believe that your combined might is even partially close enough to defeat me. It will be a pleasure to grind your skulls into dust and water the earth with your blood."

Veta growled and said, "Attack!"

Veta and his fellow Dracones soared toward the demon, while the Horanian archers immediately aimed their bows at Ankem and the demon again. They let loose a volley of arrows that struck the demon head on, but the arrows merely bounced off the demon's scales, not even scratching it.

That didn't discourage Veta and the Dracones, however. They opened their mouths and unleashed four burning streams of fire that struck Ankem and the demon at the same time. Red, white, and blue flames completely engulfed Ankem and the demon, while the Dracones flew in a circle above their heads, pouring more and more fire on Ankem and the demon than Keo had ever thought Dracones could create. The heat of the flame was so strong that Keo could feel it even behind the barrier that Jola maintained, while the Horanian archers retreated to escape the worst of it.

The Dracones continued to circle the demon and breathe fire on it for at least a minute before they cut off their attack. Then they landed around the blazing inferno that their fires had created, which was so hot that it had even melted a few nearby Dracone skeletons and the earth around it. The flames burned so brightly that it was impossible to tell if there was anyone still standing within it, though Keo doubted that anything could survive such an onslaught.

Then a roar, distorted by flame, issued from the fire, a roar that was all too familiar by now. Veta and the Dracones started when they heard that roar, but before they could do anything, a huge stream of black and red flame shot out of the fire. It spun in a circle, cutting down every Dracone it touched. It cut through their throats, causing the Dracones to fall to the ground, gasping and spasming. The only Dracone who managed to dodge the fire stream was Veta, but even he wasn't quick enough to avoid it entirely. The stream burned through one of his wings, causing him to roar in pain and fall down to the ground, stunned by the pain from the blow.

As soon as all of the Dracones were down, two huge wings extended from the flames and, with a mighty *woosh*, completely extinguished the flames surrounding the demon. When the flames vanished, it showed Ankem and the demon standing where they had before. They didn't even look slightly darkened from the flames, like they had not been burned alive by the hottest fire Keo had ever seen in his life.

"Surprised?" said Ankem, perhaps noting the shocked expressions on the faces of Keo, his friends, and the Horanians. "Don't be. There is a reason the King of Demons chose to give one of his demons the body of a Dracone. It is because Dracones can nonetheless withstand their own fire much better than non-Dracones; combined with the dark magic of the demons and you can see that this is a truly devastating weapon that completely changes the dynamic between demons and Dracones, in the demons' favor, of course."

Tananeen gulped. "But if we Dracones cannot kill it, then how can anyone else kill it?"

"Precisely," said Ankem. "I have to admit that I was worried at first that the King's theory would not work, seeing as there has never been a demon/Dracone hybrid before, but this first test exceeded even the King's wildest expectations. No doubt the King will ask me to steal more eggs so he can create more of these hybrids later."

Tananeen stepped forward, glaring angrily at Ankem. "Don't you dare harm any more unborn with your evil power. If you do, then no power in the world will be capable of protecting you from the wrath of the Dracones."

"On the contrary, if I did that, there is nothing that you or any other Dracone could do to stop me," said Ankem with a shrug. "But anyway, I can't steal more eggs if I don't first eliminate all of you. And with most of the other Dracones already dead ..." Ankem gestured at the now-still corpses of the Dracones that had attacked him, although Veta still seemed to be alive, if just barely, "... killing the rest of you humans ought to be easy."

Tananeen let out a truly monstrous roar before transforming into her own dragon form. Her throat glowed with a red light, causing Keo, his friends, and the Horanians to scatter as she unleashed a huge stream of blue flame at the demon.

Ankem pointed at Tananeen and the demon opened its mouth and unleashed its own stream of black and red fire. Both streams collided midway, creating an absolutely deafening explosion that left Keo's ears ringing.

Tananeen and the demon's stream pushed back against each

other, like two streams of water. They shoved back and forth, seemingly equal. Tananeen's eyes were full of absolute animal rage, while Ankem was smirking, with his arms crossed over his chest like he was amused.

But then Tananeen's stream, slowly but surely, started to push back the demon's. Ankem's smirk immediately vanished and he snarled at the demon, "Dumb beast! Don't let her win!"

A second later, the demon's fire stream suddenly started pushing back against Tananeen's. Tananeen increased the output of flames pouring from her mouth, but it was pretty clear that she was about to meet her limit. The demon's flames pushed back Tananeen's farther and farther until, with a final heave, the demon's fire stream pushed Tananeen's fire back into her face.

The resulting explosion sent flame flying everywhere, forcing Keo, his friends, and the Horanians to duck to avoid being hit. Tananeen was knocked flat on her back from the attack, her face smoking from the fire, her form as still as a rock.

"Mother!" Keo shouted. He ran up to Tananeen's face, despite the heat radiating off it like a furnace. "Mother!"

When Keo reached Tananeen's face, he saw that it was blackened by the demon's flame and smelled like fried leather. One of her eyes seemed to have been melted shut, while the other looked completely fried. She didn't seem to be breathing.

"Mother, wake up!" Keo shouted. He tried to touch her face, but he jerked his hand away because he almost burned it touching her skin. "Please don't be dead. Please."

But Tananeen did not move or make any noises.

Anger rose in Keo as he whirled around to face at Ankem and the demon. Ankem, as usual, looked quite smug, as if he was proud of what just happened.

"She went down a bit easier than I expected," said Ankem. "Then again, she appears to be an older Dracone, so I imagine that she couldn't handle pain as well as her younger counterparts. Or maybe I'm just that powerful."

"You monster," said Keo. Gildshine exploded into golden flames, this time without Keo even thinking about it. "You killed my mother."

"She was your mother?" said Ankem. "So you are the son of Riuno *and* the son of a Dracone? I did not know that, but it is good to know. Once I kill you and return home, I will be able to boast to everyone that the Brothers White Blood successfully killed the *shelmai* himself, which will cement our reputation once and for all as the best assassins in Lamaira and in all of the world."

"Do you think I give a damn about your reputation?" said Keo. "I am going to kill you for what you did to my mother. And it won't be painless, either."

"You speak rather tough for someone who just saw me take down five fully-grown Dracones in less than ten minutes," said Ankem. He held out his hands toward Keo. "But come and fight me anyway. The mission I was given is the same as always: Kill Keo of the Sword and his friends and return to South Lamaira to claim my fee. Although it will be with the added bonus of avenging my deceased brothers, who you killed, if you don't remember."

"I remember," said Keo, his voice shaking with anger. "I remember quite well. And I remember that I should have killed you with them."

"Then that is a mistake you will simply have to live with," said Ankem. "For the five minutes that you have left to live, anyway."

Keo stepped forward, but then heard someone shout, "Keo!"

Keo looked to his left and saw Rackan and the other Horanian archers running toward him. They stopped several feet from Keo, with Rackan in the lead.

"What?" said Keo.

"We want to fight alongside you," said Rackan, pointing at Ankem and the demon. "After seeing him so effortlessly kill the Dracones, we've realized that we cannot let him live, otherwise he might attack our village again."

"Didn't your god say that I'm a liar and deceiver?" said Keo.

"He did, but that doesn't mean we cannot work with you to kill a much bigger threat to us all," said Rackan.

Keo looked at Ankem and the demon again. "No. You guys cannot fight alongside me and my friends. If you do, you will only get killed. You don't have the weapons or skill necessary to even harm Ankem, much less kill him."

"But we want to fight," said Rackan. "How else can we ensure that our people will be safe?"

"Just trust us to kill him," said Keo, gesturing at himself and his friends. "The rest of you can go back to your village. Warn them of what has happened. If we fail and Ankem comes after you, then at least you and your people will be prepared for it, if nothing else."

"But—"

"You saw how your arrows didn't work against him earlier and how you couldn't even scratch him when he attacked your village yesterday," said Keo. He pointed over Rackan's head. "Now go!"

At first, Keo was certain that Rackan was just going to continue to argue about staying, but then, much to his surprise, Rackan nodded. "All right. We will return to our village and warn the villagers about what we have learned."

"Good," said Keo. "May your god protect you and your people."

Rackan nodded again and then turned and ran, with the other Guardsmen following close behind.

Ankem, on the other hand, said, "Oh, no you don't!" and the demon had smoke rising from its nostrils, which told Keo that it was about to shoot flame.

Just as the demon opened its mouth to breathe fire, Keo pointed Gildshine at the demon and shot a blast of golden flame at it. The blast struck the demon in the side of the face, the impact making its head swing to the side. But it didn't stop the demon from unleashing its fire breath, only this time the flame missed its intended target and harmlessly struck the ground instead.

The demon, however, was only off aim for a moment. It recovered from Keo's attack and glared at him, which gave Rackan and the other members of the Village Guard enough time to escape.

"Bah," said Ankem, glancing in the direction of the fleeing Guardsmen. "It doesn't matter if they escape. There's nothing they can do to stop me, even now that they know who I am. I might as well finish what I started; that is, killing you."

Ankem said that while pointing at Keo, who didn't even flinch at Ankem's threat. He looked at the others. Easan had Shadowbane out, which was burning with its own golden flames.

Maryal had her hands up, like she was about to cast a spell, while Dlaine had his fists raised, even though there was nothing Dlaine could do to help at the moment, since he lacked a magical weapon of his own and was not a Magician. As for Jola, she was as invisible as always, but Keo bet that she was preparing a spell of her own to use to harm the demon.

"All right, everyone," said Keo. He nodded at the demon. "For the Kingdom of Lamaira and my mother!"

# Chapter Twenty-One

KEO, EASAN, AND JOLA unleashed a combined blast of magical fire at the demon. The fire blast hurtled through the air at an astonishing speed, but the demon didn't even flinch. With a flap of its wings, it sent a powerful gust of cold wind that put the fire out immediately.

Without missing a beat, the demon unleashed another stream of black and red fire directly at Keo and his friends. Keo and the others scattered immediately, avoiding the fire breath just in the nick of time. As they ran, Keo fired another burst of flame at the demon, but then Ankem appeared in the spot where the demon would have been hit and swirled his hands. A magical barrier immediately appeared in front of Ankem, blocking the golden flame, which left the demon itself completely unscathed.

*What?* Keo thought, watching in shock as the barrier vanished. *He can still use his magic from when he was a Magician?*

The demon turned its massive head to face Keo and opened its mouth and unleashed another stream of black and red fire, which hurtled through the air toward Keo. Keo leaped to the side, dodging it, but just barely. He felt the heat of the flames as they passed by, making him break into a sweat instantly.

Just as the demon tried to turn its head to aim at Keo again, Easan appeared out of nowhere and stabbed it in the leg. The demon let loose a roar of pain and kicked at Easan, but this time Easan dodged it and followed up his stab with a burst of golden flame that struck the demon's wound. This made the demon roar even louder, causing it to whirl around to face Easan, but then burning hot flames appeared around the demon's feet. The flame —which glowed white hot—seemed to have been made by Jola, because Keo had not seen Maryal cast that spell.

Nonetheless, the demon flapped its wing and flew back into the air, avoiding getting its feet burned off by the fire. But just as it took off, Maryal thrust her hands forward and a massive gust of wind tore through the air, hitting the demon's wings. The demon immediately crashed to the ground, but it got back up just as quickly, like the crash hadn't even hurt it.

Then the demon looked back at Easan instead of Maryal, which seemed like an odd thing to do to Keo, until he noticed Ankem on the demon's neck had turned around to face Maryal. Ankem slashed his hands through the air, causing Keo to shout, "Maryal, watch out!"

Maryal tried to dodge, but she was too slow. She was struck by Ankem's slashing spell, which cut through her chest and face and knocked her flat off her feet. Blood seeped through her clothes, but she did not appear dead, just knocked out.

Nonetheless, Keo shouted, "Maryal!" He looked over at Dlaine, who was standing around looking rather useless. Keo pointed at Maryal and said, "Get Maryal out of the fight. Try to heal her wounds if you can. Easan, Jola, and I will deal with the demon."

Dlaine nodded and ran toward Maryal without another word. Meanwhile, Keo ran toward the demon, which was now trying to slash Easan into ribbons with its claws, although it was having little success, seeing as Easan kept jumping out of its range or deflecting its claws with his sword. Keo did not see Jola anywhere, but he knew that she had to be somewhere nearby planning an attack of her own.

Ankem, however, was clearly not going to let Keo get close enough to help Easan. He slashed his hands through the air, but Keo managed to dodge the slashing spell just in the nick of time. He responded by firing another burst of golden flame at Ankem, but the Magician summoned that same magical barrier in front of him again, which deflected the flame burst.

But Keo kept advancing, running toward the demon as quickly as he could. Ankem slammed his fists together, causing them to catch fire, and shot bursts of black and red flame at Keo, which Keo deflected with Gildshine.

But then it became clear that the fire bursts had been a mere distraction, because as Keo deflected the bursts, Ankem slashed his hands downwards again. This time, Keo was not fast enough to dodge the slashing spell, although he tried anyway.

The slashes cut through Keo like swords. Keo screamed in pain as he staggered backwards from the blow. His wounds bled harshly, causing him to fall to his hands and knees, dropping Gildshine onto the ground as he gasped for breath. He heard someone yell his name and looked up to see Easan still fighting for his life against the demon, although it was pretty clear that Easan stood no chance against the demon on his own, especially now that Ankem was turning his attention to the demon.

Keo tried to stand, but the wounds he had suffered from Ankem's slashing spell made that all but impossible. He gave up, thinking that it was impossible to do. He tried to fight the pain, but it was too much even for him.

*But if I don't get up and help Easan, he'll die, and so will everyone else,* Keo thought, although it was hard to think rationally due to the blood loss and pain. *But I can't get up, not in this condition. I'm in too much pain.*

*Keo, are you okay?* said Jola's voice in his head. *Do you need my help?*

*No,* Keo replied. *Go help Easan. He needs your help more than I do.*

*But you look like you are about to die,* said Jola. *Let me—*

*I said, go help Easan,* Keo repeated, although his thoughts felt quite delirious now. *Now.*

Jola did not respond to that, probably because she sensed the authority in Keo's voice. He felt her presence retreat from his mind, but now he realized that he had just made a terrible mistake.

*No,* Keo thought. *I can figure out how to save myself. But how?*

That was when Keo remembered his training with Tananeen and what she had discovered by linking their minds. She had said that Keo's dragon form looked different from others, which made Keo wonder if it was possible to access it and if it might help him save the others from Ankem and the demon.

*But I didn't succeed in our training earlier at all,* Keo thought. *How can I do it now?*

Regardless, Keo had no other options. He tried to imagine

himself transforming into his dragon self, but all this quick practice session did was remind him why he failed. It felt pointless and without direction, like he was wandering lost in a forest.

That made Keo think he was going to die for sure, but then he remembered something. Every other time he had discovered new powers or abilities, he had been undergoing extreme stress and anxiety. That was how he had discovered his ability to coat Gildshine in golden flame and how he had unleashed his other fire powers against the Brothers White Blood a few days ago. Could he do it again?

He looked up at Easan, who was still fighting off the demon, while Ankem was conjuring barriers around himself that deflected fire spells that seemed to come from nowhere (though they probably came from Jola). It was pretty clear that neither Easan nor Jola were going to defeat Ankem and the demon, even by working together.

*I have to get angry,* Keo thought, scowling and wincing at the pain. *Must use my pain to transform. But even seeing my friends losing—and knowing what will happen to them if they lose—isn't enough, at least for the moment.*

Then Keo smelled burned flesh and, glancing over his shoulder, saw the corpse of Tananeen lying as still as ever on the ground. The mere sight of his mother's corpse was enough to make the fire burn deep within his soul, burn so hotly that he could feel his hands and face start to heat up. He was angry that Ankem had killed his mother, his only surviving parent, and he was angry that he had only known her for a few days and would never get to learn more about her ever again.

Suddenly, the pain in his wounds started to lessen. The fire within Keo's soul grew hotter and hotter, until soon Keo couldn't even handle it. His hands burst into flames, but it wasn't just his hands. His whole body burst into golden flames, the same golden flames that normally only appeared on Gildshine.

But the flames didn't hurt Keo at all, even though he could feel their heat enveloping every inch of his body. In fact, it felt like the flames were actually healing him, because the pain in his body was rapidly fading away.

Not only that, but his body seemed to be changing. His hands became larger and his fingers as sharp as claws, while his hair turned into some kind of short, ridged spikes. He felt the flames on his back turning into an extra set of limbs, including one shooting out from his behind. His vision became clearer until he could soon see every crack and spec of dust in the dirt before him. It was a strange sensation, not in the least because it felt so natural.

Then the flames suddenly vanished. Keo blinked several times before he realized that he could stand. So he pushed himself up to both feet, but it was not nearly the struggle he had expected it to be. It was, in fact, quite easy, as if he had not been terribly wounded even just a few seconds ago.

Before he could solve that mystery, Keo heard Dlaine behind him gasp. "Keo! What the hell happened to you?"

Keo glanced over his shoulder, but found it hard to see Dlaine due to the Dracone wing that was in his way. It took Keo a moment to realize that that was not the wing of a Dracone, but his *own* wing that was attached to his body. A glance to the left showed that there was another one just like it sprouting from his left shoulder.

The sight of the two wings made Keo look down at the rest of his body. He was still humanoid—thank the ancestors—but he didn't look quite human anymore. His hands were more like the claws of the Dracones, with sharp tips that looked capable of tearing through flesh. His skin looked like scales and he saw it all in amazing detail, which made him think that he must have lost his mind or was possibly hallucinating from the pain he had suffered from his wounds.

"I ..." Keo said, but stopped before he could say anything else, because the second he heard his voice—which had a definite animalistic growl to it—he stopped. It didn't sound like his old voice, which was why he had stopped speaking.

He looked down at his body again. *Is this my transformed body?*

But Keo had no time to think about this very deeply, because he heard Easan shout in pain. Looking up, Keo saw that the demon had finally managed to slash Easan, knocking Shadowbane out of his hands and knocking Easan himself down. Easan tried to get up, but then the demon pinned him to the ground with its claw. The demon did not seem to have noticed Keo's transformation, and neither did Ankem, who was egging the demon on to finish Easan once and for all.

There was no time for Keo to ponder his new form. He just bent over, grabbed Gildshine, and then ran toward the demon. But running felt slow and awkward, particularly with his wings out, so Keo instead jumped into the air and took to the skies.

Keo soared straight through the air, which was a wonderful feeling that made him feel more alive than he had in a while.

Gildshine exploded into golden flames just as he reached the demon, which was starting to charge a fire blast in its mouth, aimed directly at Easan, who was unable to dodge it thanks to the claw pinning him to the ground.

With a roar that was more dragon than human, Keo slashed Gildshine straight through the demon's neck. Gildshine—which felt more powerful than ever—cut through the demon's neck like butter, cutting off its charged flame and making Ankem cry out in shock and anger. The demon's head fell off its neck and landed next to Easan, who stared at it in pure shock.

Nonetheless, the demon's body somehow staggered backwards from the blow, removing its claw from Easan's form. It was a disturbing sight, but one Keo did not focus on for the moment.

Instead, Keo landed next to Easan and said, "Are you okay?" His voice still sounded weird to him, but he ignored that for now in order to focus on his friend's safety.

Easan nodded shakily, but did not get up. He pointed at Keo's face and said, "What the hell happened to you? You look like a freak."

Keo wished he had a mirror so he could see exactly what his face looked like, but he had no time for that. He just shook his head and said, "Finally transformed. But that doesn't matter. Let me help you—"

A sudden roar caused Keo to look up at the demon. He was shocked to see that it had regrown its head, which now looked angrier than ever.

Easan jumped back up to his feet, dusting himself off and grabbing Shadowbane as he also looked at the demon and its regrown head. "How did it do that?"

The demon lowered its head, allowing Keo and Easan to see Ankem still sticking out of the back of its neck. With his arms folded across his chest, Ankem looked unimpressed by Keo's recent attack. Nonetheless, there was a definite look of confusion on his face as he looked at Keo, as if he was unsure what he was seeing.

"So you can transform, eh?" said Ankem. He shook his head. "It doesn't matter. You got in a lucky shot on my demon, but that was all it was, luck. And luck always runs out eventually."

The demon raised its head and fired another stream of fire. It was coming too fast for Keo to dodge, so he shoved Easan out of the way and then folded his wings over his body to protect himself, even though he wasn't sure how well his wings would stand against the flames.

The black and red fire struck Keo hard, sending him skidding backwards across the dirt, but much to his surprise, his wings shielded him from the worst of it. He didn't let down his wings, however, until the demon finally cut off its stream of fire, after which he unfolded his wings and looked back at the demon and Ankem.

Ankem was staring at Keo dumbfounded. "How did you survive that? No mortal can survive a direct attack from this demon. That's impossible."

Keo shrugged. "Then maybe I'm not that mortal."

With a flap of his wings, Keo shot through the air toward the demon and Ankem even faster than before. He tried slashing at the demon's face, but the demon dodged that and then smacked him with its claw, hitting him with enough force to send him sprawling across the dirt as Ankem laughed.

"Foolish boy!" Ankem shouted, gleeful amusement in his voice as Keo struggled to get back up to his feet, as the impact of the blow had messed with his senses. "You may be immune to our fire, but that doesn't mean that you cannot be killed. All that means is that we will have to work a little harder to take away your life."

Keo shook his head and looked up in time to see another demon claw come crashing down on him. With faster reflexes than he had before, Keo jumped backwards, using his wings to propel himself well out of the demon's reach. As he landed on the ground again, Keo knew that he would have to finish this fight quick, because he was finding it hard to maintain this form while simultaneously battling Ankem and the demon.

*Jola?* Keo said, walking backwards as the demon lifted its claw and glared at him, as if annoyed that he had dodged its attack. *I need your help.*

Thankfully, Jola heard him and said, *What do you need me to do?*

Keo quickly outlined his plan to her. Jola didn't ask any questions about it and, after affirming that she understood it, disconnected from Keo's mind. He knew he could count on Jola, although he worried that Ankem might be able to counter it anyway.

*That's why we've got to be careful,* Keo thought, stopping a good distance from the demon. *Speed is of the essence and we can't let Ankem even suspect what we're about to do.*

But Keo got rid of all of the doubts in his mind. He let out another inhuman roar and flew toward the demon as fast as he could. The demon looked briefly surprised at his move, but started charging another fire breath attack anyway. He saw Ankem smirk over the dragon's shoulder, like he thought that Keo was being stupid for attacking them head on like that.

Just as the demon opened its mouth and unleashed a burst of red and black fire, Keo's world briefly vanished as Jola's teleportation magic took effect. But it was only for the very briefest of moments that he was gone. In the next second, he was standing in the back of the demon, which was still breathing fire, although since Keo was not in its path it hit nothing but the dirt in front of it.

Ankem turned around, a shocked expression on his face as he said, "How the hell did you—"

Keo didn't even think about it. He just stabbed Ankem straight through his chest and into the back of the demon's neck. Gildshine's golden flames rapidly enveloped Ankem, who cried out in sheer agony, while the demon let out a roar that was neither human nor Dracone. Ankem's skin rapidly melted away underneath the sheer heat of Keo's fire, making him look like some kind of walking dead. Ankem tried to grab Keo's hands and push Gildshine out of his chest, but he was too weak to force the burning blade out of his body.

Then Keo yanked Gildshine out of Ankem's chest and jumped backwards, gilding on his wings briefly before landing on the ground behind the demon. The demon was stamping its claws and shaking its head in pain, while the golden flames of Gildshine traveled from Ankem down onto the body of the demon itself, until the demon's whole body was covered in the golden flames, burning and melting every inch of its leathery skin.

Through the golden flames, Keo saw Ankem desperately trying to remove himself from the demon, but their fusion must have been too perfect, because he did not budge from his place on the demon at all.

Eventually, the demon fell forward with an almighty crash. The flames immediately went out, and as soon as they did, the demon's body rapidly decayed into dust. And then, like all demons, the dust sank into the earth, leaving behind nothing but scorched, blackened dirt where the demon—and Ankem—had been standing mere moments ago.

# Chapter Twenty-Two

A S SOON AS THE last of the demon's dust sank into the earth, Keo suddenly felt the fire in his soul go out. Intense pain spread over his body as he fell to his hands and knees. He tried to scream, but his mouth was changing and he could not make any sounds. He felt his wings contracting and his limbs shrinking and his face going back to normal.

It lasted perhaps three seconds, but it felt like an eternity to Keo. When it was over, the pain left with it, although Keo still felt out of breath. He looked at his hands, which were back to normal now, with no hints of any scales or anything else on them to indicate that he was anything other than human.

Shaking his head, Keo stood up again and noticed that his boots had holes in them where the claws of his feet had stuck through. Not only that, but his clothes in general looked wrecked, hanging much more loosely on his body than before, although his pants, at least, didn't seem likely to fall off anytime soon.

Then Keo heard someone running over to him and looked up to see that it was Easan. Easan had Shadowbane sheathed, a surprised look on his face as he approached Keo. He stopped several feet away from Keo, perhaps farther than he normally would, and eyed Keo with suspicion, even though Keo wasn't behaving threateningly.

"What was that?" said Easan.

"What was what?" said Keo. He rubbed the back of his head, which ached for some reason.

Easan pointed at the blackened spot on the earth where the demon had been standing mere moments before. "What you did to that demon."

"Oh, that," said Keo, nodding. "See, I figured that Ankem was the source of the demon's regeneration abilities, since he and the demon worked hard to protect him and the demon took the bulk of the attacks without complaining. So I had Jola teleport me onto the demon's back and—"

"Not *that*," said Easan, shaking his head. "Your form. Your transformation. You looked like some sort of weird dragon humanoid thing. It was hideous."

Keo looked down at his body again, which looked as human as it always did. "But it was also strong. Far stronger than my human body, for sure."

"It didn't look like a normal dragon transformation to me," said Easan, putting his hands on his hips. "It looked like you got stuck halfway."

Keo looked up at Easan again. "My mother told me that my form was different from the dragon forms of other Dracones, but I didn't understand what she meant until just a few minutes ago."

"You mean that that hideous dragon/human hybrid thing was your dragon transformation?" said Easan. He wrinkled his nose. "Disgusting."

"You know, you *could* be a little bit more thankful that I just saved your life," said Keo, folding his arms over his chest and scowling at Easan. "So maybe a little thanks is in order here, after you get over your knee-jerk reaction to my dragon form."

"Fine, thanks, whatever," said Easan. "But why aren't you in your dragon form anymore? Do you hate it as much as I do?"

Keo patted his chest. "It takes too much effort for me to maintain that form for longer than a few minutes. That's probably due to my lack of training, however, because I've noticed that more experienced Dracones can maintain their dragon forms almost indefinitely."

Easan looked like he was about to say something about that, but then Keo heard movement nearby and looked to his right. Veta was walking toward him, but he was not in his dragon form anymore. Instead, Veta was in his human form, although he still walked with a slight limp and his armor was cracked in several places.

"Keo of the Sword," said Veta, stopping and looking at him. The young Dracone's eyes darted to the blackened patch of earth where the demon had died. "I saw you kill the demon and its human master. I wanted to help, but the demon's earlier attack left me unable to fight, so I had to rest to make sure my injuries didn't get any worse."

"Do you need any help from us?" said Keo. "One of our Magicians can heal you."

Veta shook his head. "No. I don't need human magic to heal me—which I don't even trust anyway—but thanks for the offer. I have enough strength left that I should be able to make it back to the Nest on my own with news of what happened here. The Queen needs to know about the death of her daughter." He sighed wistfully. "I just wish that I could have helped to finish Ankem and his demon off myself."

Keo looked over his shoulder at Tananeen's corpse, which had not moved from its current position. Then he looked at Veta again and said, "All right. But we are going to the Horanian village. The Horanians need to learn about what happened here as well."

"Yes, I doubt that my people will be going to war with the Horanians anytime soon, particularly after this," said Veta, shaking his head.

"And there's something else I need to check at the village as well," said Keo. "Someone who I think knows more about this situation than he let on."

"Who?" said Veta, raising an eyebrow.

"I'll tell you later," said Keo. "For now, my friends and I must go."

"Very well," said Veta. He looked around at the corpses of his fellow Dracones, the ones who had come with him to the graveyard, a sorrowful look on his face. "They all fought bravely, but I guess that that wasn't enough. Not against that demon, anyway. Now I must leave."

With that, Veta turned and walked away. As he did so, he transformed into his dragon form and took to the skies, where he disappeared among the clouds before Keo or Easan could stop him. Keo watched him go for a minute before turning and walking toward Dlaine and Maryal. Maryal, who was lying on the ground, still looked injured from Ankem's attack, but her chest seemed to be healing, probably due to Jola's magic.

"How are you doing?" said Keo to Maryal as he and Easan approached.

Maryal grimaced and felt her chest. "Better than I was earlier, but still not healed up completely. But I think I'll survive, thanks to Jola, who is healing me with her magic."

"Good," said Keo, nodding. "I was worried for you for a second there."

"Yeah, great, but what was that earlier?" said Dlaine. He pointed at Keo's shoulders. "You had wings and you became larger and you looked like a dragon but except as a human. That was amazing."

Keo felt his shoulders, although he could not feel the spots where the dragon wings had emerged from. "Oh, it was nothing. It was just my dragon form, which is different from the dragon forms of the other Dracones. But that doesn't matter. What matters is that we need to get to the Horanian village, and fast."

"Why?" said Dlaine. He looked down at Maryal. "Maryal is still resting and healing. She can't go anywhere just yet."

"Yes, I can," said Maryal. She sat up, but it clearly took a lot out of her. "I may not be as healed as I should be, but I'm not as bad as I look."

"Jola can hover you around," said Keo. "But in any case, there's someone we need to see at the village. Someone who I think will try to flee if we don't get there fast enough."

"And who is that?" said Dlaine.

Keo scowled, thinking of the aged face that looked so much like what the face of his father would have looked like if he hadn't died. "Zamel. Let's go."

Due to the distance between the Dracone graveyard and the Horanian village, Jola had to teleport them all there. Keo was surprised that Jola had the strength to do it, seeing as she had already teleported them all just the day before, but Jola assured him that she could do it and not to worry about her.

So Jola teleported them back to the village itself, right inside the entrance, where they found themselves standing before two members of the Village Guard. The Guardsmen, taken by surprise by their sudden appearance, raised their bows to shoot at Keo and the others, but before they could, Keo held up his hands and said, "Wait! It's us. We're on your side. Don't shoot!"

The two Guardsmen hesitated when they saw Keo and the others, but then looked like they were going to shoot them anyway. That told Keo that Rackan and the others either had not gotten here yet or had not told the Guardsmen about the demon.

But before either Guardsmen could shoot Keo and his friends, a familiar voice shouted, "Keo!" and Nobia pushed past the two Guardsmen with a smile on her face.

Keo sighed in relief. "Nobia. Good to see a friendly face."

"Where did you guys come from?" said Nobia, glancing to the left and to the right. "The guards at the village entrance didn't warn us that anyone was coming."

"It doesn't matter how we got here," said Keo, shaking his head. "Did Rackan and the others return?"

"Just a few minutes ago," said Nobia, nodding. "They told us you guys are okay and that the Dracones aren't responsible for yesterday's attack." She looked at the two Guardsmen on either side of her. "You two can lower your bows. These people are on our side."

The two Guardsmen didn't seem to trust Keo and the others entirely. Still, they must have held Nobia's opinion in great esteem, because they lowered their bows and seemed unlikely to shoot Keo and his friends.

"Anyway, what happened back in the graveyard?" said Nobia. "Is the demon gone?"

"Yes," said Keo, nodding. "We killed it and it won't return, but we'll fill you in on the details later. Right now, we need you to take us to the Temple. Specifically, to Brother Zamel."

"Brother Zamel?" said Nobia, exchanging puzzled looks with the other Guardsmen. "Why him?"

"Because I suspect he had something to do with the demon attack," said Keo. "Now, take us to him right away. We have no time to lose."

Thankfully, Nobia seemed to understand, because she nodded and said, "Okay. You guys just follow me. The Temple isn't far from here, so it shouldn't take long to get there."

With that, Nobia turned and walked between the two Guardsmen, who stepped aside to allow her to pass. Keo and his friends followed, although Keo was worried at first that the Guardsmen might shoot them in the back as they passed. Thankfully, neither Guardsman did, which made Keo feel a little safer, although not by much when he considered the upcoming confrontation.

They reached the Temple within only a couple of minutes and Keo was the first to enter after Nobia. There they found the other three elders—Osina, Shinisa, and Hanoc—lying on the floor, with large bruises on their heads from where they had been attacked. Rackan was kneeling over them, along with another Guardsmen, and appeared to be trying to awaken them, though with little luck.

"Brother!" said Nobia in shock as she, Keo, and the others entered the Temple. "What happened to the elders? Where is

Brother Zamel?"

"Zamel attacked them just seconds ago and went out the back," said Rackan, pointing to the back door of the Temple that led to the courtyard. "We only got here just in time to see him leave."

Keo didn't even wait for Nobia to ask another question, nor did he say anything to anyone else. He ran past Rackan and the fallen elders and through the door to the courtyard outside. Dashing through the open doorway, he saw Zamel—with a small bag over his shoulder that seemed to carry whatever possessions he owned—running away, but Keo was not going to let him get away.

Unsheathing Gildshine, Keo pointed the sword and fired a ball of golden flame over Zamel's head. The fire ball didn't hit Zamel, but it made him stop and turn around to face Keo. The old man's face paled as soon as he saw who had shot that fire ball and started backing up as quickly as he could, while Keo advanced on him.

"Ah, Keo," said Zamel, who sounded like he was trying—and failing—to sound congenial and surprised. "What a pleasant surprise. I hadn't expected to see you again so soon. I heard about how you and your friends killed that demon. Very good, I say."

"How could you have known about that when we just got back?" said Keo.

Zamel gulped as he backed up. "I, uh—"

"Don't answer that question," said Keo, not hiding the hostility in his voice. He pointed Gildshine at Zamel, making the old man cringe. "I know who you are. You aren't a wise old elder of the Horanians, trying to protect and lead your people to peace.

You're the brother of King Riuno, which makes you my uncle. Don't even bother to try to deny it."

Zamel kept backing up until he hit the lip of the dry well, at which point he had to stop or else he risked falling in. Nonetheless, he looked scared, like he wanted to run, although he had no way to escape now.

"All right," said Zamel with a gulp. "You guessed correctly. I don't know how you knew, but it doesn't matter. I'm indeed the brother of your father. Now will you please spare my life or—"

Keo pointed the tip of Gildshine at Zamel's throat, causing the old man to freeze.

"How did you survive the fall of the Kingdom of Lamaira?" said Keo. "How did you get here, to the Horanian village? And why?"

Zamel looked like he was too mortified to speak, so Keo pressed the tip of his sword against Zamel's neck ever-so-slightly.

That made Zamel suddenly say, in a hurried, high voice, "Because I was afraid! I was afraid that I would be killed. I thought that my brother would not be able to protect me from my enemies, so I fled as far from Tain as I could. I came here because I knew that no one would ever follow me here due to the fear of the Dracones."

"Still doesn't explain how a foreigner like you became an elder of the Horanians," said Keo. "How'd you manage that?"

"Through trickery," said Zamel, still speaking quickly. "I told the Horanians that I was the son of one of the Horanians that had gone to explore Lamaira ages ago, who had returned to rejoin my people and find my roots. They believed me and, after several years of proving my loyalty to the Horanians, they gave me a leadership position."

Keo raised an eyebrow. "They gave a leadership position to a foreigner that easily?"

Zamel shook his head. "It wasn't easy. It was hard. And I will admit to doing a little bit of manipulation and trickery to get this far, but I did do it, even though I don't have a drop of Horanian blood in me."

"Uh huh," said Keo. "And is that the whole reason you came here? Because my father wasn't alive to protect you anymore?"

"That wasn't the *whole* reason," said Zamel. "It wasn't just my political enemies who wanted to kill me. You see, I also was afraid that your father's loyalists would find out who had actually arranged for his death."

Keo's eyes widened in shock and anger. "Hold on. Are you implying that *you* summoned the demon that killed my father?"

Zamel looked like he was about to deny it, but then his eyes darted to the sword at his throat and he said instead, "Yes."

At that point, Keo was just about ready to take Zamel's head off and end the bastard's life then and there. But Keo still had some questions he needed answering, so he ignored his desire for revenge for the moment in order to get what he wanted.

"Why?" said Keo. He didn't hide the anger in his voice because he thought it would help make him seem more threatening to Zamel. "Why did you do it? Why did you kill your own brother? My father?"

"Because *I* deserved to be King," said Zamel, bitterness in his voice. "Not Riuno. Riuno was unfit to be King. He was too weak, too kind to others. I summoned the demon because I believed that I, the stronger of the two, would ascend to the Throne after his death."

"But you didn't," said Keo. "What kept you from doing that?"

"Chaos," said Zamel simply. "When news got out to the people that Riuno had died, the Kingdom immediately fell into civil war. No one listened to me, not even when I tried to assert my right over the Throne. Everything went wrong and failed to work out the way I had hoped."

"So, like a coward, you fled," said Keo. "You thought that my father's loyalists would figure out that you killed him and would want revenge, right?"

Zamel's lips trembled, like he was about to cry. "I did, I did. I had no loyalists of my own to protect me, so I came to the Upper Mountains to hide. I originally intended to return after things had calmed down, but I was too scared to leave and have been here ever since."

"Did you know who I was when we first met?" said Keo. "Did you know that I am my father's son?"

"I did," said Zamel. "You look very much like Riuno did in his younger years, albeit with shorter hair. I was shocked because I didn't think I'd ever get to meet you, so when you showed up, I couldn't believe my eyes."

"I see," said Keo. "Now, why did you try to kill me and my friends earlier?"

"What are you even babbling about?" said Zamel. "I never laid a finger on you. Are you talking about the Great Mountain Man's revelation that you are liars and deceivers?"

Anger shot up in Keo and he was just about ready to finish off Zamel here and now, but he fought down his anger just long enough for him to say, "Don't lie to me. That wasn't the Great

Mountain Man, was it? It was a trap you made to get me and my friends killed."

Zamel at first looked like he was going to continue to deny it, but then Keo pressed the tip of Gildshine against Zamel's throat again and Zamel said, in an urgent voice, "Yes, yes, okay, I faked it. That wasn't the Great Mountain Man who had spoken. That was the demon."

"So Ankem and the demon *were* working for you," said Keo. "I knew it. Did you order them to kill us, too?"

Zamel gulped. "Working for me? I was working for *them*. I had intended to live out the rest of my life in these Mountains, away from the demons that had ruined my life, but their King sought me out. He threatened to reveal my existence to the peoples of Lamaira, particularly to the people of the Old Kingdom, who still love my dead brother, if I did not help him get rid of you and your friends."

Keo almost called him a liar, but stopped himself because Zamel seemed to be telling the truth. He realized that Zamel was far too much of a coward to boss around Ankem or the demon.

So Keo said, "How did you fake the Great Mountain Man's words, then?"

"The demon did it," said Zamel. He patted the lip of the dry well. "It hid at the bottom of the well and mimicked the ancient language of old that the Great Mountain Man was said to speak. Those demons can do lots of different things like that, which makes them both amazing and terrifying at the same time."

"What was your ultimate goal?" said Keo. "What was the point of all of this? Just to kill us?"

"That was what I hoped would happen, yes, but the King of

Demons wanted to have the Dracones and Horanians fighting each other," said Zamel with a gulp. "He said that he did not want the Dracones to ally with you, so he had the Brothers White Blood steal seven eggs from the Dracones to make the Dracones hate humans even more and make it harder for you to convince them to work with you."

"But it failed," said Keo. "We're still alive and now both the Dracones and the Horanians know the truth, or will know it soon."

Zamel gulped. "What are you going to do to me, then?"

"I want to kill you," said Keo. "Because of your actions, I've lost both my father and my mother. I have every right to take your sorry life. But I won't."

"Won't?" said Zamel, a little hopeful. "Why not?"

"I'm going to have the Dracones take you to Tain, where the Keepers can put you on trial for your crimes," said Keo. He took a deep breath to calm himself. "Killing people like you in cold blood would not be right. I believe that the people of Tain—and of Lamaira—deserve to see justice themselves, rather than be deprived of it by me."

Zamel sneered. "You sound just like your father. Which is good, because it was always easy to manipulate your father whenever he talked about that."

Suddenly, Keo felt a knife stab into his abdomen. Gasping in pain, he looked down to see a knife stabbed into his stomach, a knife in Zamel's hand, which Zamel appeared to have pulled out of nowhere.

Keo looked up at Zamel, who now had a murderous look in his eyes as he drove the knife deeper and deeper into Keo's stomach.

"I should have killed you the moment I saw you," said Zamel, his voice full of wrath. "But regardless, at least when you die, you will be reunited with your weak father and neglectful mother. Won't that be grand?"

The pain from the knife was almost overwhelming, especially because Zamel was jabbing it in there with surprising strength for a man his age. Keo gasped for air, but rather than fall backwards, he redoubled his grip on Gildshine and slashed across Zamel's chest.

Zamel let out a cry of pain and staggered backwards. But Zamel tripped over the lip of the dry well and, swinging his arms, fell backwards into the well with a shout. Keo, despite the pain in his abdomen, rushed over to the lip of the well and looked down it in time to see Zamel vanish into the shadows below, a look of terror and pain on his face as he fell.

Keo waited, trying to hear Zamel's body hit the bottom of the well, but he heard nothing. Not that he actually had time to listen, because the pain from Zamel's knife—which was still embedded in his abdomen—caused him to stagger backwards. He grabbed the knife and yanked it out, causing blood to flow freely from his wound.

Keo hurled the knife to the side and fell to his knees, folding both hands over his bleeding wound and gasping for breath. He found it harder and harder to maintain consciousness due primarily to the blood loss and the exhaustion of the day finally catching up with him.

His last thoughts as he drifted into unconsciousness was that he hoped that he would not bleed to death here.

# Chapter Twenty-Three

**K**EO AWOKE IN A bed in an unfamiliar room. He thought at first that he had died and awakened in some sort of afterlife, because everything was quite silent and the walls appeared to be made out of gold and silver.

But then Keo blinked and realized that the walls were not made of gold or silver. Rather, they were made of stone and were simply bathed in the sunlight streaming in from the windows outside. Keo had simply misunderstood what he was seeing, although with his vision becoming clearer, he hoped not to make that particular mistake again.

The room he lay in was medium-sized and rather plain. It appeared to be one room of a larger building, because he saw a stone door at the other end of the room that appeared to lead to another room. The temperature was cold, although the thick blankets he lay under kept him toasty. He also saw Gildshine leaning against the foot of his bed, which made him feel a lot safer, as he had wondered where his sword had gone.

Keo looked at the bed he was lying upon. It was soft but also a little bumpy, although it was far superior to the bedrolls that Keo had slept on ever since he and his friends left Tain for the Upper Mountains. He was not wearing a shirt and a quick pat of his abdomen told him that his wound from Zamel's knife had been patched up, though by who, he didn't know.

*Someone must have found me in the courtyard and took me to this bed to heal me,* Keo thought. *But how long have I been out? And where am I? Am I still in the Horanian village?*

Just as Keo decided to leave his room to figure out where he was, the door at the other end of the room opened and Dlaine stepped through it. Dlaine carried a large bowl of some kind of hot stew on a tray, but he stopped when he saw that Keo was awake.

"Ah, Keo," said Dlaine, smiling when he saw him. "Good timing. I was just coming in to give you this stew for lunch. Thought I'd have to wake you up myself."

Keo rubbed his forehead, which hurt for some reason. "Thanks for the food, but where am I? How did I get here? How long have I been out?"

"You've been out for only a day," said Dlaine. "As for where you are, you are in the house of Rackan and Nobia. They agreed to let you rest and heal here from Zamel's attack on you earlier. They're really thankful for your help in killing that demon, which is why they wanted you to live here with them until you get better."

"Well, that was nice of them," said Keo. "Did they bandage my wound, too?"

"Yep," said Dlaine, nodding as he kicked the door closed behind him and walked over to Keo. He placed the tray down on the stone chest next to Keo's bed and then sat down on a stool beside the bed. "Nobia did, actually, because apparently she's really good at bandaging wounds. She said you should recover from the wound as long as you get plenty of rest and don't overexert yourself."

Keo sighed in relief. "That's good to hear. But what about Zamel? I saw him fall into the well. Has anyone found his body?"

"Nope," said Dlaine, shaking his head. "The well is too deep for anyone to climb down. As far as we know, Zamel's body is still down there, rotting away like it deserves."

Keo frowned. "The last time people said Zamel was dead, he turned up here. If we can't find his body, what's to stop him from escaping to get revenge against us another day?"

"You'll have to convince the Horanians to check the well, then," said Dlaine, putting his hands on his knees. "And that's going to be hard, because they treat that well like a sacred place and aren't thrilled about the idea of sending someone down there to get a corpse."

"I guess there's nothing we can do about it, then," said Keo with a sigh. "We'll just have to hope that Zamel really did die this time."

"I don't see how anyone could survive getting slashed in the chest by a big sword and then falling down a bottomless well," said Dlaine with a shrug. "Probably not worth worrying about, in my opinion."

Keo disagreed. Zamel may have been a coward and a cheat, but he also held grudges, and if he survived falling down the well and somehow escaped, then Keo had no doubt that Zamel would come after him and his friends again. When and how, Keo didn't know, but he knew that Zamel would, though Keo decided not to argue the point for the moment.

"How is everyone else doing?" said Keo.

"Pretty well," said Dlaine. "The others are staying in other huts nearby, since Rackan and Nobia's hut is too small for all of us. The Horanians have been treating us all much better ever since they learned about Zamel, Ankem, and the demon. No more suspicious glares from people who hate us. It's been great."

"What about the Dracones?" said Keo. "Heard any word from them?"

"Unfortunately, we haven't," said Dlaine, "which I suppose is good, because the Dracones—"

The door to Keo's room suddenly burst open, causing Keo and Dlaine to look at it as Nobia ran into the room. She came to a stop, looking like she was in a hurry.

"Nobia?" said Keo. He sat up, despite it being uncomfortable. "What's the problem? You look like you've seen a ghost."

"The Dracones have arrived and want to speak with you," said Nobia, jerking a thumb over her shoulder.

"The Dracones?" said Keo. "How long have they been here?"

"Just got here a few seconds ago," said Nobia. "And you *really* gotta come. Their leader, Queen Sayot herself, is among them."

Keo and Dlaine exchanged puzzled looks. What was the Queen doing here in person? Keo wondered if this had something to do with Tananeen's death.

"All right," said Keo, looking at Nobia again. "I'll get up and go speak with her. I need a shirt, though, and my shoes."

"Are you sure you feel up to going?" said Nobia. "You still need lots of rest if you are going to recover from your wound."

"I feel fine," said Keo, waving off Nobia's concern. "Besides, I'm just going to be talking with them. That's not exactly a taxing thing to do, is it?"

Nobia frowned, but she said, "Okay, I'll go find a shirt and shoes for you to wear. Please be patient."

With that, Nobia left the room, leaving Keo and Dlaine alone, with Keo wondering why Queen Sayot had come to visit him. Whatever it was, Keo had a feeling that it wasn't going to be any good.

With a new clean shirt, his old boots on, and Gildshine attached to his side, Keo stepped out of Rackan and Nobia's hut with Dlaine by his side and Nobia behind him. The cold winter air made him shiver slightly, but he stopped as soon as he saw the Dracones.

A dozen Dracones stood in the street outside the hut. Some of them were in their human forms, their arms folded across their chests and scowls on their faces that showed their displeasure at being in a human village, while others retained their dragon forms, although they looked just as displeased as their fellow Dracones about being here.

Two dozen or so Horanians were also gathered, forming a loose circle around the area. Many were pointing and muttering about the presence of so many Dracones, while many more looked angry, even though the Dracones did not seem to be causing any trouble. A few members of the Village Guard could be seen on rooftops or among the people, their hands on their bows in case they should need to attack the Dracones. Keo's friends—Easan, Maryal, and Jola—were also among the people, but quickly walked over to Keo when they saw him.

But what caught Keo's attention the most was Queen Sayot. In the light of the sun, she looked even weaker and older than ever, the sunlight showing her cracked scales. Yet she still had a certain majesty about her that Keo could not deny, an air of authority accumulated from centuries of experience. She was sitting on the earth in her dragon form, her tail wrapped around her feet, seemingly oblivious to the pointing and muttering humans all around her.

As Keo's friends joined him, Keo walked up to the Queen, who raised her head when she heard him approach. The other Dracones took notice of him as well, while the Horanians stopped talking when they saw him approach Sayot.

"Queen Sayot," said Keo, stopping a few feet from her. "I didn't expect you to leave the Nest and come here."

"Keo of the Sword," said Sayot. She sounded as grumpy as ever, although not quite as bitter as the last time Keo had spoken with her. "I didn't expect to be here, either, but recent events have forced me to leave the Nest for the first time in years. I heard from Veta about how you slew the demon and the evil human who helped it, as well as Tananeen's death."

Keo caught a hint of sadness in Sayot's tone when she mentioned Tananeen's death, sadness that Keo understood well.

"I realize that I was foolish to underestimate the threat of the demons to my people," said Sayot, with obvious reluctance. "I had assumed that the demons today were the same as the demons of old, but if their King is using his power to corrupt our unborn to make stronger demons, then it is clear that the demons are a far worse threat than I first thought. I doubt they will leave us alone from this point. They will not be satisfied with my daughter's death. Eventually, they may even try to kill me."

Keo nodded. "I'm glad you understand that. Does that mean you are willing to reconsider my earlier offer?"

"Yes," said Sayot. "Not with joy, not with glee, but with understanding that I must do what I must do to ensure the survival of my people. And I believe that the demons are a far worse threat to my peoples' survival than any human could ever hope to be."

"Including the Horanians?" said Keo.

Sayot sighed, like she didn't want to say this, but she said it anyway: "Yes. I have declared a truce with the Horanians' elders, who, as I understand, were also affected by the demon. For now, the ancient hostilities between our peoples must be put aside and we will work together to stop the demon threat until it is destroyed."

Whispers of surprise and shock scattered among the Horanian spectators, while the Dracones looked like they already know about this truce. They didn't look any happier about it than the Horanians, though.

"Well, that's good to hear," said Keo. "Anyway, while you and the Horanians do that, my friends and I are heading south as soon as I am better. We need to make contact with the Divinians, who are the only people in Lamaira who we haven't spoken with yet about the reunification of the Kingdom."

"That is what I wanted to speak with you about," said Sayot. "I do not want you to leave the Mountains just yet."

Keo looked at Sayot in surprise. "Why not?"

"Because you still need training," said Sayot. "I heard that you managed to transform into your dragon form during your fight with the demon, but I am correct in assuming that you do not have complete control over it yet."

Keo nodded again. "Right. I can't change form at will just yet or maintain it for long."

"I knew it," said Sayot. "That is why I am offering to train you. I have trained many, many younglings in transforming in the past and I believe I could do the same for you."

"Why?" said Keo. "I thought you didn't like me."

"For Tananeen," said Sayot. She sounded sad again. "I thought my daughter highly foolish, but now I understand that she was trying to do what all good Dracone parents try to do. It is ordinarily the parents who teach their children how to transform, but with Tananeen dead, that means that the duty of teaching you how to transform falls to me, your closest living relative, if you accept my offer."

"That's a kind offer, but—" said Keo.

"Think of it as honoring your mother's death," said Sayot. "By training her son, I can honor my daughter in a way I failed to do when she lived. Does that sound acceptable to you?"

Keo bit his lower lip. He could not deny that Sayot had a good point. For that matter, Sayot was his only living relative that he knew of, assuming Zamel hadn't survived the fall into the well. Even if she still hated him, he didn't think it would be right to ignore her offer for help. But he also needed to speak with the Divinians, who needed to know about the return of the *shelmai*.

Then Dlaine rested a hand on Keo's shoulder and said, "Keo, I've got an idea."

Keo looked at Dlaine, puzzled. "What idea?"

"About how to reconcile your grandmother's offer with our journey," said Dlaine. "Here's the idea: You stay here and train with your grandmother for however long it takes for you to master your transformation abilities, while the rest of us go to West Lamaira and prepare the country for your arrival."

"But that would mean we would have to be separate," said Keo.

"Yeah, but not forever," said Dlaine. "I think it's necessary because the demons are getting stronger, like Sayot said, and you need every weapon and ability you can get to fight them. Won't learning how to transform from human to dragon and back, at will, be useful?"

"Yes, but what do the others think?" said Keo. He looked at Maryal, Easan, and Jola. "Do you agree with Dlaine's idea?"

"Sure," said Maryal. "It makes sense to me. It's hugely important that you learn how to control your dragon form. And besides, we shouldn't have any trouble with the Divinians, who I'm sure are going to be happy to hear that the *shelmai* is back."

"I agree," said Easan. "We don't really *need* your help, anyway. I think we can get the Divinians on our side by ourselves. We know what to say."

*I support this idea, too,* said Jola in Keo's head. *If this is what we'll have to do to beat the demons, then we should do it.*

"Looks like everyone agrees," said Dlaine. "That means we're going to do it."

Keo bit his lower lip again, but he honestly didn't see many problems with the plan. The only issue was that they had only two months until the demons came back, but he doubted that Sayot would train him for too long, so even that wouldn't be an issue as long as they were quick with the training.

So Keo nodded once again and said, "All right. I'll stay here and train with Queen Sayot, then, while you guys go ahead of me and travel to Western Lamaira to contact the Divinians. We'll meet again in a month."

"A month it is, then," said Dlaine with a smile. "Good luck with the training."

"Thanks," said Keo. He looked up at Queen Sayot. "When do we begin?"

"Whenever you feel ready," said Sayot calmly. "But the sooner the better, of course."

"We can start tomorrow," said Keo. "By then, I should be feeling well enough to train."

"And we'll leave tomorrow for West Lamaira as well," said Dlaine. "Right, guys?"

Easan and Maryal nodded, while Keo figured that Jola was probably nodding, too.

"Okay, then," said Keo. "Now I need to return to bed and rest, but I'll be up first thing in the morning to start the transformation training."

"Good to hear," said Sayot. "We shall all return to the Nest now, but in the morning we will send someone to pick you up at first light."

With that, Sayot and the other Dracones took flight, their collective flaps sending large gusts of air and dust into everyone's eyes. That didn't stop Keo from looking up and watching them all fly away, hoping that he would be able to learn how to control his transformation to stop the demons.

# Continued in: Kingdom of Gods

Having completed his training among the Dracone, Keo travels south to the country of the Divinians, intending to reunite with his friends, who he had sent ahead of him to prepare the country for his arrival.

But then Keo learns that his friends have been captured by the country's people, who intend to execute them for daring to announce Keo's arrival. In addition, Keo has only a week to reach the country's capital and save his friends, which means he has no time to waste.

To save his friends, Keo must travel to the country's capital before the date of the execution, battling demons, enemy soldiers, and other obstacles that attempt to stop him from preventing the execution of his friends. With the shadow of the demons growing ever larger, Keo cannot afford to fail to save his friends and convince the Divinians who the real enemy is.

Now available wherever books are sold!

# About the Author

Timothy L. Cerepaka writes fantasy as an indie author. He is the author of the Mages of Martir fantasy novels, the Two Worlds science-fantasy series, and the Tournament of the Gods fantasy novels. He lives in Texas.

Find out more at his website at www.timothylcerepaka.com.

# Other books by
# Timothy L. Cerepaka

Prince Malock World:

*The Mad Voyage of Prince Malock*

*The Return of Prince Malock*

*The New Era of Prince Malock*

*The Coronation of Prince Malock*

Mages of Martir:

*The Mage's Grave*

*The Mage's Limits*

*The Mage's Sea*

*The Mage's Ghost*

Two Worlds:

*Reunification*

*Alliance*

*Allegiance*

*Retaliation*

*Desinence*

Tournament of the Gods:

*Gathering of the Chosen*

*Betrayal of the Chosen*

*Invasion of the Chosen*

*Ascension of the Chosen*

The War-Torn Kingdom:

*Kingdom of Magicians*

*Kingdom of Heirs*

*Kingdom of Dragons*

*Kingdom of Gods*

Standalones:

*The Last Legend: Glitch Apocalypse*

www.ingramcontent.com/pod-product-compliance
Lightning Source LLC
Chambersburg PA
CBHW060433030726
47495CB00003B/854